The best way to stay in touch is to subscribe to my newsletter. Go to *www.shirleendavies.com* and subscribe in the box at the top of the right column that asks for your email. You'll be notified of new books before they are released, have chances to win great prizes, and receive other subscriber-only specials.

Courage Canyon

Redemption Mountain Historical Western Romance Series

SHIRLEEN DAVIES

**Book Eight in the
Redemption Mountain**

Historical Western Romance Series

Books by Shirleen Davies

Historical Western Romance Series

MacLarens of Fire Mountain

Tougher than the Rest, Book One
Faster than the Rest, Book Two
Harder than the Rest, Book Three
Stronger than the Rest, Book Four
Deadlier than the Rest, Book Five
Wilder than the Rest, Book Six

Redemption Mountain

Redemption's Edge, Book One
Wildfire Creek, Book Two
Sunrise Ridge, Book Three
Dixie Moon, Book Four
Survivor Pass, Book Five
Promise Trail, Book Six
Deep River, Book Seven
Courage Canyon, Book Eight

MacLarens of Boundary Mountain

Colin's Quest, Book One,
Brodie's Gamble, Book Two
Quinn's Honor, Book Three
Sam's Legacy, Book Four
Heather's Choice, Book Five, Coming next in the series!

Contemporary Romance Series

MacLarens of Fire Mountain

Second Summer, Book One
Hard Landing, Book Two
One More Day, Book Three
All Your Nights, Book Four
Always Love You, Book Five
Hearts Don't Lie, Book Six
No Getting Over You, Book Seven
'Til the Sun Comes Up, Book Eight
Foolish Heart, Book Nine
Forever Love, Book Ten, Coming next in the series!

Peregrine Bay

Reclaiming Love, Book One, A Novella
Our Kind of Love, Book Two

Burnt River

Shane's Burden, Book One by Peggy Henderson
Thorn's Journey, Book Two by Shirleen Davies
Aqua's Achilles, Book Three by Kate Cambridge
Ashley's Hope, Book Four by Amelia Adams
Harpur's Secret, Book Five by Kay P. Dawson
Mason's Rescue, Book Six by Peggy L. Henderson
Del's Choice, Book Seven by Shirleen Davies
Watch for more books in this series!

Book conversions by Joseph Murray at
3rdplanetpublishing.com

Cover design by Kim Killion

ISBN: 978-1-941786-54-3

I care about quality, so if you find something in error, please contact me via email at
shirleen@shirleendavies.com

Description

Courage Canyon, Book Eight, Redemption Mountain Historical Western Romance Series

Dirk Masters, ex-Union Cavalry Captain, traveled hundreds of miles to put his past behind him. Finding Splendor and getting a job at Redemption's Edge seems the perfect opportunity to start over. His new life is predictable and peaceful...until a feisty young woman creates chaos in his orderly existence.

Rosemary Thayer has overcome more than one obstacle to achieve her dream of becoming a nurse. After a rough start, the people of Redemption's Edge have accepted her into their family—all except the rude and arrogant foreman who seems to enjoy making her life miserable. Soon, she'll have earned enough to leave the ranch for a place of her own.

But trouble continues to plague Rosemary. The unwelcome news of an escaped convict threatens to stall her plans of an independent life.

After months of anticipating her departure, Dirk is given an assignment he doesn't want, but can't turn down. Guard Rosemary from not one, but two possible threats. Could his life get any more complicated?

The last person she wants disrupting her future is now a part of it—every day, morning and night.

Not only is the escaped convict certain to come calling, another danger is inching its way toward Splendor, threatening young women, and no one can identify the attacker.

Worse, Dirk is fighting not only the threats, but his own internal desire. They're oil and water, meant to be as far apart as the Pacific from the Atlantic. So why does he crave her touch, seek any excuse to get close?

Courage Canyon, book eight in the Redemption Mountain historical western romance series, is a full-length novel with an HEA and no cliffhanger.

Visit my website for a list of characters for each series.
https://www.shirleendavies.com/character-list.html

Acknowledgements

Many thanks to my husband, Richard, for always being by my side during this wonderful adventure. Your support, insights, and suggestions are greatly appreciated.

As always, many thanks to my editor, Kim Young, proofreader, Alicia Carmical, Joseph Murray, who is superb at formatting my books for print and electronic versions, my cover designer, Kim Killion.

Courage
Canyon

Prologue

Third Battle of Winchester
October 1864

"Continue firing." Union Captain Dirk Masters gave the order as the Confederate infantry brigade, led by Colonel George Patton, began their retreat.

Holding his rifle in one hand as he reined his horse around, Dirk glanced across the field where dozens of men lay wounded or dying. He yelled out when one of his men rode past in pursuit of the retreating soldiers.

"Corporal!"

The young man stopped his horse, pivoting it toward Dirk. "Yes, sir."

"Find the ambulance wagon. There are men out there who need help."

Nodding, the corporal turned west toward the spot they'd left the supply wagons and medical personnel.

Charging forward on his large roan gelding, Dirk led his division across the wide expanse of open field and into the brush where hundreds of Confederate infantry fled, their legs no match for the Union horsemen. No matter how fast they ran, most wouldn't be able to escape.

Dirk yelled a series of commands, his well-trained division herding Patton's men into a tight cluster. Seeing the Confederates raise their rifles, fumbling with ammunition in a feeble attempt at a last stand, Dirk rode straight toward them, knowing his men's weapons were aimed at the enemy.

"Drop your guns, soldiers. There's no reason to die today." Another signal and the horses tightened the circle around the Confederates, his men shouting the same command to drop their weapons.

Looking to his right, Dirk spotted Captain Robert Crandall leading his cavalry division, along with what appeared to be over one hundred prisoners. Joining up, they merged the Confederates into one group, estimating they had close to three hundred captives.

"Where is Colonel Patton?" Robert asked, scanning the prisoners for the man in charge of their brigade.

Reining his horse to a stop, Dirk glanced down at a Confederate private. "Do you know where Colonel Patton is?"

The young man glared at him, shaking his head. "Wounded. That's all I know."

The news didn't surprise Dirk. It had been a hard-fought battle on the outskirts of Winchester, Virginia. Kicking his horse to catch up with Robert, he wondered how much longer the Confederate Army would continue to fight. The tide of the war had begun to turn, the Union winning one victory after another. He had no stomach for grinding them into the ground, but he'd follow orders until the war ended.

Reaching camp, the captives were added to the growing number of prisoners before Dirk and Robert reported to Brigadier General Wesley Merritt, a man well-respected throughout the Union Cavalry ranks.

Merritt nodded at them as they approached. "The Confederate Army is in full retreat, gentlemen. You've managed to crush their left flank. Well done."

"Thank you, sir." Dirk removed his gloves, shoving them into his back pocket. "We heard Confederate Colonel Patton was wounded. He wasn't part of the prisoners we brought in."

"That may explain their hasty retreat. I'll pass the word up to Major General Sheridan. No other orders for now, gentlemen." Merritt turned away, dismissing them as he spoke to his aid.

Robert clasped Dirk on the back. "I've got a flask of whiskey in my saddlebag. Care to join me?"

Hesitating for an instant, he nodded. "One swallow, then I need to see to my men."

"Agreed. Our divisions did well today, Dirk."

The two men had become close over the last year. As fellow cavalry officers, they'd shared many stories of growing up in Pennsylvania families with long histories in horse breeding. The similarities between them were so strong, they sometimes wondered if they might be brothers, separated at birth. Even as adults, the parallels continued. Each had a wife waiting back home. Neither had children, but looked forward to when the war ended and they could start their families.

"The war is winding down. I heard news it may come to an end before next summer."

Dirk listened as Robert spoke, hoping what his friend speculated might be true. Summer was a long way off. Anything could happen, but he'd come this far and wouldn't back out now. Some volunteers had started returning home, unable to be away from their families any longer.

No matter how much he missed his wife, Dirk vowed to stick it out, knowing Griff, his older brother, protected Melissa in northern Pennsylvania. When the war ended, he'd return to Melissa and the horse ranch he and his brother dreamed about since they were young boys. They'd follow their grandfather's and father's paths, breeding, training, and selling high-quality horses.

As the day darkened to night, he retreated to the comfort of his bedroll, feeling good about what they'd achieved at Winchester. He didn't like war, but he hated the thought of a nation divided. Whatever it took, he'd do all he could to bring it back to being the strong union it was before the strife over slavery alienated what had once seemed an unbreakable, sovereign nation.

Stretching out, he rested an arm across his eyes, thinking of Melissa. He'd loved her since they were children, vowed to marry her as soon as her parents gave their permission. The wedding had been a joyous event, bringing out everyone in their tight-knit community.

Blowing out a slow breath, an image of Melissa riding next to him, laughing, settled in his mind.

Not much longer, sweetheart, Dirk thought an instant before he fell into a deep sleep.

Chapter One

Splendor, Montana
March 1869

"I can't explain it, Dax. There are more men guarding the herds than we've ever had, yet there are ten head missing. I've had men ride the entire ranch and there's no sign of them." Dirk Masters, one of the two foremen at Redemption's Edge, ran a hand through his hair, staring out the window of Dax's study toward the barn. "A few from each pasture. If it's rustlers, that kind of planning takes effort. Most rustlers take cattle from one location and hightail it out of there. Not this time."

Dax Pelletier and his brother, Luke, owned Redemption's Edge, the largest ranch in western Montana. "It isn't the first time we've had cattle missing from different pastures."

Dirk snorted, knowing Dax referred to the time Rosemary Thayer, her brother, and two other orphans stole a few head from different herds. Dirk and Bull Mason, the other foreman, tracked down the kids, hauling them in front of Dax, Luke, and Sheriff Gabe Evans. They resolved the issue by having the young rustlers repay their debt by living and working at the ranch. The four had become part of the extended family that included just about anyone associated with the Pelletier family.

"That was different, Dax. Rosemary and the others were blackmailed into stealing the cattle. The fact they got away with it for so long was nothing but pure luck."

The orphans would find a few stray head at different locations on the ranch and gather them up. When they had at least ten, they'd hand them over to Boyden Trask. He'd butcher them and sell the meat for a tidy profit in his restaurant in Big Pine, the territorial capital several hours from Splendor. The last anyone knew, he sat in a prison cell miles from town.

Dax rubbed his chin, his eyes crinkling in amusement. "I don't know, Dirk. Rosemary and the boys were pretty darn smart about how they went about it." He knew Dirk still had a hard time accepting how long it had taken them to catch the thieves. Finding out they were led by a teenage girl and included three young boys still chafed his foreman's pride. "It all worked out. Rosemary is now working at the clinic and Trask is in jail."

Dax's wife, Rachel, had been a nurse in the Union Army, moving to Splendor to join her uncle, Doctor Charles Worthington, in his medical clinic. As the town grew, her uncle hired Doctor Clay McCord, then started to look for another nurse. With one young son and a second child on the way, Rachel had been surprised and pleased when Rosemary told her she'd like to learn nursing.

"I know you don't like losing any cattle, Dirk, but ten head isn't a great deal. No matter how hard you search, there are places on the ranch they wander off to, only to show up again a week or two later. The snow is a hindrance to finding them. Plus, there's a wolf pack along our border that's picked off cattle in the past." Dax scratched his chin. "According to our agreement with the Blackfoot, Running Bear may have sent men to take a couple head. Although he usually sends word to me beforehand." He saw the disgruntled look on Dirk's face and held up his hand. "But you're right. We need to figure this out."

Nodding, Dirk scowled. "It doesn't matter what happened in the past with Rosemary and the boys. It's *now* I'm worried about. I want to find the cattle, or whoever took them. At least that young woman is no longer underfoot, turning the heads of my men. She's a distraction they don't need. Having her at the clinic was a good decision."

"Don't tell me you're grousing about Rosemary again, Dirk." Rachel grinned as she walked into the study holding two cups of coffee, handing one to Dax and the other to their foreman. "Drink this. It might improve your mood."

Taking a sip, he let the scowl fall from his face. "Your coffee's always good enough to improve anyone's mood."

Rubbing her lower back, she sat down in one of the leather chairs. "Rosemary is a fine young woman, works hard at the clinic and still helps here when she has time. I don't know why the two of you can't get along."

Dirk looked at her, knowing he shouldn't let himself be drawn into a discussion about Rosemary. "She's stubborn, willful, obstinate, and too dang pushy."

Glancing at Dax, Rachel worked to hide a smile. "Seems you could be talking about me or Ginny...or even Lydia," she said, referring to Luke's and Bull's wives.

"You three are different," Dirk muttered, taking another sip of coffee.

"I don't know about that. It takes a different kind of woman to make it out here in the middle of nowhere. You ought to give Rosemary a little credit for all she's done."

He didn't respond. Finishing his coffee, he set the cup on the desk before looking at Dax. "What do you want me to do about the missing cattle?"

"Merge them into two herds. It's time to bring them closer to the house anyway, and it'll take less men to guard them."

"Sounds good." Dirk turned to leave.

"And triple the number of men on watch at night."

"Sure thing, Dax."

Rachel watched Dirk leave, waiting until he'd closed the front door. "What's he got against Rosemary?" Rubbing her back again, she tried to rise.

Dax stood and walked around the desk, reaching out his hand to help Rachel up. Drawing her up next to him, he settled an arm across her shoulders.

"They never have gotten along. Rubbed each other wrong from the beginning and it's never changed." Studying her face, he stroked a hand down her cheek, cupping her chin. "You look tired, sweetheart. Might do you good to lie down for a while."

Covering his hand with hers, she laughed. "When have I ever taken a nap in the middle of the day?"

Directing her out of the study and into the living room, he looked out the window, seeing their almost two-year-old son, Patrick, running around while Lydia watched him, holding her infant son, Joshua. "Seems to me you took a few naps before Patrick was born. Lydia will watch him, and Ginny will be over in a bit to help out." Leaning down, he placed a kiss on the tip of her nose.

"You know Ginny's about as far along as me. Luke said she may start staying with us in a few weeks."

Dax nodded. "He told me. It's a good idea. Most of the men at the other ranch house are out with the cattle each day. There's no one around if the baby decides to come."

Dax and Rachel lived in the original ranch house, while Luke and Ginny lived in the house they'd purchased, along with the Tolbert ranch, after King Tolbert died. His cook and housekeeper now worked for Suzanne and Nick Barnett at the boardinghouse in town, leaving no one at the ranch house with Ginny when Luke left each morning.

Continuing to stare out the window, Rachel watched as Dirk rode off, tipping his hat to Lydia.

"There's so much about Dirk we don't know."

Dax glanced down at her, his brows furrowed. "Such as?"

"He worked for King Tolbert as a foreman before staying on to work for us. Besides that, I know he was a captain in the Union Cavalry, but nothing else."

Shrugging, Dax watched as the man disappeared down the trail. "Not much else you need to know. He works hard and keeps to himself. A lot of people are the same, especially those who fought in the war. If Dirk ever wants to share his past with us, he will." Turning her toward the stairs, he accompanied her to their bedroom, giving her a kiss and a slight nudge. "Get some rest. Ginny will wake you when she arrives."

Dirk stayed alert, eyes vigilant as he rode back to the main herd. He'd be thankful when Bull finished his obligations in town and was back at the ranch. A talented designer, Gabe Evans and Nick Barnett had asked him to plan the new clinic, which meant he spent his time in town most days. With spring coming, the men Bull hired would start building, allowing him to spend more time at the ranch.

At first, Dirk had no interest in sharing the foreman job with someone else. As he'd gotten to know Bull, he'd changed his mind. They worked well as a team, their individual skills complementing each other. It helped that Bull had served as a lieutenant in the Union Army and was a crack shot, a role Dirk admired, even if his friend seldom mentioned it. Other than Dax and Luke, there wasn't another man at Redemption's Edge he'd want guarding his back.

Reaching the herd, he spotted two longtime ranch hands. Tat Whalen and Johnny Grove had been with the Pelletiers almost as long as Bull. Dirk guessed both to be somewhere between twenty-five and thirty, but never considered asking. They worked hard, played harder, and along with Travis Davis, were the best wranglers on the ranch.

"Boss." Tat rode up, slipping his hat off to run a hand through his hair.

"Dax wants us to merge the cattle into two herds in the pastures closest to the house. We'll be tripling the night guards, and I want extra men posted during the day.”

“I’ll tell Johnny and the others.” Tat swiped an arm across his forehead. “You know, Boss, ten head isn’t a lot to lose in a herd this size.”

Dirk glared at him, remembering a similar comment by Dax. “Missing cattle means less profit for the ranch and less need for men like us. We either find where they’ve wandered off to or figure out what happened.”

Setting his hat back on his head, Tat nodded. “We can circle around again, maybe pick up tracks we didn’t see on our first try.”

“Take Johnny and two others. I’ll handle getting the herds moved while you boys search.”

Tat nodded, reining his horse around. “We’ll get right on it.”

Watching him ride off, Dirk wondered if Dax and Tat were right. Maybe he was making too big an issue over ten head in a herd of several hundred.

He’d been a trusting soul before the war, believing people were basically good and tried to do right by others. Like most who’d served the North or South, he returned home with a more jaded perspective. Watching death and destruction on a daily basis would change anyone. He still looked for the good in people, but wasn’t surprised when they failed him.

Dirk hadn't been back in Pennsylvania long before his entire life changed. Trust transformed to cynicism, forcing him to make the hard decision to move west. He'd briefly worked for a couple other ranches before making the journey to Splendor and King Tolbert's ranch. When he died and the Pelletiers took over, Dirk wasn't sure he'd stay. A few months working for Dax and Luke solidified his decision. Although both served the South, Dax as a general, Dirk had formed an unexpected bond with them, trusting them more than many Northerners he knew back home.

Although he'd finally found a new home, it didn't change the fact he'd become skeptical of most people, trusted few men and fewer women, and discussed his past with no one. It colored the way he viewed life. When the cattle went missing, he assumed they'd been stolen. These days, he always anticipated the worst, being somewhat surprised when proven wrong.

"Hey, Boss."

Dirk blinked, clearing his mind of the depressing path his thoughts had taken, looking up to see one of the men riding up alongside him, a look of panic on his face.

"Johnny's down. His horse lost its footing and stumbled, throwing him off. Tat's with him now. Thinks he has a broken leg."

Mumbling a curse, Dirk nodded, indicating for the young rider to lead the way. The last thing he needed was one of his best men out for a few weeks or months.

Dirk barely acknowledged Rosemary as he shoved open the clinic door. "Where's Doc Worthington?" He didn't look at her as he spoke.

Rosemary's features hardened, back rigid as she clasped her hands in front of her. "He rode out for an emergency at the Murton ranch. Doctor McCord is eating his meal. I'll get him." She started to move when she heard an agonized groan, seeing two of the Pelletier men carrying Johnny into the clinic. "Good heavens. What happened?"

Dirk didn't spare her a glance. "Thrown off his horse. Broke his leg."

Pointing to the examination room, she held the door wide. "Set him on the table." She looked up. "Dirk, Clay is in Doc Worthington's house out back. Get him for me...please."

Glaring at her, he hurried out the back door, returning with the doctor a minute later. Dirk's eyes widened when he saw Rosemary bending over Johnny, using a knife to cut away the leg of his pants to expose the break.

Clay stepped up to the table. "I'll take over, Rosemary. Please get me some warm water, rags, and chloroform."

Johnny groaned, shaking his head. "No...chloroform."

Doc McCord looked down at him. "It's going to hurt like hell when I reset it."

Johnny shook his head again. "Whiskey."

Glancing up at Rosemary, Clay nodded. Grabbing it from a cupboard, she opened the bottle, holding it to Johnny's lips. She gasped when his hand shot out, gripping her wrist.

"I'll do it," Johnny rasped out, taking several big gulps before looking at Clay. "I'm ready, Doc."

"Dirk, I'll need you and the others to hold him down. Even with the whiskey, it's going to hurt. With luck, he'll pass out."

"I ain't passing out..." Johnny's voice turned to a groan when one of the men took hold of his good leg while the other helped steady the broken one. Dirk stood at the head of the table, holding down Johnny's shoulders.

Looking at each man, Clay didn't give any warning before a quick pull straightened the bone. Dirk let out a breath, certain Johnny's scream could be heard on the street before the cowboy's eyes rolled back and he passed out.

"Best for him to be out," Clay said as he and Rosemary worked on the leg. "Why don't you men wait out front? This will take a little time."

Dirk looked at the others. "Leave the wagon and you two head back. I'll wait here. And find Tat. Tell him to go ahead with what we talked about this morning."

Both nodded, walking out and shutting the door. Without asking, Dirk sat down in a chair against the wall, watching as Clay and Rosemary cleaned the injury and set the leg. Her hands were steady, eyes full of compassion as she worked, never once looking at him. Not that he wanted her to. Dirk would be happy if he never had to be anywhere around her.

"Get the laudanum, Rosemary. He's going to need it when he wakes up." Turning toward Dirk, Clay leaned a hip against the table. "It's going to be a while. Rosemary hasn't eaten. Why don't the two of you grab a meal and I'll come find you if he wakes up."

"No." They replied in unison, their rigid responses surprising Clay.

Dirk shot a look at Rosemary, seeing her glance down at her feet, then moved his gaze to Clay. "I've got business at the bank, then I'll be at the Dixie, having a drink with Nick."

"I assume you have a wagon."

"Out front. When he's ready, I'll need your help getting him in back."

Clay pulled a sheet up to cover Johnny's legs. "Bring Nick when you come back. We could use one more set of hands."

Standing, Dirk took one last look at Johnny before leaving the clinic.

Clay crossed his arms, a slight grin playing across his face. "Do you want to tell me what's going on between you and Dirk?"

Rosemary covered her surprise by turning away. "Nothing."

"Nothing? I can't remember a time you two had a normal conversation."

Tossing out the soiled rags and dumping the water down a drain, she rubbed a finger over her brow. "Does *anyone* have a normal conversation with Dirk?"

Clay's brows scrunched together, but he didn't answer.

She let out a breath. "I'm sure you've seen it. The man's obstinate, egotistical, and rude."

Chuckling, he straightened, dropping his hands to his sides. "Except for rude, I would believe you were talking about most of the men in Splendor."

Her face flushed, knowing Clay had a point. Rosemary didn't know why she had such a strong reaction to Dirk. Every time she saw him, ice formed in her stomach, her chest squeezing until it became hard to breathe. All she wanted was to live a peaceful life, visit her brother and Rachel at the ranch, learn nursing, and forget about her past. His presence pushed it all aside, creating tension she didn't need.

"Your relationship with Dirk is none of my business, Rosemary." Washing his hands, he grabbed a towel. "Go ahead and eat. I'll stay with Johnny."

"I'll be over at McCall's. Betts wanted me to try her new potpie recipe." She smiled over her shoulder. "If it's good, I'll bring you back one."

Stepping into the afternoon chill, she wrapped the shawl around her, crossing the street to McCall's. The small restaurant was owned by Betts Jones and her husband. Most townsfolk still tended to gravitate to Suzanne's boardinghouse for regular meals, or the St. James Hotel for fancier fare. Rosemary loved Suzanne, but often preferred the quiet atmosphere of McCall's.

Entering, she glanced around, her gaze lighting on the one person she didn't want to see. Turning to leave, she stopped at the familiar deep voice.

"Don't leave because of me."

Shifting back around, she steeled herself to face him. Standing, Dirk pulled out a chair at his table, gesturing for her to sit down.

Sighing, Rosemary saw no way to gracefully refuse, not with the other diners staring between them. Walking toward him, her eyes sparked, a grim smile on her face.

“All right, but my presence just might spoil your appetite.”

Chapter Two

Dirk tossed the frayed rope into a pile in the corner of the barn, muttering under his breath as he ran a hand through his thick, dark hair. Slamming his hat onto his head, he stared out the doors leading to a large corral, unaware he wasn't alone.

"Are you talking to me, Boss?" Tat set his saddle on a rack a few feet away.

Shaking his head, Dirk scrubbed a hand down his face. It had been a mistake inviting Rosemary to join him at McCall's. She'd been right. Her presence had spoiled his appetite.

Three days had passed since he'd returned with Johnny in the back of the wagon and he still couldn't push the bad decision out of his mind. They'd sat there like total strangers, him doing his best to start a conversation, her ignoring every word. After a couple attempts, he got the message.

Shoving down their meals in silence, she returned to the clinic and he headed for the Dixie, anger simmering as he headed for the bar. Two shots of whiskey hadn't improved his mood.

"How's Johnny doing?"

Tat lowered his lean body onto a well-used bench, stretching his long legs in front of him. "As you'd expect. Furious at himself, his horse, and everyone else right now. He hates being laid up.

Can't say as I blame him." Grinning, he shook his head. "He can't stop talking about Rosemary, though."

Dirk shifted, focusing all his attention on Tat. "What do you mean?"

"It's no mystery, Boss. She's turned into a beautiful woman with a passion for helping others. I might just consider courting her myself."

A low growl escaping, Dirk took the few steps to stand in front of Tat. Crossing his arms, he looked down at him, noting the cowboy's eyes widen. "I don't need you, Johnny, or any of the other men filling your heads with any ideas about Rosemary. You focus on work here at the ranch and keep away from her." Turning, he picked up another frayed rope, seeming to study the damage before tossing it on top of the pile. "Bull came into the Dixie while I was in town. He knows we're looking for a few men to get us through the spring and summer. He'll pass word around."

Standing, Tat walked toward the door, looking back at Dirk. "You're the boss here and I respect that, but don't go thinking you can tell me or any of the men what women we can or can't see. Just because you two can't tolerate each other doesn't mean Rosemary isn't a fine woman." He didn't wait for a response before heading in the direction of the bunkhouse.

Staring after him, Dirk's anger rose another notch as he mumbled a string of curses.

"Should I come back later?"

He'd been so intent on Tat's comments, he hadn't noticed Rachel enter the barn, hands clasped in front of her. "Apologies, ma'am," he breathed out, steadying his nerves. "Were you looking for me?"

Taking a few steps toward him, she nodded. "I thought it might be best to have Johnny stay in the house until Doctor McCord comes out and says he can move around. We have crutches ready, but he's still having a hard time leveraging himself up. Between me, Ginny, and Rosemary, we can watch after him for a few days."

"Rosemary?" Dirk smirked. "I thought she was staying at the boardinghouse."

"Bull's bringing her back this afternoon for a few days while Dax and Luke ride over to Big Pine. My uncle or Clay will send word if they need her. We all talked about it when Dax took me into town yesterday. With both me and Ginny pregnant, and Lydia caring for baby Joshua, Dax and Luke feel better having Rosemary close by."

A muscle quivered at his jaw, but he didn't comment.

Seeing the pile of rope, Rachel picked up a piece, holding it out to Dirk. "There's no reason Rosemary can't work on these while she's here. As I recall, Tat was teaching her how to repair them before she started to learn nursing. I'm sure he'd be willing to work with her again."

"I'll teach her." He grimaced, not knowing why he'd made the offer.

She bit her lip to stifle a grin. "That's a fine offer, Dirk. I'm just not certain Rosemary would be willing to learn from you. Tat might be a better choice."

His brows slanted into a frown. Rachel didn't have to explain further for Dirk to pick up her meaning. Seemed everyone knew he and Rosemary were always at odds, avoiding each other as much as possible.

Pushing his hat back from his forehead, he nodded. "You may be right. I'll talk to one of the men about helping her." He purposely avoided mentioning Tat, having no desire to stoke a fire already simmering between the ranch hand and Rosemary. "I'm heading out again to check on the herd."

"I understand the men found six of the strays."

He let out a breath. "They did, plus the remains of another one. Who knows what happened to the rest."

"They still might show up." Tossing the frayed rope onto the pile, she turned to leave, then stopped. "Would you mind having a couple of the men help Johnny to the house? I'd like to get him settled before supper."

Touching a finger to the brim of his hat, he nodded. "I'll talk to them before I ride out."

Walking to the corral, he retrieved his horse, making short work of saddling Banshee before leading him to the bunkhouse. Giving the men Rachel's message, Dirk mounted the impressive stallion that had been his constant companion since joining the cavalry. He had every intention of using the beautiful horse as a stud when the war ended, seeing him as the cornerstone of his and his brother's breeding program.

Instead, Dirk found himself riding the stallion across country, wearing his bitterness like a second skin as he traveled through one state, then another. Taking the job with King Tolbert had been a temporary reprieve before continuing to California, a state full of disenchanted dreamers and those seeking a new life.

Accepting a foreman job with the Pelletiers after Tolbert's death had been the one good thing to come out of the last few years, and he meant to hold onto it with both hands.

Dirk had done his best to set aside his distrust and cynicism, yet they continued to haunt him until he accepted they were as much a part of him as the air he breathed. Unlike most men on the ranch, he had no further desire for the dreams of his youth. Love, marriage, and a family no longer mattered. A warm bunk, decent food, and bosses he respected were what kept him going, not the recurring images of a feisty, long-haired beauty he'd never allow himself to trust.

"Are you and Doc Worthington certain you won't need me for a few days?" Rosemary hesitated next to the door, looking at Clay McCord, as Bull waited on the boardwalk.

"It's more important for you to be with Rachel and Ginny while Dax and Luke are out of town. We'll be fine until you return."

"Well, as long as you're sure."

"I am. You're needed at the ranch, and I'm certain you'd like some time to see your brother. It's been a couple weeks since you've been back, right?"

"Almost three." Three weeks of being in town without her brother—or the uncomfortable encounters with Dirk. She missed Ben, but not the surly ranch foreman. Seeing him earlier in the week had turned into another disaster, the same as always when the two of them were anywhere near each other.

She didn't understand why her throat constricted, chest tightened, and stomach clenched with each encounter. No other man affected her the same way.

"Are you ready, Rosemary?"

Startling at Bull's voice, she turned to see him waiting by the door. "Yes, I'm ready. I'll be back in a few days, Doctor."

Standing, Clay walked toward her. "Take whatever time you need."

Grabbing the bag from her hand, Bull set it in the back of the wagon, helping her onto the seat. Checking the reins of his horse tied to the back, he climbed in beside her.

"I bet you're anxious to see Ben." Slapping the lines, he turned the wagon toward Redemption's Edge. "I know he misses you."

"I miss him, too. I'm trying to save enough money for a horse so I can ride out to see him more often."

Bull shifted in the seat, his gaze narrowing on her. "There's no need to buy one. You can use any of the extra horses at the ranch any time you want."

Clasping her hands in her lap, she lifted her chin. "I don't want to impose."

Bull let out an exasperated snort. "You wouldn't be imposing on anyone, Rosemary. Ask Dirk which horse to take and he or one of the boys will saddle it for you."

"No."

Slapping the lines to get the wagon moving along, he glanced at her. "No?"

"No. I don't need Dirk's help. If it's all right to use one of the horses, I can take care of the tack myself."

"Of course you can...for one of the mares or smaller geldings. What if the only horse available is one of the bigger geldings? You'll need help with the saddle, even if you can take care of the bridle."

She looked at him. "Rachel and Ginny don't need anyone's help."

Bull's mouth curved into a smile. "Of course they do. Besides, there's no sense being stubborn about it when there are people to help." Leaning back in the seat, his smile widened. "Sounds to me like you don't want *Dirk's* help. I'm guessing you wouldn't refuse anyone else's. Am I right?"

Crossing her arms, Rosemary's lips twisted into a grim smile. "Maybe."

They rode in silence a few minutes, Bull thinking over her reluctance to speak with Dirk. Turning the last corner, he heard her sharp intake of breath when the ranch house and barn came into view.

"It's only been three weeks, yet I'd forgotten how beautiful it is out here."

Bull nodded. "Different from being in Splendor. I like the work I'm doing for Gabe and Nick, but I'm ready to get back to ranching."

Her eyes lit up at the look of anticipation on his face. "I'm sure you're more than ready to be closer to Lydia and Joshua."

Smiling, he slapped the lines once more. "That I am."

"Here's the roast, Rosemary." Rachel handed her the platter of sliced meat, wiping her hands down the apron, glancing out the kitchen window to see Patrick playing quietly in the dirt. "Seems we'll have a full table tonight."

Rosemary grinned. "I'm sure it's always full."

"Luke and I are here almost every night." Ginny leaned against the table, a hand on her expanding belly. "I love it when Bull and Lydia come over. Will Dirk be here tonight, Rachel?"

Rosemary stiffened. "I thought he'd ridden out to stay with the herd."

"To *check* on the herd." Rachel set a bowl of potatoes on the table, looking around. "Where are the others?"

An instant later, the front door opened, Bull standing aside to allow Lydia, holding a sleeping Joshua, to step past him.

"It smells wonderful in here," Lydia said as Dax and Luke followed them inside. She handed Joshua to Bull. "I'm going to see if I can help Rachel."

Dax started toward the kitchen. "I'd better find Patrick and get him cleaned up for supper."

Luke clasped Bull on the shoulder. "I heard you're almost done in town."

Shifting Joshua in his arms, he nodded. "The men start laying the foundation next week. I found a real good man from back east to supervise the construction. If he's as skilled as I think, I'll only have to ride to town once a week to check on the progress. It'll be good to get back to my *real* job."

Luke watched Bull stroke the cheek of his infant son, feeling his chest squeeze. He and Ginny had tried to have a child before, only to lose it a few months into the pregnancy. She'd gone longer this time, and every day he prayed they'd have a healthy child.

"Dirk's ready for your return. Even with Dax and me helping out, there's a lot of ground to cover on a ranch this size. I guess he told you we need a few more men."

Bull nodded. "I put the word out in town. I thought we might be able to use John and Joe Smith, but Beau's going to need them at his place."

"Aren't they working for Caro at her place?" Luke asked.

"For another few weeks, then they'll be at Beau's. With Beau and Caro marrying in a few weeks, they'll be combining their properties. Might even need more men if Beau decides to run a full herd of cattle."

Scratching his jaw, Luke's brows furrowed in a thoughtful expression. "We may need to look for men farther out. Dax and I leave tomorrow morning for Big Pine. We'll pass the word around there."

"Supper's ready." Ginny walked toward Luke, reaching up to kiss his cheek. "Rachel's made enough for the entire ranch. Hope you're both hungry."

"Starving." Luke put an arm around his wife, escorting her to the table.

Everyone took their seats, waiting as Dax got Patrick settled next to him, then said a prayer.

"Please, don't wait." Rachel reached for the bowl of potatoes, handing it to Rosemary as the front door opened.

"Sorry I'm late."

Rosemary's stomach knotted at the sound of the familiar voice. Scooping out a small portion of potatoes, her hand shook as she handed the bowl to Bull. Taking it, his gaze narrowed on her, his mouth tilting up in an encouraging smile.

"We didn't know if you were going to stay with the herd or come back this evening." Dax nodded to the empty chair next to Rosemary.

Dirk's footsteps faltered, spotting Rosemary for the first time. Hesitating, he glanced at Rachel. "You sure there's enough for one more?"

"There's more than enough," Rachel replied. "Sit down and fill your plate."

Pulling out a chair, he edged it as far away from Rosemary as possible before taking a seat. Piling food onto his plate, he did his best to ignore the woman next to him, preferring to concentrate on filling his empty stomach.

"I heard you found some of the strays," Bull said.

"Six alive and one dead. Don't know about the others, but we'll keep looking. The men are doing a count each day, and I'm still keeping extra guards posted." He shoveled a forkful of meat into his mouth, chewing slowly.

"You missed the biscuits, Dirk." Ginny passed the bowl to Rosemary, who reluctantly handed it to Dirk, her fingers brushing his hand. An immediate and unfamiliar sensation passed through her when he took the bowl, touching her arm before he jerked his hand away.

"Do you still need the extra men?" Bull asked.

"We will if the meetings in Big Pine go well." Dax looked at Luke. "There's no reason to think they won't."

"We're meeting with a buyer from the army and another from Salt Lake City," Luke said. "Agreements with either would mean shorter drives than taking the herd to Omaha."

"I'm all in favor of shorter drives." Bull covered Lydia's hand.

"We'd all like that, as long as the terms are acceptable." Luke leaned back in his chair, draping an arm across Ginny's shoulders. "What do you think, Dirk?"

Setting down his fork, he glanced across the table at Luke. "Whatever's best for the ranch."

Rosemary snorted, drawing everyone's attention, especially Dirk's.

"What?" He glared at her, his jaw tensing.

She looked at her lap, shaking her head. "Nothing."

Dirk turned to face her. "If you've got something to say, then say it."

Glancing up, she felt her face heat as all eyes seemed fixed on her. Swallowing, she lifted her chin, giving Dirk a bland expression, keeping her voice low.

"I think everyone wants what's best for the ranch, Dirk."

"And?"

Rosemary bit her lip, wishing she'd kept her mouth closed. "Well, I believe Luke asked you for your opinion, not for you to tell him what he already knows."

Ginny covered her mouth with a hand, while Rachel glanced at Dax and back at Rosemary, her eyes dancing in amusement.

Crossing his arms, Dirk leaned back in his seat, a slight smirk on his face. "Is that so?"

"Well...yes."

"Fair enough." He looked at Luke. "If you're asking for my opinion, I'd have to say until I hear the terms they're offering, there's not much I can say. However, we don't know the trail to Salt Lake, but I've heard it can be tough to travel over the mountains. I've also heard the Indian tribes along the trail to Salt Lake aren't as hostile as those between here and Omaha."

Dax looked at Luke, raising a brow. "All good points, Dirk." Moving his gaze to Rosemary, his features softened. "Don't ever be embarrassed to speak what's on your mind."

She didn't dare look at Dirk, knowing she'd probably made things much worse between them.

Luke glanced between Bull and Dirk. "As soon as we have some information, we'll send a telegram with what we've learned. You reply as soon as possible, but keep in mind we want to strike a deal if either one of them makes any sense."

The men nodded their agreement as Rachel stood. "Rosemary, would you mind helping me bring out the dessert?"

She couldn't have been more relieved at the request. "Of course." Before she knew what was happening, Dirk stood, pulling out her chair. "Thank you."

He didn't respond to her quiet remark, but for the first time since she'd met him, his lopsided grin was focused on her.

Chapter Three

"The men found another carcass. That makes three in less than a month. Tat is certain we have a wolf pack attacking the herd." Dirk leaned against a stall, watching Dax groom his chestnut stallion, Hannibal, as the sun crept up the eastern sky. It was the same stallion the ex-Confederate general rode during the war against Dirk's Union troops. The fact they'd formed such a strong bond still surprised him.

"Does he have any estimate on how many are in the pack?" Dax placed the saddle on Hannibal's back, tightening the cinch.

"His guess is eight to ten, judging by the amount of time between kills." Leaning down, Dirk picked up a piece of straw, rolling it between his fingers. "We're going to need every head to fulfill the contracts you and Luke agreed to in Big Pine."

Leaning his arm against the saddle, Dax looked at him. "We'll fulfill the contracts. We already have more than enough cattle for the drive to Salt Lake, and the army doesn't want their order until late summer. There's still a chance we'll be driving a smaller herd to Omaha. Suzanne will buy a few head for the boardinghouse, as will the St. James. Next year..." His voice trailed off, his expression thoughtful. "If all goes well with these contracts, we'll need another bull to fulfill the obligations next year."

"I heard the Murtons have one they're looking to sell. Do you want me to talk to one of the brothers?"

Dax nodded. "Rosemary's ready to go back to town and I have an order you can give Noah. Afterward, you should still have time to ride out and speak with the Murtons."

Noah Brandt owned the livery and blacksmith shop. A former sharpshooter in the Union Army, he'd come to Splendor with his closest friend, Gabe Evans, the local sheriff. Following a tumultuous courtship, he'd married Abby Tolbert after her father, King Tolbert, was murdered.

"I'll have time to ride to the Murton's and get back here before dark." Dirk concealed his displeasure at spending time with Rosemary. Although the last few days had gone well, he'd spent most of his time traveling between herds and checking on the men.

"Rosemary can take one of the horses and stable it at Noah's livery. That way she can ride back here whenever she wants."

"Alone?" Dirk couldn't hide his incredulous tone.

"As long as it's light out, she should be fine."

"I don't like the idea of Rosemary going between the ranch and town without someone with her." His expression clouded. "The same as you wouldn't want Rachel or Ginny doing it."

Mounting Hannibal, Dax held the reins in his lap, looking down at Dirk. "You're right. Set up some kind of schedule so you can accompany her to town some days and back to the ranch on others."

Dirk opened his mouth to protest, shutting it when Rosemary walked into the barn. Dax reined Hannibal around, stopping next to her.

"Dirk will get your horse ready and ride to town with you. I want you to work out a schedule with him so you aren't riding back and forth alone."

"That's not necessary, Dax. I can ride alone."

His eyes narrowed as he looked at her. "You *can*, but you won't." He glanced at Dirk, noting his clenched jaw and narrowed gaze. "I need to get riding. Figure something out with Dirk." Kicking Hannibal, Dax rode out, lifting a hand when he saw Rachel standing on the front porch.

Dirk didn't wait for Rosemary to complain further before he walked out the back of the barn, a halter in his hand. He returned a few minutes later with Lydia's horse, Angel. Without speaking, he groomed and saddled her, then did the same with Banshee.

"Ready?"

Rosemary wanted to shake her head, change her mind and stay another night. It would've been an easy decision if she hadn't already been gone from the clinic several days. Nodding, she stepped up to Angel, tying her small bag behind the saddle.

Her heart pounded as her fingers fumbled with the leather ties. They had little interaction the last few days. She'd spent her time making certain Johnny was following Doc McCord's instructions, helping Rachel in the house, and visiting with Lydia and Ginny. With two pregnant women and another caring for an infant, she felt conflicted. A part of her wanted to stay, knowing they'd appreciate her help. The other, more insistent part encouraged her to flee, put as much distance between her and Dirk as possible.

"Do you need help?"

Lost in her own thoughts, she hadn't noticed Dirk approaching. Shaking her head, Rosemary placed her left foot in the stirrup and mounted.

Dirk watched until she was settled in the saddle before swinging onto Banshee's back in one effortless move. "Let's go."

Rosemary didn't mind riding alone, getting lost in her own thoughts. The solitude gave her time to think about her and Ben's future. She'd spent more time with her brother in the last few days than she had in the last few months. They sat together at breakfast, but he preferred taking his other meals with the men and the other *ranch orphans,* as the townsfolk referred to them. Homeless boys and girls who called Redemption's Edge their home. Even at twenty, Rosemary still felt like one of them. She thought of each one, a smile curving the corners of her mouth.

Jimmy and Teddy Odell were orphans who lived with Rosemary and Ben in a rundown shack outside of Splendor for months before the Pelletiers took them in. At seventeen and sixteen, they'd become like older brothers to twelve-year-old Ben.

Seventeen-year-old Sam Rinehart and thirteen-year-old Selina were Lydia's younger brother and sister who lived with her and Bull.

At eighteen, Billy Zales lived at an adjoining ranch Dax and Luke purchased from older, widowed brothers who'd decided to sell. It had become the location of their horse breeding operation run by Luke and Travis Davis. An approximate two-hour ride, Billy didn't often make it back to the main ranch to see his younger sister, ten-year-old Margaret, which meant she spent most of her time with Selina.

None of them would ever be able to repay the Pelletiers for their kindness in taking them in, making them a part of their extended family.

"I want to take a detour to check for any missing cattle."

Dirk's gruff voice cut into her daydreams, a habit she'd acquired while spending so much time worrying about the future. It was a hard habit to break.

Nodding, she followed him along a narrow trail still covered in a light dusting of snow. After a while, the trail merged with the original route, allowing enough space for them to ride next to each other.

"I thought you found all the missing cattle."

"There are always some that wander off." He kept looking around, checking for strays or other dangers. "They aren't the brightest animals in the world, but they're what keeps the ranch going."

Swallowing, she shifted in the saddle, letting out a slow breath. "Did you raise cattle back east?"

Glancing at her, he shook his head. "No."

"What did you do?"

Focusing on the trail ahead, he shrugged. "It's not important."

Catching her bottom lip between her teeth, she frowned, taking a quick sidelong glance at him. "Why would Dax and Luke hire you if you didn't have experience?"

He blew out a frustrated breath. "I had experience."

"Where?" She winced the instant the question came out.

Shifting in the saddle, he smirked. "For a woman who doesn't like me, you sure are curious."

Letting out a breath, she gripped the reins tighter. "I like you well enough."

Snorting, he focused his gaze straight ahead. "I guess that's something." They rode in silence for a short while, a question churning in Dirk's gut. "Why do you care about my background? My work at the ranch has nothing to do with you." He ground the last out, hoping his brusque voice made it clear he had no intention of sharing anything about his past.

When she didn't answer, he mumbled a grateful prayer, thankful for the silence as they covered another mile. In another minute, they'd be able to see Splendor.

"I don't know."

His brows furrowed, confused at her comment. "What?"

Lifting her chin, she glared at him. "I don't know why I'm curious about you, but I am."

His lips twisted into a wry grin. Even if he didn't trust her, Dirk appreciated the fact Rosemary always spoke her mind.

Seeing the town come into view, he exhaled a relieved breath. "Appears you'll have to hold onto your curiosity, darlin'."

"Darlin'?" she gasped, ready to lay into him until she saw Beau Davis riding toward them. "I am *not* your darlin'," she hissed out.

"No, *darlin'*. You certainly aren't."

If Beau weren't so close, she would've, well...she wasn't sure what she would've done. No man had ever called her any type of endearment, not even her father. It was always Rosemary or Rosie Girl, never sweetheart, or dearest, or…darlin'.

Smiling, Beau looked at Rosemary, touching the brim of his hat. "Ma'am, Dirk. What brings you to town?"

"I'm on my way to the clinic, Deputy." She barely glanced at Dirk as she moved Angel past Beau.

Dirk's mouth quirked into a slight grin as she rode away, appreciating how she looked in the saddle. If he were being honest, he appreciated the way she looked all the time. He'd just never let her know.

Beau looked at Dirk. "I've never known Rosemary to be quite so feisty." Pushing his hat back on his forehead, he leaned on the saddle horn. "What'd you say to her?"

Dirk shook his head. "It doesn't take much. At least not when she's around me." Shaking his head, he turned toward Beau. "Are you heading out to your ranch?"

"Not yet. I'm riding out to Redemption's Edge, then heading to Caro's place," he said, mentioning his fiancée, Caroline Iverson. "She's getting the house ready for the wedding…which can't come soon enough."

Not much for talking about weddings, deaths, or anything personal, Dirk nodded.

Beau took a quick look to see Rosemary dismount and head into the clinic before continuing in his deep, southern drawl. "Did you hear about Boyden Trask escaping?"

Dirk's head whipped toward him. "Say that again."

"Trask escaped about a week ago."

"And you waited this long to tell anyone?" Dirk mumbled a curse.

"Hell no. Gabe received the telegram yesterday. That's why I'm going to see Dax and Luke. To warn them about Trask."

"He'd be a fool to come back to Splendor, or even Big Pine. If he's running, my guess is he'd head north to Canada."

Beau snorted. "The man's already demonstrated he's not the brightest person around these parts."

"Which is why he's such a threat."

Beau nodded. "He's a vengeful sort, and Rosemary was the main witness at his trial. Nothing he does would surprise me."

Dirk rubbed his jaw, doing his best to ignore the tightening in his chest. "Including coming after Rosemary."

"There's something else, but it may not mean anything. Gabe received a letter a few months ago from a family friend in St. Louis. The man is thinking of moving his family out this way and wanted Gabe's advice." Beau paused, adjusting his grip on the reins.

Dirk lifted a brow, his mind still whirling on the news about Boyden Trask escaping. "What'd it say?"

"Seems there's been a string of murders following a path from Boston to St. Louis."

A muscle in Dirk's jaw twitched, his throat thickening as a ball of ice formed in his stomach.

Beau continued, not noticing his friend's reaction. "We didn't think much about it when the first letter arrived. Murders occur all the time. A second letter arrived a few days ago from the same friend. He'd traveled to Kansas City on business, learning another murder, similar to the others, had occurred. He met with a friend who works for Pinkerton. The agent believes all the killings are connected." Beau drew in a breath. "Young women in their early twenties go missing. Their bodies are found a week or more later." He scrubbed a hand down his face. "They were all tortured before being strangled."

Dirk cursed under his breath. "Does Gabe think whoever is doing this is headed our way?"

"He has no idea. Kansas City is a long way from Splendor. If the murders are connected, the odds whoever is doing this would travel our way instead of west or south are pretty slim. If he's after young women, there are bigger towns elsewhere."

Dirk nodded, although he didn't share Beau's optimism at Splendor being too far away to attract a killer. "Does Gabe plan to spread the word around town?"

"Not about the murders, but Cash, Mack, and Caleb are letting people know about Trask." He mentioned the other deputies. "They'll also be riding to warn people outside of town." Beau looked at him, his face grim. "We're taking the news of Trask seriously. Not much we can do about what's happening back east. No need to panic everyone when the murders are hundreds of miles away."

"I'm headed out to speak with the Murtons. I'll stop at the jail and tell Gabe that I'll let them know about Trask, although they're a good distance outside of Splendor." Dirk would do what he promised Dax—talk to the Murtons about their bull. What he wanted to do was plant himself outside the clinic to make certain if Trask came back to Splendor, he got nowhere near Rosemary. For a woman he didn't particularly like, he couldn't push aside the overwhelming need to protect her.

"Appreciate it, Dirk. I'd better get going." Beau reined his horse north, taking the trail toward Redemption's Edge.

Watching until he disappeared around a bend, Dirk rode into Splendor, pausing outside the clinic, wrestling with the idea of going inside to warn Rosemary. Deciding the news could wait until after he met with the Murtons, he rode on.

Leaving Banshee outside the jail, he glanced around, a sense of foreboding washing over him. Boyden Trask might not be the smartest criminal, but he had a long memory and a heart for vengeance. No doubt the man had a list of those he blamed for his fall from respected businessman to convicted felon, coercing Rosemary, Ben, Jimmy, and Teddy into committing crimes, with him as the sole beneficiary.

It was Rosemary's testimony that persuaded the jury to sentence him to time in the territorial prison. He'd screamed out his anger as the deputies hauled him out of the Wild Rose, the saloon used as the courthouse until the town could build one. His protests about believing the word of a girl over his fell on a jury of twelve men already convinced of his guilt.

Trask hadn't helped his cause by defending himself, expressing his indignation with vulgar outbursts and deranged ramblings. By the time the judge pounded the gavel, indicating the time had come for deliberations, everyone had witnessed the man's crazed eyes and belligerent attitude. It would've been a shock if the verdict had come back as anything except guilty.

Shoving open the door of the jail, Dirk spotted Gabe standing in the corner where an old stove kept a perpetual pot of thick coffee ready for anyone who entered. Glancing over his shoulder, the sheriff nodded at him.

"You must have heard the news."

Dirk nodded, lowering himself into one of the chairs across from where Gabe sat down behind his desk.

"I saw Beau on his way out to see Dax and Luke. What are your plans for protecting Rosemary?"

Gabe blew across the hot liquid in his cup before taking a sip, wincing at the bitter taste. "We have a number of young women to protect in Splendor, not just Rosemary." His mind had gone straight to his younger half-sister, a woman he hadn't met until months before. Nora Reeser Evans journeyed to Splendor at the insistence of their father, a man who'd betrayed Gabe's mother by having an affair not long after Gabe's birth. Nora's mother had been unaware of his married status, believing his words of love.

Dirk shook his head. "I'm talking about Trask, not some lunatic killer who may never find his way to Splendor."

"I have nothing new on Trask. He escaped, but hasn't been seen since." Gabe set down his cup, leaning his arms on the desk. "Do you honestly believe he'd be foolish enough to come back this way? He must know we'll be watching for him."

"What I *know* is he's not right in the head. A man like him will do anything for revenge, and we both know Rosemary is who he'd come after."

"I agree. My advice is she stay at the ranch until we hear more about Trask. I've sent telegrams to lawmen I know in Idaho, Wyoming, and the Dakotas. He'll show his face somewhere."

Dirk rubbed his chin. "Rosemary won't take well to being told she should stay at the ranch. She's serious about her work at the clinic."

"Guess it all depends on how big a target she wants to be. Even Trask isn't stupid enough to go after her at a ranch where she's surrounded by people who'll protect her." Standing, Gabe picked up his cup, opening the back door to the jail. Tossing the contents outside, he turned toward Dirk. "You or one of the ranch hands could escort her to town each morning."

"Dax already has me doing that," Dirk grumbled, his mouth forming a thin line. "He wants her close by if Rachel or Ginny need her."

Gabe nodded, understanding the protective nature of the Pelletiers, as well as most families in Splendor. "Trask knows she works at the clinic."

Standing, Dirk's jaw tensed. That was where Trask found her the day Gabe and a few other men had set a trap for the man. Dirk had been one of the men.

"Trask won't get to her again, Gabe. You have my word on that."

49

Chapter Four

Omaha, Nebraska

"Hear that?" The older ranch hand leaned forward in his saddle, trying to hear the sound again, stroking his graying stubble.

The man beside him lifted a brow, nodding. "Seems we found the missing cattle."

Reining their horses in the direction of the bawling animals, they rode through thick brush before finding the ten head of cattle they'd been searching for all morning huddled around a small pond, oblivious to their arrival.

"They're all here. The boss will be real happy about this. Let's get them back with the rest of the herd." The older man circled to the right while the other ranch hand cut through thick brush to the left of the cattle.

"Ah hell." The younger man reined to a stop. Dismounting, he took a few cautious steps, getting a better look at the crumpled form covered in dirt. "You'd better come see this," he yelled in the direction his friend had ridden. Pulling away several fallen branches, the man's face blanched before he turned away, retching into the bushes.

"We need to get…" The gruff voice faded away as he stopped next to the other horse. Sliding to the ground, the older man's eyes widened. "Good Lord," he breathed out, his stomach rebelling at the sight of what appeared to be the body of a young woman. "Looks like someone beat her before she died."

"Before she was murdered, you mean." The younger of the two wiped a sleeve across his mouth. "What should we do?"

"I'll grab a blanket. We'll wrap up the body, then take her to the boss."

"Are we leaving the cattle?"

The older man untied the blanket from behind his saddle, closing his eyes for a moment before turning back to look at the body, letting out a pent-up breath. "Nope. We get them back with the herd, then find the boss."

Splendor

"Excellent work, Rosemary. I'll talk to the family while you finish in here." Clay McCord dried his hands, tossing the towel on the counter before heading for the waiting room.

Pausing until the door clicked shut behind him, she looked down at the face of the boy who'd fallen off a ladder, breaking his leg below the knee. Still sleeping from the effects of the chloroform, Rosemary took a moment to study his serene features, allowing herself to wonder what it would be like to have a family of her own. Rarely did she let her mind wander to such frivolous thoughts. Lately, though, they'd come a little more often.

Until the Pelletiers had taken her, Ben, and the Odell boys in, her dreams had consisted of keeping everyone safe, scavenging enough food for the four to make it through one more day. Rosemary seldom worried about those things now.

Brushing hair off his forehead, she used a damp cloth to finish cleaning his face before organizing the instruments Clay had used to set the leg, hearing the child's soft moan. Reaching for a bottle in the cupboard, she poured some of the liquid into a small container. Neither Clay nor Doc Worthington were comfortable administering laudanum to children. In this case, however, Clay decided the pain would be too great for the boy to bear without help.

Finishing her task, her gaze moved to the closed door as it creaked open, Clay walking in.

"Dirk is out front to escort you back to the ranch. I'll finish with the boy."

She grimaced, shaking her head. "I'm going to stay at the boardinghouse tonight."

Clay shook his head. "You'd better let Dirk know. He seems set on taking you back with him."

Her brows furrowing, lips drawing into a thin line, she wiped her suddenly damp palms down the front of her skirt. Steeling herself for the battle to come, she took one more look at the sleeping boy before confronting Dirk.

Closing the door behind her, she spotted him leaning against a wall, his arms crossed, features unreadable. Casting a brief smile at the boy's family, she nodded for Dirk to follow her outside. Not allowing him an instant to talk, she whirled around to look up at him.

"I'm staying at Suzanne's tonight."

He glared down at her. "Afraid that won't happen tonight, or any night soon. Get what you need and let's get going."

Refusing to budge, she crossed her arms. "Are you deaf? I said I'm staying at the boardinghouse tonight."

Glancing around, he reached out to grasp her elbow, drawing her into the narrow passageway between the buildings.

"Let go of me." Struggling against his hold, Rosemary gave up when his hand tightened.

"Calm down. There's been a change. I've got news you aren't going to like." Dropping his hand, he took another look toward the boardwalk.

She rubbed her arm, not because of any pain he'd inflicted, but to rid herself of the strange feeling his touch caused. "I already don't like the way you're treating me."

"This is worse, sweetheart."

"I am not..." Her voice trailed off when he held up a hand.

"Boyden Trask escaped."

His comment stalled any further complaints, her jaw dropping. "Escaped?"

"Gabe got the news yesterday that he escaped a week ago."

Placing a hand on her stomach, she forced away the ball of dread lodged in her throat, refusing to voice her fear.

Dirk's eyes softened. "No one knows where he went, Rosemary. He may be hundreds of miles away by now."

She looked up at him, trying to control the trembling in her voice. "You don't believe that or you wouldn't be insisting I return to the ranch."

There'd be no point in scaring her further by telling her he believed Trask would seek revenge on Rosemary and the boys before leaving the territory. "I'm a cautious man, as are Dax and Luke. We can keep you safe while you're at the ranch, and Gabe will make sure someone's watching for Trask while you're at the clinic. He knows you've stayed at the boardinghouse. If you go back there, you'll be putting yourself and Suzanne at risk. Is that what you want?"

She couldn't dispute his logic. Trask would have no qualms about using Suzanne to get to her. Rosemary also believed Suzanne wouldn't hesitate to place her own life in danger to save a friend. Shaking her head, her shoulders slumped as she let out a slow breath.

"Let me get my coat."

A slight scowl crossed his face. "The horses are in front of the clinic. If we hurry, we'll have time to reach the ranch before sundown."

Nodding before turning away, her eyes reflected the fear he knew she wanted to keep hidden.

Dirk felt an unfamiliar wave of relief when she failed to fight him any further. What bothered him most was his body's reaction to her. He didn't like the way his breath caught at the sight of her slender hips swaying in the soft cotton dress, or the way his chest tightened, his protective instincts flaring when he saw her bottom lip tremble at the news of Trask's escape. He told himself he'd feel the same if any woman were threatened, especially one included in the Pelletier family. The catch in his heart told him he might just be fooling himself.

Omaha

"The telegram from St. Louis confirmed the injuries to their victim are much the same as the ones inflicted on this young woman." The aging doctor pointed to a series of cuts along the arms and legs, then looked up at his younger colleague. "I witnessed a good many atrocities during the war, but I've never seen anything like this."

"This, my friend, is nothing less than torture." Looking closer at the injuries, the younger doctor shook his head before straightening. "Does the sheriff know who she is?"

"Thinks she's the daughter of a farmer a few miles north of here. Recognized her from church. He has a deputy riding out to talk to the man and his missus."

"You said there were other cases like this one and the one in St. Louis."

"The Pinkerton agent told the sheriff he knows of at least four others, starting in Boston. There could be more. All with the same strange pattern of cuts on the arms and legs. All strangled and left to the elements. No one should die like this."

"Wish there was more we could do."

"It's up to the Pinkerton agent and the law to find out who's murdering these young women."

The younger man rubbed his jaw, his gaze focusing on a series of cuts on the right arm. Leaning closer, he traced a finger over the slashes.

"It's as if whoever did this is leaving a clue."

Tugging at his graying beard, the elderly doctor's eyes narrowed. "What do you mean?"

Pointing to the right arm, the younger man traced the cuts. "I think whoever did this is spelling out a word. Can you make out what it says?"

Adjusting his spectacles and holding his beard out of the way, the doctor leaned closer, his brows scrunching in concentration. "Well, now that you mention it, this right here might be the letter O, or maybe a D. The rest just looks like random scratches to me. Probably should let the sheriff know. He said to tell him about anything we found."

"It's not much, but it could be a start at finding the man responsible." Pulling the cover over the woman's face, the young doctor thought of his wife. Not much older than the deceased, with hair a similar shade of wheat blonde, he thanked God it wasn't her lying on this table. "Let me study these a little longer, then I'll get the sheriff."

Patting his colleague's shoulder, the older doctor turned to leave. "Take as much time as you want. This young woman has nowhere else to go."

Moosejaw, Montana

The man's hand trembled as he lifted the glass of whiskey to his lips and took a sip. His stomach clenched in hunger. He hoped the amber liquid would ease the emptiness for a couple more hours.

His ill-fitting, tattered clothes fit right in with the others in the ramshackle bar on the eastern frontier of Montana. The tin sound of the piano and raucous laughter at a few tables reminded him of any of the hundreds of small frontier towns scattered around the western region of the country.

"Don't know that I've seen you in here before."

Taking one more sip, he glanced at the stranger sitting next to him at the bar. "First time in town." His gaze moved lower, noticing the tarnished badge. He didn't worry too much about being recognized. The wanted poster showed him clean-shaven with short hair. The scraggly beard and hair below his collar rendered him unrecognizable to even his closest friends. He snorted at the thought, unable to think of one person he could call a friend.

"Something funny?"

Glancing at the lawman, he shook his head. Downing the last of the whiskey, he set the empty glass on the bar, turning to face the door. "You know of anyone hiring?" He needed money for food. His belly couldn't tolerate another meal of roasted squirrel.

The lawman studied him a little closer, coming to some conclusion. "Not much here in Moosejaw. If you're headed east, there might be work in Bloody Basin."

"How far?"

"Twenty miles, in the Dakota Territory."

Too far on an empty stomach. Still, he nodded. "Thanks. I guess I'll be heading east."

Stepping into the afternoon sun, he pushed his hat lower on his forehead. He had no intention of riding east. His goal was to reach Splendor by the end of the week. Unless he could shoot a rabbit, it looked like another night of roasted squirrel.

Redemption's Edge

Rosemary clenched her hands in front of her, fuming as she paced back and forth in the living room of the Pelletier home, waiting for Dax and Luke to finish talking with Dirk. She knew he had news about the bull they wanted to purchase from the Murtons. Even so, she thought Trask's escape was more important than anything else.

He wasn't a man to forget the smallest slight. She'd heard of him shooting one of his men when the man had questioned one of Trask's orders. As the main witness against him at his trial, she'd been the focus of his hateful gaze for hours, feeling a slight bit of relief when the jury had found him guilty. The hateful gaze had turned to deadly rage, a vengeful promise in his eyes, telling her she'd never be safe as long as Trask lived. In her heart, Rosemary knew his hate wasn't focused only on her. His twisted mind would seek revenge on all those he believed had betrayed him, including Ben, Jimmy, and Teddy.

"Rosemary?"

Turning, she smiled as Rachel approached with cups of tea. "Sorry. My mind was somewhere else."

"I heard Dirk mention Trask before the men went into the office. Do you have news on him?" Rachel motioned for her to sit down next to her on the sofa. Leaning forward, Rachel stuffed a small pillow behind her back.

"Gabe received news he escaped."

"That isn't good. I imagine they're searching for him."

Rosemary shook her head. "During the ride from town, Dirk told me Gabe doesn't believe there's a search. They're sending word to the lawmen in the territories, including Montana, Idaho, and the Dakotas, to keep watch for him." Her hand trembled as she held the cup to her mouth. "I'm worried he'll come after the boys."

"It's more likely he'll come after you, Rosemary. It might be best if you stay here at the ranch until he's captured."

"What will the doctors do without either one of us?"

Rachel chuckled. "As much as it's hard to admit, I'm certain they'll do fine. My uncle was here by himself for several years before I came west. Now he has Clay. Although I'm certain they'll deny it, those men can handle things without us. Remember, most small towns don't even have one doctor. We're fortunate to have two."

Rosemary let out a breath. "I suppose."

Rachel reached out, placing a hand on her arm. "Ginny and I can use you here. Our babies could come at any time."

Biting her lower lip, Rosemary looked at her. "I've only assisted with two births."

"If Ginny's baby comes first and neither of the doctors are available, I can tell you what to do."

Her lips twisted into a grim smile. "And if your baby comes first?"

"Then I'll have to stay calm enough to talk you through it."

Rosemary's eyes crinkled at the corners. "I've never known you to be anything except calm."

"That's because you weren't around for Patrick's birth." Rachel looked up when the door to the study opened.

Dax walked over, holding out a hand to help his wife up, then doing the same for Rosemary. "We should all talk."

Waiting until the ladies were seated, Dax began. "Dirk told us the news about Boyden Trask. Until he's caught, we need to decide how best to keep Rosemary and the boys safe."

Dirk didn't wait to voice his opinion. "She should stay at the ranch."

After speaking with Rachel, Rosemary believed it would be best to stay at the ranch. Still, the fact Dirk was trying to force the decision on her thrust her anger to the surface.

She glared at Dirk, then looked at Dax. "What about my work at the clinic?"

"We know how important your work is to you, Rosemary, but we have to do what we think is best to keep you and the boys safe. I'll speak with Doc Worthington. I'm certain he and Clay will understand." Dax glanced at Rachel before returning his gaze to Rosemary. "You know, we'd all feel more comfortable with you here. The herds are closer to the house, which means we can spare a couple men to stay here during the day. Plus, all the men will be alerted to what's happening. It's doubtful Trask could get within a hundred yards of the house."

"You shouldn't have to go to so much trouble for me, Dax. It isn't right."

Luke stood, walking to the window, looking toward the barn. "The fact Trask may be coming after you isn't fair, either. It's the way life is and we're prepared to do whatever it takes to keep everyone safe. No matter the skill of Gabe and his deputies, it isn't as easy to protect you in town."

Rachel looked at Dax. "Johnny's leg is healing, but he won't be able to ride for a few more weeks. As far as I know, he's still able to handle a gun."

Dax nodded. "Good idea. We'll rotate men each day." He looked at Dirk. "You and Bull decide what's best."

"We have to make some decisions about the drive to Utah," Dirk said. "If Trask isn't captured by the time we leave, it may be best for Rosemary to go with us."

Her head whipped toward Dirk. "I don't know the first thing about being on a drive. Besides, I'm needed here until the babies come."

"The drive isn't for several weeks, Rosemary," Dax said. "It's something we can consider as it gets closer."

Crossing his arms, Luke walked to the desk, leaning a hip against the edge. "I'll send a telegram to Dutch McFarlin, find out if he's done with his last assignment. If so, he might be interested in working for us as extra protection for Rosemary."

Rachel placed a restraining hand on Rosemary's arm when she opened her mouth to protest.

"I think that's a good idea, Luke," Rachel said. "That will free up the ranch hands and give him time to decide if he might want to settle in Splendor permanently."

Luke's brow raised. "How'd you know Dutch was considering settling down here?"

Rachel smiled. "I heard he might take time away from Pinkerton. It would be wonderful if he made Splendor his home."

Dax slapped his hands on the desk and stood, bringing the discussion to an end. "It's settled. Rosemary stays at the ranch."

Chapter Five

Dirk couldn't shake the feeling someone was watching him. Holding his Sharps rifle in one hand, he continued his journey around the barn, stopping every few seconds to focus on the surrounding pasture. He could hear the bawling of the herd, knowing it wasn't the sound of animals who sensed danger.

Coming around the corner to the front of the barn, Dirk lowered himself onto a bench, stretching out his long legs. Placing the rifle next to him, his gaze moved in a wide sweep from the bunkhouse to the front of the Pelletier house, then to the trail from town. Nothing unusual caught his attention.

Besides the men who watched the herd at night, he and Bull selected two others to guard the house. The men had been told of Trask's escape and reminded of the danger to Rosemary and the boys.

At the sound of a door opening, his gaze returned to the house, seeing Rosemary step outside. Dirk watched as she took a deep breath and looked around. He saw the instant she spotted him, could almost feel her struggle whether to be courteous and acknowledge him or retreat back inside the house. To his surprise, she tightened the shawl around her before approaching him.

"Good evening, Dirk."

Standing, he took off his hat. "Rosemary." Picking up the rifle, he gestured to the spot next to him.

Hesitating a few seconds, she lowered herself onto the bench, looking up at the sky. "It's beautiful out tonight."

Even with his senses on high alert, Dirk had taken the time to notice the cloudless sky covered by a thick blanket of shimmering stars.

"That it is." Taking a seat next to her, he settled his hat on his head.

Leaning the rifle against the bench, he crossed his arms, his gaze vigilant as he scanned the area around them one more time. The same sense of being watched assaulted him, yet he saw no sign of danger.

He knew his two men had positioned themselves in the trees behind the house, and even though Bull hadn't said anything, Dirk figured he'd be sitting beside a window inside his own place, a rifle across his lap.

When the original foreman and his wife had retired, Dax and Luke offered Bull the foreman's job. It included a small house a few yards from where Dax and Rachel lived, plus meals at the main house. When Dirk arrived, he'd turned down their offer to build him a place, preferring to bunk with the men.

"Do you truly think the boys and I are in danger?"

Her question surprised him. Rosemary, more than anyone, knew the threat Boyden Trask posed. The man had gone from respected restaurant owner in the territorial capital of Big Pine to convicted felon. The choice to commit crimes was his, but it had been Rosemary's testimony that convicted him to years in prison. It didn't take any amount of effort to figure the man would be heading in their direction, looking to retaliate.

"I was in the clinic with you and Doc McCord when Trask came looking for you."

Pulling her shawl tighter, a slight shiver ran through her. "I remember."

"The look on his face when Gabe arrested him was pure hate, Rosemary...hate directed at you." He stayed silent a few moments, allowing his words to take hold. "I believe he'll be looking for revenge."

Nodding, she glanced toward the bunkhouse where her brother, Ben, slept near Jimmy and Teddy. "Do you think Trask is alone?"

"Gabe sent a telegram to the prison asking if anyone else escaped with him."

Two of the men who rode with him were convicted within days of his trial. Rosemary had testified against each of them. All three were shipped to the territorial prison in Deer Lodge, several days' ride east through thick, mountainous forests. Dirk believed Trask, and any other escapees accompanying him, would take the easier trail north.

It would require them to travel through Blackfoot territory, but it was a chance he believed the man would be willing to take in order to avoid the treacherous journey over the mountains. What Trask didn't know about was the strong bond between Chief Running Bear and the Pelletiers. The Blackfoot leader also had a special place in his heart for Bull and Lydia.

When Rosemary remained silent, he glanced over at her, his chest tightening at the tears glistening in her eyes and rolling down her face. Without thought, he reached over, brushing the moisture from her cheek with the back of his rough fingers. Her startled response didn't surprise Dirk. Leaning into him to lay her head on his shoulder did. Stilling, he didn't move at first, then he felt her tremble, heard a soft sob. Draping his arm around her shoulders, he pulled her close, feeling her body relax against him.

"We aren't going to let anything happen to you, Rosemary." He didn't know what possessed him to do it, but he kissed her forehead, lingering a moment before pulling away. Her response was a deep sigh as she snuggled closer.

"Uh, Dirk?"

Dax's voice had Rosemary jerking away, then standing. She cast a furtive look at Dirk, not meeting Dax's gaze.

"I'd better get back inside."

The men watched as she hurried up the steps to the front door, closing it behind her. Turning back to Dirk, Dax raised a brow.

Standing, Dirk picked up his rifle. "Don't make more of it than what you saw. She's scared, worried about the boys."

"Understandable. I'm hoping Gabe will have word tomorrow about anyone else who may have escaped with Trask. It would be good to know how many men we're going to face." Turning in a circle, Dax studied the area, finding nothing to concern him. "There's a chance he'll ride out of the territory."

Dirk shook his head. "Doubtful. He may take the northern trail, taking him through Running Bear's territory."

"I was thinking the same. I'm going to send Bull and a couple other men up to the Blackfoot camp tomorrow, let Running Bear know what's happening. Not much else we can do until Trask decides to show his face."

Cradling the rifle in his arms, Dirk's face took on a fierce expression. "If he does, he's dead."

Red Dog, Montana Territory

Huddling behind the only hotel in the tiny frontier town east of Big Pine, he fished in his pockets for the last of his money. He'd used a few coins to stable his horse, making sure the animal was well attended. Now he stared at the money in his hand, hoping it would get him through the rest of the day and night.

Weeks had passed since he had a decent meal and a clean bed. He knew the chance he took that someone would recognize him from a wanted poster, assuming one had been put out on him. Rubbing his palms into his tired eyes, he made a decision before he could change his mind.

Standing, he did the best he could to brush off the dirt and straighten his clothes. As he'd done so many times over the past month, he wondered how his life had turned so bad. At one time, he'd had a sister and brother-in-law, worked on their farm in Tennessee, and looked forward to establishing a place of his own. Circumstances forced him to move on, and a series of questionable choices put him where he was today.

A friend once told him vengeance wasn't the answer to his problems, yet he believed differently. Now he snuck around like a beaten animal, desperate in his need to regain the life he'd lost. First, he had to survive the trip to Splendor.

Hesitating, he looked up and down the short, muddy trail that served as Red Dog's main street. Counting the few people milling about, he reasoned there couldn't be more than fifty people in the entire area. More importantly, he saw no sign of a jail, which meant if a wanted poster did exist, it wouldn't be displayed here.

Stopping at a horse trough, he splashed water over his face, wiping it away with the sleeve of his shirt. Running shaky hands through his hair, he glanced around. No one seemed to care about his presence, going about their business as if he didn't exist.

If luck were with him, he'd wolf down a quick meal, sleep a few hours, then ride to Big Pine. He figured it would take several days to get there, then another to reach Splendor. If his information was accurate, he'd find the person he sought, then go from there.

Straightening, he settled his hat back on his head, inhaling a deep breath. A grim smile crossed his face. It wouldn't be long now. All he had to do was make it through a few more days.

Splendor

"The stage just left." Cash Coulter, one of Gabe's deputies, walked into the jail late in the afternoon, tossing a week-old newspaper from Big Pine onto Gabe's desk. Even though Splendor had a newspaper run by Lewis Gibson with the help of his son,

Franklin, it mainly carried weddings, births, deaths, territory news, and information obtained from other newspapers. Lewis did run a short article about Boyden Trask's escape, which caused at least a dozen people to stop by the sheriff's office.

Gabe glanced down at the paper, lifting a brow. "Is there something specific in there you want me to read?"

"Remember the letters you received from your friend about the deaths of young women?"

Gabe nodded.

"There've been more. The latest near Omaha. At least that's what this paper says. There could be more by now." Cash lowered himself into a chair opposite Gabe, steepling his fingers under his chin. "I don't like it."

"Omaha is still a long way from Splendor." Picking up the paper, Gabe read the article, his brows furrowing. "The article cites a quote from a Pinkerton agent." He glanced up at Cash. "Guess they're still investigating the murders."

"Which means they believe they're connected."

Standing, Gabe grabbed his hat, looking at Cash. "Do you mind staying here and keeping an eye on the cells?" Cash and Beau had brought in two rowdy drunks the night before. So far, no one had shown up to claim them.

"Sure. Where are you going?"

"To send telegrams to the sheriffs in Omaha and Ogallala. If the murders are connected, the next logical place would be the Nebraska cattle town."

"You might want to send one off to Cheyenne. Ask them to get word to you if any young women go missing."

Gabe sucked in a breath, nodding.

"Gabe?"

He looked at Cash before walking outside. "Yeah?"

"You're probably right about Splendor being out of the way. The murders seem to follow the path of the railroad. To reach Splendor, whoever is doing this would have to ride horseback or take the stage. I'm not sure it makes sense when they could simply continue west."

Gabe's jaw worked as a ball of dread formed in his stomach. "Let's hope you're right."

"Glad you came in, Sheriff. I have a telegram from the territorial prison." Bernie Griggs, the man who'd run the telegraph and mail office since before Gabe came to Splendor, held out a piece of paper.

Taking it, Gabe scanned it quickly, pursing his lips.

"Do you want to send a reply, Sheriff?"

Shaking his head, he stuffed the message into his pocket. "Not now. I do want to send a couple other telegrams." Grabbing a piece of paper, he penned telegrams to the sheriffs in Omaha and Ogallala, adding Cheyenne and Denver. Digging into a pocket, he put money on the counter as he handed the paper to Bernie, who read it over.

"I'll get these right out."

"Thanks." Walking to the door, Gabe glanced over his shoulder. "I'd appreciate getting any responses right away."

"Will do."

Stepping into the early evening air, Gabe made his way along the boardwalk toward the Dixie Saloon. His wife, Lena, would be working in the office, their eight-year-old son, Jackson, working on his homework at a small desk in the corner. Nodding at the bartender, he skirted several tables as he walked to the back and through the office door.

Jackson glanced up from his work and smiled. "Hi, Papa. I'm almost done with my homework, and Mama told me she'd be ready to go home when you got here."

Ruffling his son's hair, Gabe moved to where Lena worked, bending down to kiss her before leaning his hip against the edge of the desk.

"I have to ride out to see the Pelletiers."

She looked up at him. "Is something wrong?"

"I received a telegram about Boyden Trask. Two other prisoners escaped with him."

Glancing at Jackson, she lowered her voice. "The men who were convicted when he was?"

"Yes. It means Trask will have help if he decides to come after Rosemary or the boys. I have to let Dax, Luke, and Dirk Masters know. I'll stop at the jail first to tell Cash, but I wanted to make sure you'd be all right to get home."

Although they'd planned a big home on property Gabe had purchased before they married, their work made it more realistic to have Noah build them a small house at the edge of town. As the sheriff and co-owners, with Nick and Suzanne Barnett, of two saloons, a boardinghouse, and the St. James Hotel, neither he nor Lena could afford to be more than a few minutes away. Both still planned to build the home they fantasized about. It would just take a little more time.

Laughing, she reached for his hand. "Jackson and I can manage just fine. You go ahead. They need to know what you found out as soon as possible."

"And let Nick know." He drew her up, wrapping his arms around her waist before giving her another kiss, this one longer, scorching, until it drew Jackson's attention.

"Eeuwww."

Chuckling against Lena's mouth, Gabe pulled away. "Sorry, son, but I thought you'd be used to it by now."

Jackson shook his head. "Never. I'm never kissing a girl."

"Of course you aren't." Lena smiled at Gabe, walking him to the door. "I'll see you back at the house. And tell the Pelletiers we'll all be watching out for Trask."

Chapter Six

"Are you sure you won't stay and have supper before riding back?" Dax looked at Gabe, who'd delivered the bad news to a full table, including Rosemary and Dirk.

Gabe glanced around the table, seeing the somber expressions, knowing each person had their own thoughts about the two men who'd escaped with Trask. "Thanks, but I need to get back to Lena and Jackson."

Walking him to the door, Dax glanced over his shoulder at the people who meant the most to him, his gaze settling on young Patrick. Lowering his voice, he leaned closer to Gabe.

"Send word if you hear anything at all about Trask."

"You know I will." Gabe fingered the brim of his hat before settling it on his head. "You do the same. If you see any sign of him or the other men, have someone ride to town."

Dax nodded, watching as Gabe stepped into a night turned chilly by the wind and thick cover of dark clouds. He waited until Gabe mounted his stallion, Blackheart, before closing the door, taking the few steps back to the table.

"Increase the number of men on guard at night?" Luke asked, reaching over to cover Ginny's hand with his own.

Shaking his head, Dax sat down. "No. We already have men covering the herd and two watching the house at night." He looked at Luke before his gaze moved to Bull and Dirk. "The four of us will alternate shifts at night." Keeping his voice low, he explained the plan, seeing the men nod.

Dirk rested his arms on the table. "Bull and I will start tonight."

Glancing at Rachel, Dax saw the look of resolution on her face and relaxed. She'd always shown extreme faith in him, perhaps more than he deserved.

He looked back at Dirk. "Sounds good. Luke and I will take tomorrow. We'll alternate nights, but all four of us should plan on spending every night here until Trask and his men are found."

"I know how to handle a rifle. I can sit by a window and keep watch."

All eyes went to Rosemary, four male voices replying at the same time. "No."

Sitting next to her, Dirk saw her features harden as she sat up straighter in the chair. "I don't know why not. I'm as capable as anyone else. There's no reason I can't help." Her gaze shot to Rachel, looking for support. "I'm the reason he might come here. It's only right I should be a part of this."

Placing a hand on her stomach, Rachel drew in a breath, letting it out in a slow whoosh. "She has a point, Dax. What harm would it do to have her at the window? Another pair of eyes will only help."

"I agree with Rachel." Ginny tightened her grip on her husband's hand. "Rosemary's bedroom is upstairs, which is a good place to watch. I can go up and sit with her."

"So can I," Rachel said, seeing Dax's jaw twitch.

"You'll be in bed, Rachel. The baby is due anytime, and I won't have you putting yourself at more risk."

"I'd only be watching out a window, Dax."

"He's right, Rachel." Rosemary sent her friend a pleading look. "You and Ginny need your rest. Neither of you need to do anything that could hurt your pregnancies."

"And Rosemary doesn't need to have a rifle." Dirk's stern voice had everyone looking at him, a mutinous look on Rosemary's face.

"Of course I'll be armed. What's the point if I can't fire a shot at the men threatening me?"

"Dirk's right, Rosemary. You can keep watch, but no gun. I don't want Trask and his men to know you're here. Can you tell me with one hundred percent certainty you won't shoot the man if you see him?" Dax asked.

Huffing out a breath, she clenched her hands in her lap. Biting her lip, she shook her head. "No. How do I let the men know if someone is approaching?"

Dirk looked at Dax, who nodded for him to respond. "You'll light a candle, placing it in the window. Then you'll notify whoever is in the house and light more candles so any of the men on watch can see."

Crossing her arms, she glared at Dirk. "Then what?"

"You'll stay with Rachel, Patrick, and Ginny in one room until we take care of Trask. And each of you should have a gun for protection." When Rosemary began to protest, Dirk raised a hand. "Toting around a rifle will slow you down. Light candles and get in with the others. They'll have a gun waiting for you."

Locking her gaze with Rosemary's, Rachel nodded. "He's right. Let the men take care of Trask and anyone with him. If one of them gets into the house, he'll have to deal with the three of us. Selina and Margaret will be inside Bull and Lydia's house," she said, mentioning Lydia's younger sister and another orphan who both sat at the supper table, their eyes wide, remaining quiet. Rachel looked at Dax. "What about the younger boys in the bunkhouse?"

"Sam, Jimmy, and Teddy have their own rifles. The men in the bunkhouse will watch out for them.

We may want to bring Ben into the house with the women." Dax glanced at Rosemary, a question in his eyes.

After a moment, she shook her head. "No. He's twelve and knows how to handle a gun. He'll want to stay with the other boys."

Everyone quieted as they thought through the plan, the younger girls and Patrick squirming in their chairs.

"If we're finished, I'd like to get Lydia and the girls settled in the house." Bull stood, offering his hand to his wife.

"I'll get the guns ready for the women. Might as well be prepared." Luke helped Ginny up. Even with the threat, his body remained relaxed, features unreadable.

"Dirk, I'd like you to speak with the men on watch and those in the bunkhouse."

Pushing away from the table, Dirk stood, nodding at Dax. "I'll do it right away. Is there extra ammunition?"

Dax nodded. "I'll get the boxes. You can take them with you now." He extended his hand to Rachel, seeing the determination on her face, a look he'd come to count on over the years.

"Rosemary, Ginny, and I will take care of the dishes and pull out the candles. From tonight on, we'll be ready if that miscreant is foolish enough to come around here."

He pulled her into a hug. "That's what I needed to hear." Stepping back, he looked at Dirk. "Let's get the ammunition for the boys."

Dirk finished speaking with the men in the bunkhouse, mindful of the reactions of the younger boys. Sam and Jimmy were seventeen, and Teddy sixteen. He didn't worry too much about them. All three were good shots and had their own rifles. Jimmy might be a little hotheaded at times, but Dirk felt certain the boy would be able to do what was needed if Trask showed up. At twelve, Ben was a bit of an unknown. Dirk didn't know how he'd react if under attack.

"Ben, you might want to consider coming back to the house with me."

The boy shook his head. "No. I'm staying here with the others."

Dirk shot a look at Tat and Johnny, two ranch hands he trusted as much as he trusted anybody. Each gave him a slight nod of understanding.

"You're almost a man, Ben. The decision is yours."

Nodding at Dirk, a solemn expression crossed Ben's face. "Will Rosemary be all right in the house?"

"You have my word. I won't let anything happen to her." Dirk winced at his words, not knowing why he would promise such a thing. Rosemary wasn't his responsibility, and she wouldn't appreciate it if she'd heard what he'd said.

Tat stepped forward. "Me and the men have been talking, Boss. We think all of us should take turns watching the house at night. Ain't that right, boys?"

Dirk noted how each man nodded. "If that's what you want, I'll talk with Bull about including everyone." Turning toward the door, he glanced back at them for a moment before heading outside. Stopping, he settled his fists on his waist, looking around as he inhaled a deep breath, his chest squeezing.

The sensations running through him were unwelcome and all too familiar. Once before, he'd possessed a strong desire to protect another woman, a woman he vowed to love, cherish, and honor. He'd taken his pledge seriously, discovering too late she hadn't done the same.

His gut clenched as the stabbing pain rolled through him. It had been almost four years. The raw ache felt as fresh now as it did the night he'd stared at her lifeless body—before he'd learned the truth of her actions and the depth of her betrayal.

The sound of the herd over a mile away drew his attention back to the present. Shaking his head to clear the uneasy images of the past from his mind, Dirk swept his gaze from the house to the barn. The dense cloud cover obliterated the moon's glow, making it hard to see. Taking a few steps forward, he halted at the sound of someone moving about inside the barn. Settling a hand on his gun, Dirk walked forward, making little noise as he approached the entrance.

Resting his back against the side of the barn, he waited, hearing the sound again. All but two of the men were in the bunkhouse. The Pelletiers, Rosemary, and the younger girls were in the house. He glanced in the direction of Bull's place, seeing no candles lit. He knew his friend would be getting as much sleep as possible before relieving Dirk for the second shift. A rustling noise drew his attention back to whoever was inside the barn.

Pulling the gun from its holster, he sucked in a calming breath before pushing away from his position to look inside. The interior was too dark to make out anything except a lone figure leaning against one of the stalls. Moving closer, he made little sound, hoping to catch the person unaware. Pointing the gun at the intruder, he halted.

"Keep your arms at your sides and move away from the stall."

The person whipped around, letting out a startled scream.

"Rosemary?" Dirk stepped closer, seeing her hand move to her chest. "What are you doing in here?" Holstering the gun, he walked toward her.

"You scared me to death." She let out a breath, her heart still racing.

Crossing his arms, Dirk narrowed his gaze. "I asked what you're doing out here alone? You should be in the house where it's safe."

"Don't glare at me." Wiping her palms down the hem of her dress, she took a couple steps back, creating a small measure of distance.

Dirk didn't back down. Instead, he moved toward her, eliminating the space she'd created. "Then don't do things that put yourself in danger."

Swallowing her annoyance, Rosemary lifted her chin. "I'm a grown woman, Dirk."

"Then act like one." He moved closer, leaning to within inches of her face. "This business with Trask is serious. It not only jeopardizes you, but everyone on this ranch, including the children." He sucked in a breath, but didn't move away. "If you need to go outside, one of the men should be with you. You should never be alone. Not until Trask is caught and sent back to prison." Straightening, he turned around, pacing several feet away before looking back at her. "This isn't just about you, Rosemary."

She blinked several times, not meeting his gaze. Dirk's words stung. More so because she knew he was right.

After he'd left the house, her anger simmered until she needed to get away—outside where the darkness could surround her, providing an odd sense of peace and freedom. Rosemary had lived her life being controlled by men—their motives, desires, wishes—all for their own selfish purposes.

Until living at Redemption's Edge, seeing how women were supposed to be treated, she thought all men acted the same as her father. Dax, Luke, Bull, Dirk...none of them were anything like the man who'd raised her. They were good men, risking their lives for someone they barely knew, yet had taken into their home. The same with the men in town. Doctor Clay McCord, Gabe, Cash, Beau, Noah, and the others were better than her father could ever hope to be.

She sighed, wishing the past didn't distort her future. "I know."

He moved toward her. Seeing the pain in her eyes, hearing her shaky response, his voice softened. "Do you?"

Taking in a ragged breath, she nodded. "I appreciate everything you and everyone else is doing for me. I just needed some room to breathe."

Lifting a hand, he stroked his fingers down her cheek, knowing he should step away. Instead, his hand cupped her chin, lifting it until their eyes met.

"I know how you feel."

Her eyes widened. "You do?" She refused to look away. Something in his voice, the pained sadness in his eyes, kept her gaze focused on him.

He nodded an instant before lowering his head, brushing his lips across hers. Both stilled at his action, but neither pulled away. He kissed her again, taking more time, feeling the softness of her lips as her hands moved to rest on his shoulders. Dirk groaned as she moved into him, allowing him to deepen the kiss.

There'd been women since his wife died. Quick, impersonal, meaningless. No one stirred his blood—until Rosemary. Sweet and innocent. Everything he wasn't.

The reality of what they were doing shoved through his hazed mind enough for him to break the kiss. Resting his forehead against hers, he forced himself to back away.

She stared at him, confusion clear in her expression.

He glanced behind him, glad for the dark night. "I'm sorry. That wasn't supposed to happen."

Rosemary didn't know how to respond. The last thing she expected when entering the barn was for Dirk to join her. His stern manner, arrogance, and overbearing ways had irritated her from their first meeting. She hadn't liked it...hadn't liked him. Then he'd kissed her. Touching a finger to her still tingling lips, she could feel her face flush.

"It's all right." And it was. She enjoyed the kiss. More than she should.

He shook his head, all arrogance gone. "No, Rosemary, it isn't. I'm supposed to protect you."

Pursing her lips, she walked forward, stopping next to him on her way outside. "You have been protecting me. It's all you've done since we met." Seeing the surprise on his face, she felt a slight amount of satisfaction. Continuing past him, she glanced over her shoulder. "Are you going to walk me to the house?" Seeing his jaw go slack, she stifled a laugh.

Moving up beside her, Dirk cupped her elbow. "I'd be honored."

Dirk took another walk around the barn, stopping to study the areas beyond the corrals before returning to his spot on the bench. Leaning his back against the side of the barn, he settled the rifle across his thighs. Stretching out his long legs, he sighed, replaying the events of the evening.

He still couldn't explain what had happened with Rosemary or how his body had reacted to her touch. All he understood was it could *not* happen again. If she had any idea what took place after he returned from the war, she'd run far and fast. Whatever had been left of his soul after fighting for the Union had been ground to dust when he'd learned the extent of his wife's deceit.

His gaze rose to the second floor of the house, seeing the flickering light pouring from Rosemary's window. Since learning the truth about his wife, Dirk had compared all women to her, believing every one bore a layer of deception and secrets beneath the surface. It only took the right circumstances to bring it to life. He wondered what secrets Rosemary held.

Forcing his gaze away from her window, he took another look around, seeing nothing of concern. Leaning forward, he rested his elbows on his legs, scrubbing his face, feeling tired beyond his years. He was in his late twenties. The cracked mirror hanging on the bunkhouse wall told him his real age didn't matter. Those who looked at his face would mistake him for much older.

At twenty, and considered a woman, Rosemary seemed little older than a child, a girl he had no business wanting. It had been a shock when he learned the extent of his attraction to her. Until tonight, he never intended to act on it. Now he had to figure out how to stay away from her, erase his inappropriate thoughts from his mind. His job was to protect her, nothing more. The women who worked at the Dixie and Wild Rose would fulfill his needs, the same as similar women had since he'd ridden away from Pennsylvania for the last time.

Chapter Seven

Rosemary extinguished the lantern, moving to sit by the window. The moon had found an opening in the thick clouds, allowing a ray of light to shine on the barn. Looking down, she couldn't help staring at Dirk, his strong shoulders slumped, arms resting on his legs, a rifle in his lap. She wondered what held his thoughts. Did he regret kissing her?

Her face flushed, remembering how his lips felt on hers, how much she wanted him to continue. The realization shouldn't have been a surprise. In spite of his foul moods and arrogance, she felt a strange pull to him. She had no business feeling anything.

Rosemary's mother had been a saint, working day and night on the farm while raising her and Ben without any aid from her husband. He spent his days in the fields. After supper, he'd head to town, coming home close to midnight, smelling of whiskey and other strange scents. Rosemary now understood the potent perfume came from his activities in the brothels behind the saloons.

The only words he spoke to Rosemary were harsh, unforgiving, meant to make her cower the same way his wife did. When Rosemary didn't shrink from his words, he punctuated them with his hands. Never enough to cause outward scars, his treatment forced her to see the man who'd fathered her as a threat, a man she'd never be able to depend upon or trust.

Instead, she'd given her trust to an eighteen-year-old farmhand her father hired the summer she'd turned fifteen. Rosemary had seen him as an answer to her troubles, someone to depend on when her father's treatment became too harsh. He'd been handsome and charming, filling her head with stories of how they'd live once he saved enough and they ran away. She'd believed every word, even giving him the small amount of money she'd saved. Then he disappeared, but not before changing her life in another frightening and unexpected way.

Her gaze still fixed on Dirk, she drew in an unsteady breath. He'd hate her if he knew the secret she kept hidden close to her heart. No one had known—not her parents or her brother. But she knew, and it still tortured her every day of her life.

A light tapping drew her attention. "Come in."

The door opened. Rachel, Patrick, and Ginny stood in the hall, all dressed for bed.

Standing, she walked to them. "Is something wrong?"

"Not at all. We just wanted to be sure you're all right." Rachel walked forward, holding Patrick's hand. Ginny leaned against the doorframe, a hand rubbing her stomach. Sitting on the edge of the bed, Rachel lifted Patrick up beside her. "I know you'd rather be in town, working at the clinic."

Rosemary sat beside her. "I want to be where I'm needed. Right now, that's here with you and Ginny."

Rachel rested her hand on Rosemary's arm. "You aren't a prisoner. If you want to go into town some days, Dirk or one of the men will go with you. I just don't want you to feel trapped."

She thought of Dirk's words about her being selfish. They caused a lump to form in her throat, strengthening her resolve to stay. Rosemary refused to leave those who'd shown so much faith in her.

"I don't feel trapped, Rachel. Honestly, I want to be here with my family."

Rachel's warm smile touched Rosemary's heart. "You *are* part of our family. I hope you never forget it."

Ginny walked to the window and looked out. Spotting Dirk, she turned back to Rosemary. "A family that is growing rapidly. Luke says it won't be long before we'll need a dozen houses for all the families this ranch will hold."

An image of her and Dirk sitting in comfortable chairs by a fire rolled across Rosemary's mind, causing her to still. She had no reason to think of a future with him, didn't know why the image appeared. She ruthlessly pushed the thought aside before it took root in her fantasies.

Rachel stood, lifting Patrick into her arms. Joining Ginny at the window, she glanced outside, seeing Dirk stand, grasping his rifle in his hands.

"With all the single men working here, I have no doubt the number of houses will expand." She looked back at Rosemary, her brows drawing together. "Dirk is an example. He's a good-looking man, smart, dedicated to his job. I wonder why he's never married. He must have had many opportunities."

Rosemary shook her head. She'd wondered the same many times, never having the courage to ask him outright. "Has he ever mentioned his life before King Tolbert hired him?"

"If he spoke about his past, it would have been to Dax or Luke. Maybe Bull." Rachel glanced at Ginny. "Has Luke ever mentioned anything about Dirk's past to you?"

Ginny shook her head, her hand rubbing a circle on her stomach. "Not a word. What about Dax?"

"No." Rachel looked out the window once more, seeing Dirk gazing into the distance before walking around the corner of the barn. "He's a very private man. He'll tell us of his past when he's ready."

Rosemary agreed, although it didn't stop her from wondering. Had he ever been in love as she thought she once was? She'd never seen him smile. What had changed him into a sullen, guarded man, someone bound by honor and loyalty with little ability to feel?

Rachel stepped next to Rosemary. "I need to put Patrick to bed. Dax and Luke will finish going over the books soon. We'll see you at breakfast."

"Yes, you will." Closing the door behind them, Rosemary returned to her seat by the window. Not seeing Dirk in his usual spot, she directed her attention to the sky. It had again turned dark, the thick clouds signaling rain later that night or early the next morning.

When her gaze returned to the front of the barn, Dirk had resumed his seat on the bench. This time, he sat straight, his features fixed in a stern expression. One she knew well.

Touching her lips, she felt a tingle almost as powerful as when his mouth covered hers. Rosemary never thought such a hard man could kiss with so much tenderness.

Stranger still, she'd sworn to never again surrender to the touch of a man—and certainly not one she didn't like.

Mack Mackey, one of Gabe's deputies, shook the rain from his shoulders before stepping inside the jail. "Good morning, Gabe." He tossed a newspaper on the desk.

"What's this?" Picking it up, Gabe noted the heading. "From Denver. It's almost a week old."

"Look at the story further down the page."

Spreading the paper out on the desk, his gaze caught on a specific story. Reading it, he rubbed the back of his neck. "It's about the murders Pinkerton suspects are connected. Seems another girl went missing. Her body was found outside Ogallala."

Lowering himself into a chair, Mack leaned forward. "I read it." Scratching his brow, he sat back. "I'm unclear what makes them believe the abductions and murders are done by the same person."

"There must be more to the deaths than what we read in the stories." Standing, Gabe picked up the paper, then grabbed his hat. "Dutch McFarlin returned last night. I want to speak with him, ask him to contact Pinkerton. Maybe he'll be able to learn more about the murders."

"I'm coming with you." Mack stood, following Gabe out the door and to the boardinghouse across the street.

"Good morning, Gabe, Mack. Would you like a table?" Suzanne Barnett, a partner with Gabe and her husband, Nick, in several businesses, walked up to them.

"We're looking for Dutch. Has he been down for breakfast?" Gabe asked, taking off his hat.

"I haven't seen him. His room is at the top of the stairs on the right. Would you like a key?"

"Thank you, Suzanne. I believe he'll open the door for us. Come on, Mack." Gabe pounded up the stairs, knocking on Dutch's door. "It's Gabe and Mack. We need to speak with you."

A rough voice sounded through the door. "Give me a minute."

They stood back, hearing the rustling sound of clothing an instant before the door opened. "Sheriff, Mack. It's a little early for a social call." He stood back, gesturing for them to enter.

"It's not a social call, Dutch. We need your help." Gabe walked to the window, looking outside, as Mack leaned against the wall.

"What do you need?"

Gabe explained, seeing recognition on Dutch's face. "You already know of the murders."

Dutch nodded. "Yes, I've heard about them. Allan sent me several telegrams. They were waiting for me when I arrived in Splendor."

"What did he say?" Mack asked.

"He mentioned the murders in the early telegrams. The last one asked me to be available to travel to Denver. He believes they are connected."

Mack pushed away from the wall. "The news stories say all occurred not far from the railroad."

Dutch nodded. "There's more. Each victim was strangled."

Gabe's jaw tightened. "Were the women...were they...?" He let his voice trail off.

Dutch shook his head, knowing what Gabe asked. "No. They found no evidence of them being violated." Clearing his throat, he shredded fingers through his unruly hair. "All the victims were between eighteen and twenty-three, unmarried, living with their parents, with similar features."

Gabe tilted his head to the side. "What do you mean?"

Pacing a few feet away, Dutch shrugged. "Average height, fair skin, slender, and comely. Strangely, none had a serious suitor."

"That could describe thousands of young women." Gabe pinched the bridge of his nose. "Do you know if they were abducted at night?"

"Early evening," Dutch responded. "From the little I know, I agree there is consistency between the murders."

Mack rubbed his chin, his brows furrowing. "With all this information, they still have no idea who's doing it?"

Shaking his head, Dutch grimaced. "Not that I know about."

Glancing out the window once again, Gabe folded his arms over his chest. "Common sense would tell us it's a man, maybe more than one. They either travel on the railroad or follow it."

Mack looked at Gabe. "Which would seem to make Splendor safe."

Gabe nodded, a grim expression on his face. "For now."

Big Pine

Brushing the dust off his tattered coat, he set the broom next to a bucket in the closet of the saloon. The day's work had earned him some coin, supper, and a much needed drink. The unexpected job came with a tiny room at the back of what appeared to be the most disreputable saloon in town.

He'd spent longer than intended in the territorial capital. If it hadn't been for the generosity of the aging bartender, he might've spent his last days on earth freezing at night and sweltering during the day, wedged between two leaky water barrels behind the saloon.

The owner needed a man to clean the building during the day and provide a ready gun against drunken and rowdy cowboys at night. After one particularly raucous night, in which his skills had been tested, the owner hired him.

A few more days and he'd earn enough to outfit himself for the final miles to Splendor.

Bull settled his hands on his waist, studying the progress of the new clinic, a scowl on his face. Guilt washed over him. Looking at Clay McCord, he shook his head.

"They should've been much further along by now. If only I'd seen the man's weaknesses sooner."

"It's not your fault the man supervising them turned out to be a drunk and a thief."

Bull grimaced. "I should've checked on the progress sooner."

"You had a more pressing responsibility at the ranch. Keeping your family, Rosemary, and the Pelletiers safe from Trask. Gabe and Nick agree with me, as does Doc Worthington. No one blames you."

"I appreciate your words, Doc, but I must take responsibility. My consolation is Gabe and Nick discovered the missing funds."

Clay chuckled. "During a drunken state when the man babbled about what he'd done. He now sits in jail and the money has been recovered." He clasped Bull on the shoulder. "We've lost a little time, nothing more."

Bull shifted his stance, his jaw tight. "I'll need to stay in town."

"No, you won't." Nick walked up beside them. "You've done more than what Gabe and I expected. You're needed at the ranch. And for good reason." He narrowed his gaze at Bull, daring him to argue.

"Who will watch over the men?"

Nick's face broke into a wry grin. "I will."

Bull's eyes widened. "You?"

Placing a hand over his heart, Nick feigned offense. "You don't believe I can do it?"

Bull's head fell back as a roar of laughter burst from his lungs. After a moment, he settled down, looking at his friend. "You're more capable than I am."

Crossing his arms over his chest, Nick nodded, a wide grin on his face. "I can't argue that."

Gabe walked up, shaking his head. "All right, you two. Now that we've determined you're both capable, a fact we already knew, I think it's time to develop a plan for getting back on schedule."

Nick slapped Bull on the back. "He's right. We'll meet with the men, let them know of the changes, and have the clinic finished within weeks."

Bull stared at him, one brow arched. "Weeks?"

Gabe chuckled at the incredulous look on Bull's face.

Nick nodded. "Yes, Bull. Weeks."

Scrubbing a hand down his face, Bull looked around, counting those cutting wood and pounding nails. "Then we'll need more men."

Clay, who'd stayed quiet, enjoying the men's banter, cleared his throat. "I must return to the clinic. Doc Worthington and I will be happy with whatever you three decide."

They watched him leave, Nick's brows furrowing when his daughter, Olivia, intercepted Clay partway to the clinic. Slipping her arm through Clay's, they walked along the boardwalk.

Gabe turned toward him. "Are they courting?"

Nick's attention switched from his daughter to Gabe. "No. Olivia says they are friends, nothing more."

Chuckling, Gabe watched Clay walk into the clinic as Olivia continued up the street. "Seems that's the way it started for all of us."

Railroad to Cheyenne

"Young man, you have been very quiet. Are you well?"

"Now, Sister. Can't you see he has much on his mind?" Selma Ritter touched the arm of her older sister, Davinia.

Straightening, Willard Cullin forced a weak smile. He guessed the spinster sisters to be in their sixties, although he'd never embarrass them by asking.

"No, no. It's quite all right, Miss Ritter." He looked at Davinia. "I'm afraid I'm not as stout as you two women. Traveling across country does not suit me as it does you."

"Nonsense. You are as resolute as my sister and I. I've seen it in your eyes, and those of your two companions." Davinia glanced around. "I've not seen them since we were in Ogallala."

"They seem to come and go as ghosts. Don't you think so, Davinia?" Selma's soft titter was muffled by the white handkerchief she held in front of her mouth.

Davinia nodded. "Yes, Sister. Ghost is a fitting name for Mr. Cullin's companions." She looked at Willard. "Your friends are quite elusive. Wouldn't you agree?"

A weary smile replaced the patient expression plastered on his face whenever he spoke with the elderly spinsters. "We have business in each town. After the work is done, my friends like to, uh...indulge."

Davinia quirked a brow. "Drink and whore, Mr. Cullin?"

Willard shifted in his seat. "Eat, drink, and play cards, Miss Ritter. Then, of course, they sleep much of the next day." Leaning back in his seat, he cocked his head. "I notice you stay in each town the same number of days as my companions and I do. What do you lovely ladies do in these dusty, frontier towns? Certainly, they are not up to your standards."

"Ah, Mr. Cullin. I am sure it would seem so to those who don't know us. Let me assure you, Sister and I have slept in silk sheets and beds filled with lice. We've eaten gruel in rough, wooden bowls many times. We've also dined on roasted duck served on silver plates." Straightening her skirts, she clasped her hands together in her lap. "However, to answer your question, Sister and I acquaint ourselves with what each town offers. Some have libraries, although quite sparse. Others offer fine millinery every bit as good as what is found in Boston or Philadelphia. Mostly, we rest." She touched a hand to her forehead. "Traveling by rail is quite tiresome."

"May I ask how far you're traveling? We've been on the train a good amount of time together, yet you've never mentioned a destination."

Selma's eyes widened. "We haven't?" She looked at Davinia. "We've never talked to Mr. Cullin of where we are going, Sister?"

Davinia gave her sister an indulgent smile, patting her hand. "It never came up." She looked at Willard. "Sister and I have not decided on a final destination. We may go as far as the Pacific, or stop in Denver. Now that the war is over, we decided to see the country. How much we see is in God's hands."

Willard turned his gaze out the window, a faraway look in his eyes. "I would very much agree, Miss Ritter."

Chapter Eight

"If you're looking for Dirk, he's talking to the men inside the bunkhouse." Rachel stopped grooming her horse, tossing the brush into a bucket. She'd come into the barn as the sun rose, shortly after Dax and Luke left for Splendor.

Rosemary walked up beside her, shaking her head. "If Dax were here, he wouldn't allow you to be working around the horses. The baby could come anytime."

The corners of Rachel's mouth tipped up into a mischievous grin. "My husband can't get his way all the time."

"I'd argue he'd say the same of you."

"True." Stroking the neck of her horse, Rachel let out a sigh. "I'd love to ride, but Dax and my uncle won't allow it."

Rosemary ran a hand down the horse's nose. "Of course not. Even though they might not say it, Doc Worthington and Dax are worried about you and the baby. Luke feels the same about Ginny. It won't be long for either of you."

"My uncle was here for Sunday supper. He estimated it would be less than a week for me, maybe two to three for Ginny. I'm so glad you're here to help, Rosemary."

"Good morning, ladies." Dirk's friendly greeting didn't match the serious expression on his face as he walked into the barn, followed by Mal Jolly and Tat. Mal and Dirk worked together for King Tolbert, coming to Redemption's Edge after their boss was murdered. "Can we do anything for you before riding over to meet Travis and Billy?"

The Pelletiers had purchased the rundown ranch owned by widower brothers, Frank and Hiram Frey, a couple years before, moving the horse breeding business to that location. Travis Dixon and Luke, along with Billy Zale, the oldest male orphan, were in charge of the horses. Contracts with the U.S. Army made it a profitable part of Redemption's Edge. One the brothers hoped to expand.

Rosemary glanced at Rachel, then back at Dirk. "Not unless you want to take Rachel with you. She's aching to ride."

Tat held up his hands. "Hey. I like my job at the ranch."

"Same here," Mal added. "Dax would be real mad to know Miss Rachel got on a horse right now."

Dirk's gaze narrowed on Rosemary. "She's jesting with you, boys." Walking forward, he took a lead rope off a hook, slinging it over his shoulder before tossing a blanket over his arm and lifting his saddle off a wooden bracket. "We'll be gone several hours. I'm leaving three of the boys to keep watch. Bull is checking on the herd. He should be back within an hour." A flash of concern crossed his face before he masked it.

Rachel led her horse back into a stall and closed the gate. "I'll let Ginny and Lydia know. Please, don't worry about us, Dirk. We'll be fine."

Rachel's comment didn't make him feel any better. "We wouldn't be going if it wasn't necessary." A sick feeling built in his gut. "Perhaps we should stay until Bull returns."

"There's a ranch to run. We can't sit around doing nothing on the chance Boyden Trask will come our way." Rachel stepped next to him. "You've done all you can. Dax and Luke will be back after lunch, so we'll have plenty of protection."

Rosemary watched the exchange, seeing the corded muscles flex in Dirk's neck. She'd learned the action signaled the extent of his concern. Moving next to him, she hesitated, his unique scent sparking something inside her. Swallowing away the sensations, she looked up at him.

"She's right, Dirk. We'll get Lydia and stay in the house with Ginny. She's moved her classes inside the house, so the younger children will be with us." Ginny had become the resident teacher, working with the growing number of children on the ranch.

Looking down at her, she could see his jaw working, strain showing on his face as he gritted his teeth. "If something happens while I'm gone…"

Touching his arm, she felt a connection so strong, she yanked her hand away. "Nothing will happen. The men will take care of us. Plus, each of us will have a gun nearby."

Wavering for an instant, he turned to Mal and Tat. "Saddle up, boys. We'll get our business done with Travis and be back by early afternoon."

"Yes, sir," Tat said before grabbing his tack and heading outside, Mal close behind.

Taking her elbow, Dirk steered Rosemary a few feet away from Rachel and leaned down, his voice rough. "Do not take any chances. If Trask does show up, get everyone in one room upstairs and barricade it. The men will be posted, so they can't miss anyone who rides up. It's your job to make sure everyone is together and safe."

"All right."

"I mean it, Rosemary. If anything would happen to you, I…" He shook his head, stopping himself from saying any more.

Reaching up, she cupped his cheek, then gave him a quick kiss. "I promise. I'll do everything you asked."

Stepping back, he nodded at her, then turned toward Rachel. "We'll be back as soon as we can."

Waiting until he left the barn, Rachel moved next to Rosemary. "Do you want to tell me what that was all about?"

Rosemary could feel her face heat. Swiping loose hair from her face, she moved away, hoping Rachel didn't notice her flushed expression.

"He's worried about us and asked me to get everyone in a room upstairs if Trask shows up. Um...we should probably head back to the house." Leaving the barn, she hoped Rachel wouldn't ask any more questions.

"Hmmm. It seemed there was more to it than that. I think he may have an interest in you."

Slowing her pace, Rosemary waited for Rachel to catch up. "Believe me. Dirk has no interest in me at all." Although a part of her wished it wasn't true, she knew the kiss was a one-time incident. He'd even apologized, regret clear on his face. No matter how much he worried about her, the desire she'd seen in his eyes had been fleeting, a mistake made at a vulnerable time. "You know how serious he is about his job. Dirk is a cautious man."

"I suppose you could be right." Seeing the distress on Rosemary's face, Rachel decided to say nothing more...for now.

Dirk kept his gaze moving as they continued on the trail to the old Frey place. He knew Tat and Mal were just as vigilant. Everyone on the ranch knew of Boyden Trask, how he'd blackmailed Rosemary and the boys, how her testimony had sent him and his two men to prison.

He'd felt uneasy the farther away from Rosemary they got. For all her bravado, he knew how trapped she felt, fear controlling her actions since news of Trask's escape. Dirk much preferred the feisty female who'd given him nothing but grief since he met her. The quiet, unsure young woman worried him. People living in fear for themselves or people they cared about often did things they wouldn't consider when not under stress.

Her loyalty and compassion could be used against her. His biggest concern was she'd turn herself over to Trask if it meant keeping the others safe. Dirk would never allow that to happen.

"Boss?"

Dirk shifted in the saddle to glance behind him. "What is it, Tat?"

"I think we're being followed."

Reining to a stop, he looked around, Mal and Tat doing the same. No one made a sound as they scanned the area bordering the trail and the mountains to the west. After several minutes without seeing or hearing anything, Dirk gave the signal to continue. They hadn't journeyed more than half a mile when they heard rustling in the trees somewhere behind them.

Giving a signal for Tat and Mal to continue, Dirk turned off the trail to wait behind thick, broadleaf shrubs. He didn't have to wait long before he spotted a horse and rider coming toward him. Pausing a moment to unholster his gun, he waited until the rider passed in front of him, then charged out onto the trail.

Aiming the gun at the rider's back, Dirk rode closer. "Stop and get your hands up."

The rider reined to a stop, but didn't raise his hands or turn around.

"Are you deaf? I said get your hands in the air, away from your gun."

A chuckle escaped the rider's lips before he glanced over his shoulder. "I can hear you fine, Dirk."

"Billy?" He moved closer, lowering his gun.

"Yeah. It's me."

Holstering the gun, Dirk rode up next to him. "Why in the hell are you following us? We thought you were Trask or one of his men."

Billy shook his head. "I wasn't following you. I was on my way back down the mountain and saw you boys pass by."

Dirk glared at him, doing his best to rein in his frustration. "And you didn't think to let us know you were behind us?"

Shrugging, Billy nodded at Mal and Tat as they rode up. "You all seemed real intent on staying quiet. I've never seen those two together without joking back and forth, so I knew something was going on."

Dirk closed his eyes long enough to force away the annoyance he felt. Billy had always been a loner and, in his opinion, a wild card. Of the five orphans found in a cave a few years back, his time spent with the Crow tribe, along with the sour taste in his mouth about white settlers not offering them help after their escape, had left the boy bitter, angrier than the others. It was one reason he volunteered to work with Travis miles from the main ranch. He needed space. A place where he could deal with his despair far away from his younger sister, Margaret.

"Travis told you about Trask and how he escaped."

"Yes." Billy waited, knowing there was more.

"Did he also tell you his two men escaped with him?" Dirk asked as they continued along the trail.

Billy's features stilled. He hadn't believed Trask would make the difficult journey from the prison to Splendor by himself. In his most basic form, the man was a coward. Having his men with him made a big difference.

"No. I've been gone a few days, checking the property boundaries and looking for one of the horses who jumped the corral fencing."

Dirk kept his gaze moving about as he'd done before Billy joined them. "Doesn't look like you found him."

"Not yet, but I will. We haven't lost one horse so far, and I'm not going to let it happen now."

Dirk admired his tenacity. Travis liked Billy, and so did the other men who worked at the rapidly expanding horse breeding section of the ranch. If he could get his temper and defensive attitude under control, Dirk believed he'd make a good foreman one day.

"What are you doing out here, Dirk?"

"Checking on the order we have from the army for twenty-five more horses. They need them in a couple weeks. Last time I spoke with Travis, he planned to have the herd ready by this weekend."

Billy took off his hat, scratching his head. "Well, if Travis says he'll have them ready, then he will." Placing his hat back on his head, he glanced over at Dirk. "Maybe I ought to ride back to the ranch with you today."

"You don't need to worry about Margaret. The Pelletiers will keep her safe."

"Sure they will, but she's my sister and my responsibility."

Seeing the last curve in the trail before reaching the old Frey place, Dirk reined to a stop, taking a hard look at Billy. "You want to do something for Margaret?"

Billy set his jaw, nodding.

"If you believe she's your responsibility, come back to the main ranch and learn to work cattle. Live in the bunkhouse where she can see you each day." He saw a brief flare of fire in Billy's eyes before the young man got it under control. "I know you like working the horses, but Margaret is growing up fast. She misses you, son."

Billy opened his mouth, then clamped it shut. He hadn't been anyone's son in a long time, and he sure wasn't a son to Dirk.

"If I do ask Dax and Luke, I'd want to work with Bull."

"I see no problem with that."

Bull had been the one to find the orphans, marrying Lydia, the oldest. Billy had always looked up to him. It surprised everyone when he chose to work miles away, with Travis, instead of staying near Margaret and Bull.

Billy nodded. "I'll think on it."

In Dirk's mind, that was as good as a yes.

"I've got ten good men here, Dirk, and the horses are set to move whenever you're ready. Why don't I ride back over with you and the boys? With the danger of Trask coming back, I'd feel better being close to the ranch." Travis leaned on the top rail of the fence, his legs crossed at the ankles, watching two horses chase each other. Twenty-five horses had been selected and gathered in one large corral next to the barn.

Dirk leaned against the fence, rubbing his jaw as he mulled over the idea. He was pretty certain Dax and Luke would tell him they had the ranch covered. Dirk's gut told him to ignore those thoughts and encourage Travis to do what he thought best.

"It's up to you. Worst I can see happening is they'll send you back." Staring out at the horses, Dirk had another thought. "You could drive the horses to the ranch tomorrow. The big pasture behind the barn is open."

Travis's eyes lit up. "Or we could go today. Billy says he wants to ride along, and you've already got Mal and Tat."

A half-grin crossed Dirk's face as he nodded. "I guess five men for twenty-five horses should be fine."

"I've moved fifty with me and two other men." Travis chuckled, remembering how none of them had slept during the forty-eight-hour journey. "Can't say as I'd want to do it again."

Dirk looked up at the sky, then checked his pocket watch. "It's almost noon and the sky is clear. Let's get some food in our stomachs and get these horses moving."

Rosemary stood on the front porch steps, shaking out a braided rug from the kitchen. Finishing, she folded it, looking up to see a lone rider approaching from the direction of town. Rushing back inside, she dropped the rug in the entry.

"Rachel, Ginny. There's a rider coming."

Rachel came out of the kitchen, Ginny from down the hall.

Wiping her hand on a towel, Rachel looked out the front window, then at Ginny. "Do you recognize him?"

"No. With the beard and his hat covering his face, it could be anyone."

Rachel moved to the gun cabinet, looking over her shoulder at Rosemary. "Go out back. Signal the men on guard. They've probably already seen him, but I don't want to take a chance. Then get Lydia. Bring her, Josh, and the girls in the back door. We'll be upstairs."

"He'll come to the front door," Rosemary said, taking hesitant steps to the back.

"The men will intercept him. Now go."

Rosemary didn't waste another moment. Dashing out the back, she ignored the slamming of the door as she ran around the house to where one of the men chopped wood, the other standing guard. Joe and Ellis had been working for the Pelletiers since they took over the place. Quiet and hardworking, she had little chance to get to know either since both were usually out with the herd.

She stopped next to Joe, glancing at Ellis. "Rider's coming. I need to get Lydia and the children. Rachel's getting everyone else upstairs."

Ellis pushed away from where he leaned against the house. "Saw him headed this way. Never saw the man before. Me and Joe will go out and greet him, find out what he wants, then encourage him to move along. You get moving, girl."

Rosemary let out a relieved breath, then took off to find Lydia and the children. By the time she returned, ushering them inside and up the stairs, she could hear loud voices from the front of the house. Not following the others, she slowly walked to the front window and stared out at the stranger.

The man was thin to the point of being emaciated, his salt and pepper beard in need of a good trim. With his hat pulled low on his forehead, she couldn't make out his face, but something about his voice didn't sound right.

Shifting to get a better look, Rosemary narrowed her gaze. The men who rode with Trask were clean-shaven. One had short hair, the other pulled his back into a queue. A few months in prison could change a man. Still, she thought something would be familiar.

This man's hair fell to below his shoulders, appearing not to have been washed in weeks.

Although he gripped the saddle horn with both hands, she could see them shake slightly. In her heart, she knew this wasn't one of Trask's men.

"Seems when you got to the fork in the trail from Big Pine, you rode north instead of south to Splendor. That's where you'll find him." Ellis kept his rifle ready at his side, nodding toward town.

The man looked over his shoulder, then glanced back at Ellis and Joe, his shoulders slumping even more than when he rode up. Rosemary couldn't let him ride off without at least offering him some water. Taking a chance, she hurried to the front door, throwing it open and walking to the steps.

"Miss Rosemary, you shouldn't be out here," Joe said, waving his arm for her to go inside.

Biting her lip, she ignored him to look directly at the man. "Can we help you?"

Relief flooded the man's face. He opened his mouth to speak, but the words caught in his dry throat.

"Wait here." She rushed back inside, filling a cup with water before returning. Holding it up to him, she watched him lick his parched lips, one trembling hand reaching out to take the cup. Gulping down several swallows, he wiped an arm across his mouth.

"Thank you, ma'am."

The pain in his voice almost broke her heart. "What's your name, sir?"

"Wyatt...Wyatt Jackson. I'm looking for Cash Coulter. Do you know him?"

The slight southern accent reminded her somewhat of Cash and his good friend, Beau. "Everyone around here knows Cash. He's a deputy in town."

"We already told him that, Miss Rosemary. It's time he rode on out to find him."

Handing back the cup with a shaky hand, Wyatt nodded. "They're right, ma'am. I need to move on."

Crossing her arms, she glared at Ellis and Joe before looking at Wyatt. "Not before you've had something to eat, Mr. Jackson. You get off your horse and rest on the porch a spell. I'll go in to see what we have left from dinner."

"Miss Rosemary..." Joe's voice trailed off when she shot him a withering glare. Shaking his head, he looked at Wyatt. "Might as well do what Miss Rosemary says. She'll not let you leave here before you've eaten and met the others."

Sliding off his horse, grabbing the back of the saddle for balance, Wyatt let out a ragged breath. "Others."

Ellis chuckled. "Miss Rachel, Miss Ginny, and Miss Lydia. By the time you've eaten and answered their questions, you'll be more than ready to get out of here."

Chapter Nine

The women sat around the table, children playing in the living room, as Wyatt hunkered over his meal, eating every bite. Rachel watched his movements, believing he had been close to starvation before Rosemary offered him food. She'd seen the look many times as a nurse for the Union Army.

"It might be best if you slowed down some, Mr. Jackson. We have plenty and you can eat as much as you want, but I'm concerned your stomach might not be ready for it."

He glanced up. Even with his beard, Rosemary could see his cheeks redden. "Rachel was a nurse during the war, Mr. Jackson. It's probably best if you take her advice."

Pushing the empty plate away, he leaned back in his chair, looking at Rachel. "I'm certain you are right, Mrs. Pelletier. It all tastes so good."

Rachel smiled. "Like I said, there's plenty more." She had Ellis send a man to town for Cash. It would be best for everyone to confirm Wyatt's story, know for certain the man posed no threat.

Trying to stand, he winced before dropping back into the chair. A painful chuckle escaped his lips. "Guess I'm a little weaker than I thought."

Ginny studied him, not finding it difficult at all to believe he was Cash's friend. "No need to get up,

Mr. Jackson. Sit a while and tell us how you know Cash."

"And what brings you this way," Rachel added.

"It's a long story, and not too interesting."

"Ha. That's what everyone new to Splendor says." Ginny's gaze moved to Rachel, then Rosemary. "There are some amazing stories told by the people who've come here."

His face brightened a little. "I'll bet there are, ma'am."

"My guess is you fought with Cash during the war. Am I right, Mr. Jackson?" Rachel asked.

A weary expression crossed his face. "No offense, ma'am, since you served the North, but I'm an ex-Confederate soldier. That's how Cash and I met. He was my commanding officer."

"No offense taken. My husband, Dax, served the Confederacy, as did his brother, Luke. He's Ginny's husband. Our foreman, Bull, Lydia's husband, served the North. You'll find our town is filled with men and women who were on both sides of the war. We aren't here to judge you, Mr. Jackson, just to learn a little bit more about what brought you to Splendor."

Wyatt rubbed the back of his neck, formulating a reply, when the front door burst open. Cash rushed inside, stopping abruptly at the sight of his friend.

"My God. It *is* you, Jackson. You look like hell."

Wyatt nodded. "Yes, sir, I do. But my belly is full for the first time in weeks."

Rachel stood, indicating for Lydia and Ginny to do the same. "Rosemary, would you mind getting Cash something to drink? It's time we settled the younger children in bed for their naps."

"Of course." She looked at Cash. "Coffee, whiskey, water...

"Coffee, if you don't mind, Rosemary."

Nodding, she turned toward the kitchen. "I'll just be a minute."

Grabbing a chair, Cash swung it around, straddling it to rest his arms on the back. "Tell me what happened."

"If the weather holds, we should make it to the ranch before the sun sets." Tat reined to his left, guiding a few horses back to the herd.

Billy grinned at him from a few yards away, shouting over the sound of pounding hooves on the trail. "In time for me to have supper with Margaret."

Tat moved back alongside him. They'd taken positions at the back. Riding drag was the worst place to be on a cattle drive, but not bad when moving a relatively small number of horses.

"She usually eats with Selina at Bull and Lydia's house. Both girls help take care of Joshua. Bull sure does love that little kid." Tat grinned, thinking about the look of affection on Bull's face whenever he held his son.

"What about the other boys?"

"Sam, Ben, Jimmy, and Teddy eat and stay in the bunkhouse most nights. They like being around the men. Isn't Sam about a year younger than you?" Again, Tat moved to his left, steering the same horses back into the group, muttering under his breath about stubborn animals.

"What about Rosemary?"

Tat looked at him, his brows furrowing. "What about her?"

"Travis said she's staying at the ranch because of Trask. Is someone watching out for her?"

Tat looked toward the front of the herd where Dirk had taken up a position on the right. "The boss watches after her most of the time."

Billy couldn't hide his surprise. "Dirk? I thought they hated each other."

Rubbing his chin, Tat worked to suppress a grin. "From what I've seen, they seem to be getting along real well. 'Course I don't know how long that'll last."

Chuckling, Billy shook his head. "I'd bet not long after Trask is found and sent back to prison. Can't imagine those two keeping the peace much longer than that."

Tat wasn't so certain. He'd seen the look on Dirk's face when Rosemary didn't know he was watching. They appeared to be getting along just fine.

Taking two more bends in the trail, they came to a rise, seeing the ranch sprawled out below them. "Won't be long now." Billy adjusted his hat lower on his head, picking up the pace to bring in the stragglers.

Dirk and Travis guided the herd to a pasture behind the barn, separate from where the men kept their horses. Waiting until the animals were inside, Dirk jumped down from his horse, closing the gate behind them.

"Good job, boys. Time to clean up and relax."

Grabbing his horse's reins, he opted to walk around the barn to the front rather than take his horse through the corral to the back doors. Getting close, he glanced at the house, seeing Rosemary sitting in a chair on the porch, a man he didn't recognize next to her. He didn't return her wave as he continued into the barn, making short work of removing the saddle and letting his horse into the back pasture for water and feed.

Frowning, he stomped out of the barn, taking slow, measured steps to the house. All the time, his gaze assessed the man next to her. As he took the steps, the front door opened.

Cash held out his hand. "Good evening, Dirk. I heard you were meeting with Travis."

Gripping Cash's hand in his, he nodded, glancing again at Rosemary and the stranger. "We made a decision to bring the horses for the army contract over here. Otherwise, I would've been back hours ago." He took a few steps closer to Rosemary, not liking the way the man leaned close to talk to her. "It'll shorten the trip to where we'll meet the men who will move them on to the fort."

Cash watched, not missing the foreman's protective stance. "Dirk, this is Wyatt Jackson. He served with me during the war. Wyatt, Dirk Masters. You've already met Bull. Dirk is the other foreman."

Standing on wobbly legs, Wyatt held out his hand. "Nice to meet you."

Dirk's frown remained fixed as he studied the man, his gaze flickering to Rosemary before he accepted the outstretched hand. "What brings you to the ranch?"

Wyatt opened his mouth to speak when Cash interrupted. "He helped me with a problem a friend of ours had a while back. I told him if he ever had an itch to travel farther west to stop by Splendor."

Looked more as if Wyatt had fallen on some very hard times, but Dirk kept his thoughts to himself. "Do you have experience working on a ranch?"

His eyes flashed for an instant before he shook his head. "After the war, I worked on my brother-in-law's farm. He had some cattle and horses, but nothing compared to Redemption's Edge."

Dirk watched Rosemary. She hadn't taken her gaze off Wyatt for more than a few seconds, which bothered him more than a little.

"If you're interested, we're looking for a couple more men. There'd be a lot to learn, but the bunkhouse is clean and the food plentiful."

Wyatt's jaw worked as he considered the offer. No one but Cash knew the danger that could be following him. He needed the work, could use a warm place to stay and solid food, but putting these people at risk didn't appeal to him.

Rosemary stood, eyeing Wyatt. "It's a good offer. You need a few more days for your body to recover from the long journey."

"I appreciate the offer, Dirk. I'm going to town with Cash to meet his wife. Can I think on it a couple days?" Wincing at the sudden cramping in his stomach, he grabbed the back of the chair to steady himself, Rosemary reaching out to grip his arm.

"Are you all right?" The concern in her eyes wasn't lost on Dirk.

"I'm fine. Probably ate too much." Bending at the waist, he flinched, tightening his grip on the chair.

Stepping next to him, Cash prepared to grab his friend's arm, backing away when Wyatt shook his head.

Cash knew Dirk was cautious and somewhat mistrustful, taking his time to assess people and their motives. "I'd like to show him around Splendor, have one of the doctors check him over. He'll be staying with me and Allie for a few days."

Dirk felt his chest tighten. All his instincts told him Wyatt was on the run, either from the law or something else. He preferred to have him close by, judge his interest in Rosemary, and do his best to learn what secrets the man hid.

Clearing his throat, Dirk looked at Wyatt. "If you decide you want the job, come back and talk to me or Bull." He said nothing more before heading toward the bunkhouse.

"I thought I heard Dirk out here." Dax stepped outside, looking around, his gaze landing on Dirk's retreating back. He and Luke had met Wyatt briefly when they'd returned to the ranch before sequestering themselves in the study to go over the new contracts. "Rachel mentioned you'll be heading into town with Cash."

Doing his best to straighten, Wyatt nodded. "Yes, sir."

"No need for formalities. I'd appreciate it if you called me Dax."

Cash shifted his stance, an indication he was ready to leave. "We'd best get going, Wyatt. I don't want Allie wondering where I've ridden off to."

Rosemary's gaze narrowed on Wyatt. "Are you certain you're all right to ride?"

He controlled the next stab of pain with sheer determination. "Yes, ma'am. I made it this far." Moving toward the edge of the porch, he looked back at Rosemary and Dax. "Thank you for your hospitality."

Dax held out his hand, careful not to tighten his grip too hard when Wyatt took it. "You're welcome back here anytime."

Lifting his hand to touch the brim of his hat, Wyatt nodded at Rosemary. "Ma'am."

Standing on the edge of the porch, her hand wrapped around a post, she watched as they rode off. She had so many questions whirling in her mind about Wyatt. Something had happened to cause him to ride miles in search of Cash, and she knew it had nothing to do with passing through Splendor on his journey west. He seemed so lost, alone, and unsure of his future, much the same as she did.

"What do you think of him?"

Rosemary had been so lost in her thoughts, she'd forgotten Dax stood next to her. Wrapping her arms around her waist, the corners of her mouth tipped up into a wry grin. "Besides my feeling there's more to his story than discovering Splendor?"

Dax chuckled. "Yes. Besides that."

Worrying her lower lip, she stared at Wyatt's back as he and Cash disappeared down the trail. "He's hurting. Not so much physically. He's gone too long without sufficient water and food, but he isn't injured."

"I've seen it many times in the faces of people who were in the heart of the war. It's as if they saw too much death and destruction in too short a time to accept it. I remember Cash mentioning him over a year ago when he returned to Splendor after helping a friend in Arkansas. Wyatt had gotten himself mixed up with a gang raiding local farmers. I don't remember details, other than Cash encouraging him to get out." Dax crossed his arms, noticing Dirk leaving the bunkhouse. "I'm certain there's more to learn about Mr. Jackson. Excuse me, Rosemary. I need to talk to Dirk about the horses for the army contract."

She wanted to speak with Dirk, too. They hadn't been alone since he kissed her in the barn the night before when he'd made it clear the action had been a mistake.

Knowing she shouldn't let it happen again, Rosemary still couldn't push how she felt from her mind. He'd made it clear to everyone he preferred spending his time alone, but that wasn't what she'd experienced when he held her in his arms. His touch was both desperate and gentle, not at all what she expected. She touched her face, feeling it flush, realizing she wanted more than the one kiss.

Her heart tripped over itself as she watched him speaking with Dax. When he glanced at her, his face clouded over before he looked away. She sensed the same pain in him she'd seen in Wyatt's eyes, wondering again about Dirk's past. Maybe he had lost someone dear to him during the war. Many people had lost wives, husbands, brothers, sisters, and parents. Few walked away unscathed from the brutal assaults both sides made on the other. She had her own story. It had less to do with the war and more to do with the necessity to eke out a living on a farm incapable of producing enough food for her family.

Holding a hand over her chest, she squared her shoulders and turned back toward the house. She still had to take supper to the men in the bunkhouse, set the table, and help Rachel and Ginny serve the evening meal. When they were done eating, she vowed to get Dirk alone, ask some of the questions that preyed on her mind.

Just the thought had her gut clenching. Touching a hand to her forehead, she let out an unsteady breath, seeking to relieve her anxiety. If the past were any indication, he'd ignore her questions and excuse himself. All she wanted was a chance to ask.

Dirk wiped his arm across his mouth, leaning back on the bench. He'd chosen to take his meal in the bunkhouse with the men rather than eat inside the house.

When he'd stopped to let Rachel know, Rosemary had been standing a few feet away. Seeing her shoulders slump, her eyes dim, almost had him changing his mind.

Avoiding her hadn't been easy. After their kiss, he'd wanted nothing more than to stay close to her, not let her out of his sight. The decision to ride with Tat and Mal to see Travis had been spontaneous, a way for him to create distance. He'd regretted the impulse the instant he entered the barn. The ride to and from the old Frey place had been long and tedious, his mind consumed with thoughts of Rosemary.

Standing, he picked up his plate and cup, washing and drying them before grabbing his hat.

"Where you off to, Boss?" The broad smile on Tat's face, knowing look in his eyes, almost had Dirk shoving past him. The man seemed to understand far too much.

"Not that it's your business, but I need to speak with Bull." He looked at the others, waiting for comments, but they'd already lowered their faces.

The door closed behind him as he took unhurried steps to Bull's house. Seeing no lights, he shifted his direction to the main house, hoping they'd be finished with supper and he could get Bull alone. Opening the door, he stilled at Ginny's voice.

"Even though it turned out all right, I still don't think it was right for you to just walk outside when Ellis and Joe were sending Wyatt away."

Dirk's back stiffened at her words. Taking another step inside, he kept himself hidden in the entry.

"I don't know what else I could've done. Wyatt didn't look dangerous and he obviously needed food and water. I doubt he could've made it to town in his condition." Rosemary's voice remained calm as she defended herself.

Rachel's soft voice followed. "Helping him was the right decision, but it may have been better to talk with Ellis and Joe before putting yourself in his sights. If he had been one of Trask's men, there was nothing stopping him from pulling a gun."

Dirk's throat tightened. Neither Ellis nor Joe had mentioned what happened once they spotted Wyatt. He'd assumed Rosemary had done what they'd agreed—gotten everyone, including herself, upstairs behind a barricaded door.

"I peeked out the window and saw his condition. He didn't look like a man who planned to harm anyone."

Dirk had heard enough. Removing his hat, he walked to the table, nodding at the men as he stopped behind Rosemary. Setting his hat on the empty seat next to her, he placed his hands on the back of her chair.

"I'd like to have a word with you, Rosemary."

For the second time in an hour, her heart tripped over itself. She'd heard someone walk up, but hadn't looked to see who. Hearing his voice had her throat tightening.

He looked down at her, his voice hard. "Rosemary?"

"Um...fine." Waiting for him to pull out the chair, she stood, gasping when he gripped her elbow.

"Excuse us." Grabbing his hat, he guided her out the front door and down the steps. He didn't speak as they walked to the barn. The bright moon made it unnecessary to light a lantern. Not for what he wanted to say.

Drawing her inside toward the stalls, he turned her to face him, his hands grasping her shoulders.

"Look at me."

When she didn't, he lifted her chin with his finger.

"What the hell were you thinking, approaching a stranger? He could've been anyone, planning to do anything to you and the women. Do you have a death wish?"

Swallowing, her gaze collided with his. "No, of course not."

Letting her go, he paced a few feet away, taking off his hat to shove fingers through his hair. Taking a deep breath, letting it out slowly, he turned to face her. "We agreed if a stranger approached, you'd get the women and children upstairs and stay with them. Did you forget what you promised?" His voice shook, causing her to take a step away as he began to walk back toward her.

Catching her lower lip between her teeth, she lifted her chin, crossing her arms over her chest. "I didn't forget anything." Her voice shook with indignation. "You saw him. Wyatt could not have ridden to Splendor in his condition. He could barely walk inside the house."

Resting fisted hands on his hips, Dirk stopped a foot away, glaring down at her. "But you didn't know that at the time, did you?"

She refused to budge. "He needed help."

"I'll bet you walked out there unarmed. Right?"

Gritting her teeth, she nodded. "I was in a hurry to get to him before Ellis and Joe sent him away."

"God in heaven," he hissed out before grasping her shoulders. "You cannot put yourself in danger that way." Tilting his head back, he stared at the roof, not loosening his grip. When he felt her hands wrap around his arms, he looked down.

"Aw, hell." Without thought, he pulled her close, capturing her mouth in a kiss that wasn't soft or tender. Fear gripped him as he deepened the kiss, wrapping his arms around her in a brutal embrace. Feeling her hands move up his arms to wrap around his neck did nothing to lessen the gnawing terror filling him.

Backing her up against the stall, he continued his assault, hearing her moan, feeling her struggle to get closer. Moving a hand to the back of her head, he moved his mouth along her jaw, trailing kisses down her neck, then up to the tender spot below her ear.

"Dirk..." The need in her voice matched what he felt. Her hands splayed across his back, creating a consuming heat he hadn't allowed himself to feel in years.

The need to fill the aching desire overwhelmed him. He wanted to lift her up, carry her into one of the stalls, and continue what they'd started. But he couldn't do that to her. Not here, not now.

Drawing back, his heart hammering in his chest, he sucked in a ragged breath. Opening his eyes, he waited until she looked at him, her glazed expression matching his own.

"What's wrong?"

Brushing a strand of hair from her face, he placed one more kiss on her lips. "This can't happen."

Blinking, she shrugged out of his embrace, his rejection making her feel foolish. "I don't understand."

Dragging his gaze away from the hurt in her eyes, he paced away. "There are things from my past you don't know about, Rosemary. No one knows. At least not in Montana."

Walking up to him, she placed a hand on his shoulder, only to have him shirk it off and move away. "Tell me."

The tightness in his chest threatened to suffocate him. She wouldn't want anything to do with him if she knew what happened after the war. He'd spent years pushing it all aside, learning to live with the guilt and betrayal. Bringing it up now would serve no purpose. Nothing good could come from purging his soul to satisfy the curiosity of an innocent young woman. A woman he'd come to love, knowing he'd never have a place in her future.

Turning, he cupped her face, settling his mouth over hers for one more kiss.

Releasing her, he stepped away. "Whatever we feel for each other will never work, Rosemary."

The sadness in his voice brought tears to her eyes. "Maybe if you told me..."

Shaking his head, he reached out a hand. "I'll walk you to the house. We won't speak of this again."

Chapter Ten

Rosemary tossed and turned in her bed, unable to let sleep claim her. Throwing off the covers, she swung her legs to the floor and grabbed her night wrapper. Padding to the window, she drew back the curtains, seeing Bull sitting on the bench, his rifle resting across his thighs. A wave of disappointment settled over her.

The memory of Dirk a few hours before, the passion in his kiss, heat radiating from his body, engulfed her. Swiping fingers across her brow, Rosemary closed her eyes, sucking in a shaky breath.

She hadn't imagined it. He wanted her as much as she wanted him. Nothing had ever felt so real or so right. The intensity of their embrace had overwhelmed her, fogging her mind, making her forget all the reasons they couldn't be together. If Dirk hadn't ended it, insisted they never speak of what happened again, she'd be dealing with guilt instead of lack of sleep.

Walking back to the bed, she settled against the headboard, drawing her knees up and wrapping her arms around them. Rosemary knew Dirk thought her inexperienced, and in many ways, she was. She'd made one terrible mistake and suffered the consequences. It didn't mean she knew much about passion, desire, or love.

Every instinct told her Dirk understood these emotions, making the decision to shove them aside before they could take hold. No matter his words, she'd seen the way he looked at her, felt the heat passing between them as he crushed her to his chest.

Rosemary had a decision to make. If she pushed him, somehow convinced Dirk to confide in her, she'd have no choice but to do the same. As much as she wanted to explore the passion between them, she had to protect her past. Protect the secret no one knew.

Dropping her head back, she closed her eyes, then bolted upright. An ear-splitting scream had her jumping up and racing across the room to throw the door open. A loud moan came from the room where Luke and Ginny slept.

"Oh God," Rosemary whispered, hurrying down the hall, praying it wasn't what she suspected. As she reached their door, it opened, Luke standing inside, his face ashen.

"Is it the baby?" Rosemary asked, stepping around him toward the bed. Ginny lay on her side, knees drawn up, hands covering her stomach. Her teeth clenched as beads of sweat rolled down her face. She opened her eyes, focusing on Rosemary.

"I think the baby is coming," she gritted out, feeling Luke at her back.

"I'll get Rachel." She turned, relief flooding her as Rachel entered the room. Rosemary started to speak, stopping when Rachel held up a hand.

"I heard. Get some cool water and towels." Walking up to the bed, she smoothed the hair from Ginny's face. "I've sent Dax to get a wagon ready. Although I'm certain we can handle the delivery at home, I don't want to take a chance."

Ginny's panicked gaze searched hers. "What if the baby won't wait?"

A reassuring smile crossed Rachel's face. "Then you'll have the baby here. I won't let anything happen." She sucked in a slow breath, sending up a prayer her words were the truth.

Rosemary rushed back into the bedroom, setting down the bowl of water. Saturating a cloth, she wrung it out, pressing it against Ginny's face and neck as another scream broke from her lips at the same time pounding on the stairs drew their attention.

Dirk stopped in the doorway, his gaze landing on Ginny before moving to Rosemary. "Dax has the wagon ready."

Luke stood, moving around the bed. "I'll carry her. We'll meet you down there."

Within minutes, Rosemary and Luke were in the back of the wagon with Ginny, Dax on the seat, holding the reins.

"I'll saddle my horse and catch up." Dirk started running to the barn.

"Dirk, wait. You should stay here," Dax called out.

Stopping, he turned back toward the wagon. "I've notified Bull and the other men. Lydia and the girls will stay with Rachel. You'll all be busy with Ginny. Someone needs to keep watch in case Trask shows up at the clinic."

"No sense arguing with him, Dax. Let's go." Luke cradled Ginny's head in his lap, his gut twisting with each scream.

Dax glanced once more at Rachel, concern obvious by his worried expression.

Rachel reached up to touch his arm, giving him a weary smile. "I'll be fine, Dax. You get Ginny to the clinic."

Nodding, he slapped the lines.

Rosemary stepped into the waiting area to see Luke pacing, his features drawn with worry. Seeing her, he opened his mouth, but the words lodged in his throat. Ginny had been pregnant a year before, losing the baby while Luke was away from the ranch. Although no one blamed him, he couldn't shake the guilt of being away when she'd needed him most.

Dax understood Luke's fear. Pushing up from where he sat near the door, he walked to Rosemary.

"Is Ginny all right?"

"She's exhausted, but doing great. Doc McCord expects the baby to come anytime." Just as the words came out, a loud, piercing cry came from the examination room. A slow smile spread across Rosemary's face. "Guess the baby is here."

Luke started forward, stopping when Dax grabbed his arm. "Wait until Rosemary goes back and checks with Doc."

"But—"

Rosemary interrupted him, her eyes misty with relief. "Dax is right. Let me go talk to the doctor. I'll be out as soon as he says it's all right for you to come in."

Shredding both hands through his hair, Luke nodded, wincing when the door closed behind her.

"She's going to be fine, Luke. Did you hear that scream?" Dax asked.

Luke lifted his gaze, his eyes brightening. "Pretty loud, huh?"

"Girl or boy, the baby's going to be a hellion."

Swallowing the fear that had built in his gut since her first scream before dawn, Luke nodded. "One more half-pint ranch hand for us to worry about."

Dirk had kept silent the entire time, keeping a watchful gaze out the window, taking an occasional glance at Rosemary. He knew the pain of losing an unborn child, the guilt that never disappeared, and the stress it created between a man and wife.

Luke jumped when the door opened. Seeing Clay, he walked toward him. "Is she all right?"

Clay couldn't contain his broad smile. "Ginny and the baby are doing fine. Would you like to see them?"

When Luke stood frozen in place, Dax clasped him on the shoulder, urging him along. Following him to the door, Dax peered inside, his chest tightening at the sight of Rosemary holding the baby in her arms, her gaze riveted on the tiny face. When Luke stepped forward, she reached out, encouraging him to take the bundle.

"Go ahead, Luke. You won't hurt him."

"Him?" Luke rasped out, glancing at Ginny. A nod was his only confirmation. Leaning over her, he swept damp hair from her face before placing a kiss on her lips.

"Are you all right?"

Reaching up, she touched his face. "I'm tired, but fine." She looked at Rosemary, who still held the baby. "I know you hoped for a girl..."

His features stilled as he gazed down at her. "I prayed for you to be safe. Boy or girl, it didn't matter, as long as you were all right." Giving her another kiss, he straightened, returning his gaze to Rosemary, who held out his son.

Clearing her throat, Ginny's eyes filled with tears as she watched her husband cradle the baby, staring down at him as if he were the most precious thing on earth.

"Why don't we give them some time alone, Rosemary?" Clay held the door open for her to pass by him. "We'll be out front."

Letting out an exhausted breath, Rosemary walked straight to Dirk, who didn't hesitate to settle an arm around her shoulders, pulling her close. Forgetting about Clay and Dax standing a few feet away, he brushed a kiss across her forehead.

"You did very well in there, Rosemary. I couldn't have asked for a better nurse."

Lifting her head, she looked at Clay, the corners of her mouth tilting up. "Thank you, Doctor. I was worried about her and the baby."

"You did your job and didn't let your apprehension show. That's what all good nurses learn to do." Clay patted her shoulder. "It all turned out fine." Switching his gaze to Dirk, he nodded toward the door. "Why don't you and Dax take Rosemary to the boardinghouse for breakfast? I'll stay here with Luke and Ginny."

"I'm staying here," Dax said. "You two go along."

She looked up at Dirk. "I *am* hungry."

Chuckling, he dropped his arm. "Can we bring you two back anything?"

Sitting down in one of the chairs, Clay shook his head. "Thanks, Dirk, but I'll get something later."

"Same here," Dax added.

Dirk settled his hand on the small of Rosemary's back as he looked down at her. "Do you need anything before we leave?"

"Just my coat."

She walked to the other room off the waiting area, a small place used when the doctors had more than one patient. More and more, they'd been seeing several patients at a time, confirming the need for a new clinic.

When she stepped into the back room, Clay cocked a brow at Dirk while Dax cleared his throat. "You and Rosemary?"

"We're friends, Dax."

"Yes, I can see that."

Dirk stared at his boss, gritting his teeth. "Just friends."

"Uh-huh." Clay scrubbed a hand down his face, ignoring Dirk's scowl.

"Don't worry. Neither of us will say anything. Whatever is going on is between you and Rosemary."

Dirk started to speak, closing his mouth when Rosemary came back.

Looking between the men, her brows furrowed. "Is everything all right?"

"Fine," Dirk ground out, grasping her elbow. "Let's go."

Suzanne's restaurant had been open long enough that morning to fill most of the tables. They'd taken one of the two empty ones, sitting close to each other in a back corner. Both were exhausted, talking little as they ate the eggs and ham before them.

"More coffee?" Suzanne stood next to the table, a pot in her hand.

Nodding, Dirk held up his cup. "Thanks, Suzanne."

She filled Rosemary's next. "So, what brings you two into town so early?"

Dirk locked his gaze on Rosemary, indicating it was her decision whether or not to say anything. Letting out a slow breath, she looked at Suzanne, who took a seat next to her.

"Ginny and Luke had their baby this morning. We brought them in from the ranch a few hours ago."

Suzanne slapped the table with both hands, then motioned for her husband, Nick, to come over from where he sat with two other gentlemen. He walked up, then leaned down to kiss her cheek.

"Yes, sweetheart?"

"Luke and Ginny had their baby this morning."

Pulling out a chair, Nick sat, taking Suzanne's hand in his. "That's wonderful news. Is Ginny doing all right?"

Rosemary nodded. "She's exhausted, but yes, she and the baby are doing fine."

"A boy or girl?" Suzanne asked, squeezing Nick's hand.

"A boy. Healthy and loud."

"Were you with them, Dirk?" Nick asked.

"Dax brought Luke, Ginny, and Rosemary in the wagon. I rode in with them."

"Doc McCord and I were with Ginny until the baby came." Rosemary took a final sip of coffee, setting the cup down. "Dax is still at the clinic with them."

Rubbing the back of his neck, Dirk leaned forward. "We should get back, let Clay get breakfast."

"How soon before Luke can take her and the baby home?" Suzanne asked Rosemary.

"I don't know. He may let her go home today if she and the baby are doing all right. Rachel told me that in the big cities, they make women stay at the hospital for days."

Nick shook his head. "That's not too practical out here. With Rachel at the ranch, I'll wager Ginny won't stay in town long."

Rosemary grinned. "I agree."

Standing, Nick pulled out Suzanne's chair. "I'm meeting Gabe at the new clinic."

"And I have customers." Suzanne looked at Rosemary. "Tell Luke and Ginny we'll come out to the house in a few days."

Dirk stood, pulling money from his pocket. "We'll tell them. We'd better get back, Rosemary."

Stepping outside, he took her hand, slipping her arm through his as they walked to the clinic.

"Have you been married before, Dirk?"

Stopping, he sucked in a breath, turning to look at her. His gaze darkened, a muscle in his jaw twitching as he let her arm drop from his.

"Yes." Without another word, he continued down the boardwalk.

"Dirk. Wait." Rosemary hurried to catch up. When she reached him, she grabbed his arm. "Wait...please."

He stared down at her, his face a mask.

"Are you still married?"

He narrowed his gaze at her, his mouth twisting in disgust. Shaking off her hand, he opened the clinic door. "No."

"But—"

She wasn't able to say anything more before he turned on her, holding up a finger, the veins in his neck pulsing.

"This discussion is over." Leaving her with her mouth gaping open, Dirk knocked on the examination room door.

Dax opened the door and whispered, "Come on in."

Dirk hesitated, not wanting to intrude.

"It's okay, Dirk. Ginny's sleeping." Luke walked up to him, the baby in his arms. Lifting the blanket, he looked down at his son.

"He's beautiful, Luke." Rosemary stood next to Dirk, ignoring the pain in her chest to focus on the baby. "Did you have time to choose a name?"

"Not yet. Ginny's been asleep, which is what she needed. We'll talk about it when she's rested."

"I think Dax is a good name." Dax leaned a shoulder against the wall, his eyes crinkling at the corners.

Luke chuckled. "It's a fine name, but we have some other ideas, which I'm not sharing with you right now. What does need to be decided is how long before I can take my wife and son home." He looked at Clay.

"If Ginny's doing fine later today, perhaps she'll be able to go back this evening."

"That's great—"

"I said *perhaps*, Luke. Ginny was fortunate the baby didn't take long to get here. Still, it's an ordeal and the ride to the ranch is long after what she's been through. It may be best to get a room at the boardinghouse or the St. James for a couple nights. I can check on her and the baby each day to make sure they're both doing all right."

Dax's face sobered. "The doc has a point, Luke. Rachel stayed in bed a few days before leaving the bedroom."

"You were at home, right?" Rosemary took another look at the baby.

Dax nodded. "Yes. Bull rode into town to get Doc Worthington. Charles didn't waste any time getting there." He remembered it as if it happened yesterday. "I didn't think I'd live through it."

"Neither did the rest of us." Luke grinned, rocking the baby in a gentle motion.

"It might be best to stay in town, little brother. I can go talk to Gabe about a room at the hotel, unless you'd rather stay at Suzanne's place."

"I'll speak with Ginny. My guess is she'd rather be near Suzanne. You know how close they were when Ginny worked for her. Plus, I'd be able to go down to the kitchen and rustle up some food."

"I'll go let her know, make sure she has a room." Dirk moved to the door. "Dax, do you want me to head back to the ranch with Rosemary?"

"It's a good idea. I'll borrow a horse from Noah and ride back after I've had breakfast. She'd have to ride behind you."

Lifting her chin, her shoulders drawn back, she waited for Dirk to refuse the idea.

"Fine, if Rosemary approves."

His answer stunned her to the point she shot him a shocked look.

He crossed his arms, lifting a brow. "Rosemary?"

"Yes, I'll ride behind you. I don't want to be away from Rachel too long."

"Let her know I'll be back soon."

Rosemary nodded. "I will, Dax."

"I'll check with Suzanne about a room and be back in a few minutes." Dirk focused his attention on Rosemary. "Be ready to go when I get back."

She wanted to stomp her feet at his brutish attitude. Instead, she plastered a sweet smile on her face and nodded. There'd be time to pay him back on the ride home.

Chapter Eleven

"Hold on, Rosemary. I don't want to waste time returning to the ranch." As soon as they reached the edge of town, Dirk rolled a heel into Banshee's side, moving the horse into a lope.

Doing as he asked, she tightened her grip around his waist, resting her head against his back. After a few minutes, she became accustomed to the pace, letting her hands relax a little and drop lower.

A low growl vibrated through his body, surprising her. One of his hands grabbed both of hers, pulling them to his chest.

"Keep them there."

His terse command had her lifting her head from his back and drawing away. Nothing she did ever seemed to please him, and she was getting darn tired of it. Rosemary did her best to create some distance between her body and his, but each bend in the trail seemed to pull her closer.

Trying to relax, she drew in a deep breath, glancing skyward. She took in the cloudless, blue sky, the bright sun beating down on them, allowing exhaustion to take over. Leaning forward to rest her head against his back, she let out a tired breath.

She kept her eyes open, watching as they rode past bushes and trees, finally allowing sleep to claim her, awakening a few minutes later when Dirk changed Banshee's pace. Without warning, Dirk grabbed her hands again, gripping them tight in one hand. She hadn't realized they'd fallen below his waist.

"That hurts," she yelled over his shoulder.

He didn't respond. Instead, Dirk pulled her hands to his chest, holding them there.

Anger, frustration, and exhaustion exploded within her. She had more than enough of his churlish attitude. Ripping her hands from his grasp, she pulled them to her chest, then pushed against his back. When he didn't respond, she pushed again, then began to pound.

Dirk reined Banshee to a stop, turning in the saddle. "What the hell are you doing?"

Losing her grip, she slid off the saddle, hitting the ground hard, knocking the wind from her lungs. Unable to draw a breath, she sat there, dazed, feeling strong hands slide up and down her arms.

"Breathe, Rosemary." His voice had softened, the anger gone as he studied her face. Moving a hand to her back, he rubbed in soft, soothing circles. The motion helped her relax as she drew in a slow breath, then another.

"It hurts."

Shaking his head, he wrapped his arms around her, pulling her close. "Of course it hurts," he whispered in her ear. "Falling off a horse never feels good, sweetheart. What were you thinking?"

Rosemary had no explanation for the way she acted—shoving him, pounding on his back, then allowing herself to fall. At least no explanation she wanted to voice. One moment, he was harsh and brutal in his comments. The next, he was soothing her, holding her in his arms.

Wrapping her arms around him, she relaxed in his strong embrace. "I don't know."

Drawing back, he moved one hand to her chin, lifting her face, his gaze locking with hers. "You don't know?"

Rosemary let her eyes drift closed, shaking her head. She sensed him lowering his head right before he brushed a kiss across her lips.

"Again," she breathed against his mouth.

There was no hesitation this time.

Even as he lifted her into his arms, Dirk knew their actions were foolish. No matter how he tried to convince himself otherwise, in his heart, Dirk knew she deserved better. Young, beautiful, and innocent, she needed a man without the burdens his past held.

For now, he'd take some of what she offered, allowing the comfort of her touch to cleanse him.

Walking off the trail, he placed her on a bed of bison grass, removing his hat before stretching out beside her. Running his fingers down her cheek, his breath caught when she turned her face toward him, the desire and trust in her eyes burning a path through him.

Placing a soft kiss on her lips, he sat up, running both hands through his hair. Looking down at Rosemary's confused expression, Dirk took hold of her hand, cradling it in his lap.

Sitting up, she rested her head on his shoulder, her heart all but jumping out of her chest. Touching his arm, Rosemary drew in an unsteady breath.

"What's wrong, Dirk? Please...tell me."

Tamping down the pain, which never let up, he thought through all the reasons to stay silent. Dirk told himself he owed her no explanation. The secrets of his past belonged to him and no one else.

"Perhaps talking about it will help."

He didn't see how. Nothing could undo what had happened when he returned from the war. The events of those few weeks scarred him as much as all he'd seen during years of war.

"I've never spoken of it, Rosemary. I'm not sure I can." Dropping her hand, he stood, pacing several feet away. Staring back at the trail, at Banshee standing where he'd been left, Dirk fisted his hands at his sides.

Standing, she took a hesitant step toward him. "You won't know unless you try."

Turning toward her, his jaw tight, eyes haunted, he took one tentative step forward.

"My wife was murdered."

Rosemary's gasp, her hand flying to cover her mouth, almost stopped him from continuing. Watching as surprise, shock, and confusion played across her face, Dirk knew he had to tell her everything, end her fantasies about the two of them.

"They arrested me for her murder."

Denver, Colorado

"Sister, you must read this." Selma Ritter handed Davinia the Denver Gazette, dated two days before. "It is quite interesting." Picking up her cup, she stared out the window of the restaurant, pushing aside her empty dinner plate before sipping her coffee

Huffing out an exasperated breath, Davinia pulled the reading spectacles from her reticule, settling them on the bridge of her nose. "I can't imagine what a small frontier newspaper would say that I'd find of interest." Scanning the paper, her eyes froze on a story at the bottom of the front page.

"It's about those missing young women, Davinia."

She peered over the rim of her glasses. "I can see that, Selma." Reading the article, Davinia's eyes narrowed, the only sign the news surprised her.

Tapping her fingers on the tabletop, she pressed her lips into a thin line. Looking around, she focused her attention on the street outside. "I don't believe I've seen Mr. Cullin since we arrived in Denver. Have you seen him, Sister?"

Selma shook her head. "Nor have I seen his traveling companions. I do declare, those men can disappear with the snap of a finger." She giggled at her own joke, then sobered, leaning toward Davinia. "We must be careful. I have a bad feeling about them."

Davinia waved her hand in the air, dismissing her sister's concerns. "You're suspicious of everyone, Selma. Why, just yesterday, you were certain the young man at the hotel was spying on us."

Selma sat back, crossing her arms. "That's because he was. How else do you explain him showing up at each place we visited since arriving in Denver?"

Tossing aside the paper, Davinia shook her head. "That was *not* him in the library yesterday."

Selma scoffed. "And that *wasn't* a library. It was a ramshackle hovel with dust an inch thick and books so used, one could barely read the pages."

Davinia bit her lip to stifle a laugh. Whereas she was the one who dampened spirits, forcing her sister back to reality, Selma saw enchantment in almost all things. The world she lived in held little resemblance to what others saw around them. Instead, Selma created a realm of her own design.

The one topic she took seriously was books. In her heart, they were sacred objects. She had little patience for those who didn't revere them in the same way. It had been the source of many arguments while they were growing up, causing tension between her and their cousins. The thought of their cousins conjured up an image of their parents. Davinia's heart turned cold at the thought.

"Regardless, Selma, at least there *is* one, which is more than we found in Ogallala or Cheyenne. Now, back to Mr. Cullin and his companions. I agree we should be careful around them. That is, if they do get back on the train."

"I do believe we travel back to Cheyenne before leaving for Salt Lake." Selma touched a finger to her forehead. "I am getting tired of the train, Sister. Have you considered changing our plans so we may ride a stagecoach?"

Davinia choked on the last of her coffee. "Stagecoach? From what I've heard, they're dirty, rough, and are populated by scoundrels and villains."

"I've heard nothing of the sort. Until the railroads, many people traveled by stagecoach, including women and children. It would be a nice change and, well..." Selma lifted a hand, chewing on a fingernail, the other hand fidgeting with the pendant around her neck.

"What is it, Sister?" Davinia cocked her head to one side.

Rubbing the pendant between her thumb and index finger, Selma shifted in her seat. "Well, the missing young women, those who've been murdered, are along the train route. Do you remember hearing there were Pinkerton agents on the train from Ogallala?"

"Of course I do," Davinia snorted.

"I believe they're here in Denver looking for whoever is doing this. The Pinkerton Agency believes the killer is riding the train. It may be time for us to change our plans, Sister. Perhaps take a stagecoach north."

Davinia stared out the window, her brows lifting when she spotted Willard Cullin and his companions. Her attention focused on the state of their clothing. Dirty and in disarray, she wondered what they'd been doing, and if the Pinkerton agents were on the train, were they aware of Cullin and his friends' strange behavior at each stop. Right then, she made the decision to find the agents and let them know.

Davinia folded her hands in her lap. "Perhaps you're right, Sister. Taking the stage north might be a very good idea."

The trail to Redemption's Edge

"Murder?" Rosemary took a faltering step backward. "I don't understand."

He refused to go to her, offer comfort after the shock of his confession. As harsh as it seemed, she needed to understand why they'd never be able to build a life together.

"It's simple enough, Rosemary. My wife was murdered and they arrested me for her death."

Taking slow breaths, she ignored the sharp edge to his words. "Did you do it?"

His muscles tensed, nostrils flaring as he shook his head. "No."

"Then that was the end of it."

Dirk shook his head again, his shoulders slumping. "Not really. Most in the town still believed me guilty. Store owners refused to sell me supplies. The blacksmith refused to work on my horses. Only one saloon would allow me to come in for drinks, and not a single restaurant welcomed me. Even the minister and his wife shunned me, and I'd known them my entire life." He let out a shaky breath. "No matter the lack of evidence or the witnesses who said I was with them playing cards at the time, they believed I killed her." He shifted his gaze, no longer able to look at her.

Her chest squeezed at the pain in his voice. "That's why you left."

"I couldn't stay." Crossing his arms over his chest, he fought for control, not wanting to tell her more. "Now do you understand why we can't be together?"

"Excuse me if I sound simpleminded, but no, I don't understand. You've built a life here, far away from those who doubted you. It's a fresh start, Dirk."

A low growl escaped his lips. "There's more."

Closing the gap between them, she placed a hand on his arm. "Tell me. I want to hear all of it." Turning away, she walked to a fallen tree and sat down. Arranging her skirt around her, clasping her hands together, she looked up at him. "No one is expecting us back this early. We have as much time as you need."

Pinching the bridge of his nose, Dirk closed his eyes for a moment. He'd rather be doing almost anything than standing here, baring his soul to the person who meant the most to him. Memorizing the serene look on her face, the hope in her eyes, knowing they'd be gone when he finished, Dirk began.

"Since we were boys, my older brother, Griffen, and I dreamed of building the best horse ranch in northern Pennsylvania. Fine horses the upper classes would be proud to own. We worked hard, built houses, married. Griff had a son and a daughter. Melissa and I wanted a family, but it didn't happen as easily as it did for him and his wife." Sucking in a breath, he continued. "When the war started, I enlisted to fight for the Union. Griff understood my need to play a part in keeping the country together. With two children, he volunteered to keep the ranch going while I was gone." Shaking his head, he paced several feet away. "Melissa never accepted my decision. She was a good woman, but more fragile than Griff's wife. After I left, she found out she was pregnant. I didn't hear of it until a letter found me much later...after she'd lost the baby." He looked at Rosemary. "I wasn't there for her. In her mind, I chose the country over her."

"You did what you believed was right."

"I abandoned her. That's what she told me in one of her letters." Dirk rubbed the back of his neck. "Melissa moved into Griff's house to help with the children and not be alone. At least that's what my brother's letter said. She didn't mention it in hers." He paused so long, Rosemary thought he wouldn't continue.

"I stayed until after the Battle of Winchester. I was a captain in the cavalry and felt my work was done. I'd given enough and it was time to return to my wife and the ranch."

Scrubbing a hand down his face, Dirk shook his head, searching for the best way to continue. Now he understood why he'd never spoken of his past after leaving Pennsylvania.

"Melissa moved back into our house, but things were different between us. There was no passion, no desire. She went about her day, cooking, cleaning, sometimes helping with the horses. We spoke little. The worst was when she'd shy away from my touch, didn't want me near her. I began spending some of my nights in town, drinking and playing cards. There was nothing at home." He put a hand on his chest, trying to lessen the pain of what he was about to say. "One night, I came home earlier than she expected. Griff's horse was outside the house. When I climbed the porch steps, I heard them inside." He looked at Rosemary. "By the sounds they were making, they weren't talking."

"Oh God." She covered her mouth with her hand.

"I looked in the window, saw what I needed, and rode out."

"You didn't confront them?"

His features hardened. "If I'd have gone inside, there's a chance I may have killed them both. Instead, I chose to leave, go back to the saloon, and drink. By the time I returned later that night, he was gone and she was in bed. I didn't join her. I'd made the decision to confront Griff the next day, then do the same with Melissa." Pausing, he walked in a slow circle, wishing he could forget the rest. "I'd forgotten

Griff was leaving early the next morning on business. So I waited, spent long hours in town, kept my mouth shut, and tried not to think on it too much. What was the point? I'd already figured my marriage and partnership with my brother were over. All that was left was getting my half of the ranch from him and starting over." He snorted. "Although I had no idea where I'd go."

She waited as he gathered his thoughts, not wanting to push. "Don't feel you have to tell me everything now. We can talk another time, Dirk."

"No. It's best if you hear it all now." Walking to a large pine, he leaned against it, his face clouded. "The third night after he left, I came home a little before midnight. Everything looked fine outside, nothing seemed amiss. When I walked into the house..." His eyes closed, throat working, but nothing came out for several long moments. Inhaling a deep breath, he went on. "When I walked inside, Melissa was on the floor, covered in blood." He looked up. "She was dead."

Rosemary placed a hand on her stomach, trying to lessen the nausea his words caused. She couldn't imagine the pain he must have felt at seeing his wife dead, knowing she'd given herself to his brother. He'd never have a chance to understand why.

"I rode to town, returning with the constable and doctor. The doc was still in the saloon where I'd left him at a table playing cards. If it weren't for his assertion I couldn't have been the one to kill her, the constable would've arrested me that night. Instead, it took him two days to come back for me." Weary from the tale, he sat down on a small rock across from Rosemary, rubbing a hand across his brow. "Griff had returned by then, stunned at the news of Melissa's death. I confronted him with what I knew about the two of them. He didn't deny it, admitting they'd been together for months."

Rosemary's eyes widened. "His wife didn't know?"

"No. I'd never seen my brother break down or cry, not even when our parents died. He begged me to forgive him, to stay at the ranch." He glanced at Rosemary. "I told him I couldn't do it. Not after what he'd done. An hour later, the constable came and arrested me."

Leaning forward, Dirk buried his face in his hands, his shoulders shaking as he dealt with grief he'd held inside for years.

Rosemary's heart constricted, wishing she knew how to relieve his pain. Going to him, she sat down, her hand rubbing comforting circles on his back as he'd done for her earlier.

"But they let you go?"

Nodding, he sucked in a breath. "The doctor sent for a specialist he knew in New York. A man who analyzed crimes as a scientist would also analyze a specimen. Doc had written meticulous notes, documenting everything he saw the night Melissa died. The most important part was the fact her blood had dried, already turning color, when the doctor arrived. The specialist was adamant I couldn't have been the killer. Griff spent a good deal of money, hiring an attorney from Philadelphia. Between the specialist from New York and the lawyer's arguments, the jury didn't have enough proof to convict me. Still, most of my neighbors believed I'd done it. It seems a few of them knew what was going on between Melissa and Griff." The last words were cryptic, filled with disdain.

"Did they ever find out who killed her?"

"Not that I know of. I left not long after being released. Griff sends money once in a while, paying me for my half of the ranch. Beyond that, we have no communication. To be truthful, I don't care about finding the killer. Nothing will change the past or what she and Griff did."

They sat in silence for several minutes, Rosemary processing all he'd told her. After a while, he stood, reaching out his hand to help her up. When she stood, he rested his hands on her hips.

"I've no interest in trying to rebuild the life I once had. The thought of a wife and children mean nothing to me now. I can't ask that of you, Rosemary."

"And you don't know if you can trust me."

Her words startled him. She cut through all he'd said, identifying the biggest obstacle between them. The betrayals of his brother and wife had changed him more than the destruction he'd witnessed during the war. As much as he cared for Rosemary, wanted her in his bed, he'd always wonder if she could be trusted.

Letting his hands fall to his sides, he shook his head, the sadness in his eyes breaking her heart. "No."

Taking a step away, Rosemary did her best to ignore the hurt and disappointment, refusing to let him see her cry. She'd fallen in love with him, only to learn no woman would ever hold a place in his heart again.

"I'm sorry. I had no business making you believe otherwise."

She shook her head, looking down, unable to meet his gaze. "You've always been honest with me, Dirk. I never expected to have feelings for you." Placing a hand on her chest, she turned away, refusing to let him see her break.

"And you do?"

Without looking back, she nodded. "I guess we'd better get back to the ranch. We don't want Dax getting there ahead of us."

Watching as she walked toward Banshee, he felt the most acute pain in his chest he'd ever experienced. Not even Melissa's betrayal ripped through him the way Rosemary's quiet acceptance of his rejection did.

He hadn't expected to care for her. Falling in love had never been his intention, yet it happened. He wished he could be the man she needed. One who'd love her with a complete heart, not one shattered by his wife's betrayal. But he'd never be that man.

Chapter Twelve

Both were silent during the final portion of their journey to the ranch. Rosemary's hands hooked around Dirk's waist, yet she no longer pressed her body against his as she'd done the first part of the ride. He missed the contact and her warmth.

"You aren't the only person to experience injustice, Dirk."

Her quiet comment surprised him. Glancing over his shoulder, he saw the sincerity on her face. "I know that, Rosemary."

"Most people in Splendor are here to put their past behind them and move on. You could do the same."

Letting out an exasperated breath, he didn't respond, giving her a curt nod. They had a couple more bends in the trail before they'd see the ranch house. Whatever she had to say needed to be said now. Reining Banshee to a stop, he shifted in the saddle, giving her his full attention.

"What secret are *you* trying to forget, Rosemary?"

Recoiling at his question, she dropped her hands from around his waist, gripping the back of the saddle. Although not nearly as secure, the cantle kept her from sliding to the ground.

Licking her lips, she glanced away. "I don't know what you mean."

"We all have something in our past we'd rather forget. What happened to you that you're not telling me?" His intense gaze bore into her.

She knew the time had come to confess. When Rosemary opened her mouth to speak, the words froze in her throat.

The sound of an approaching horse saved her from responding. She knew it would be a short reprieve. Dirk wasn't the type of man to give up.

"I thought the two of you would be at the ranch by now." Dax stopped alongside Banshee.

Dirk glanced at Rosemary. "It went a little slower than intended."

She swallowed, glad for the interruption. "Are Ginny and the baby doing all right?"

A smile brightened Dax's face. "They're doing fine. They'll be staying at the boardinghouse tonight and maybe tomorrow night. Doc McCord will make the decision on when Ginny and the baby are ready to come home." He looked up, noticing a few rain clouds moving toward them. "We'd best get back. Rachel's probably sitting on the porch, waiting for news." He moved ahead of them, continuing along the trail.

"Don't think this conversation is over, Rosemary, because it isn't." Shifting forward in the saddle, he waited until he felt her hands move around his waist, then followed Dax.

His dogged persistence in learning about her past worried her. She knew he'd be relentless in his questions until he was satisfied she'd told him everything. Once he learned her story, she saw little chance they'd remain friends.

Rosemary had never spoken to anyone about what happened, pushing the painful memory aside. After he'd shared his past, she knew he deserved the truth, though she wasn't certain she could speak of it now.

Trask's escape had left her with few options. Before, she'd have stayed at the boardinghouse with little worry of running into Dirk. That choice had been taken away from her and she had no idea how long her stay at the ranch would last. She couldn't avoid him, or the conversation, forever. As they made the last turn, she felt herself stiffen with resolve. If she had to speak of it, it was best it be with Dirk. He wouldn't like what she had to say, but believed he'd never betray her trust, just as she wouldn't betray his. The time had come to reveal her past.

"We should've headed north, like Herb said." Rufus Ickert sat huddled near the fire, chewing the last of the hardtack they'd stolen from a farm two days before.

Herb Yandell nodded. "It might've taken longer, but we wouldn't be lost in these woods without food. At least there are farms and ranches to the north."

Boyden Trask finished the water in his canteen, then stood. "Neither of you know what you're talking about. Heading north would've taken us into Blackfoot territory, a risk I'm not willing to take. I hear they're mostly peaceful, but I'm not willing to bet my life on it. Besides, we'd be tromping through a helluva lot more snow than what we see on this trail." Turning his back on them, he walked toward the creek.

"Where you headed?" Rufus asked.

"To fill my canteen." Trask cursed as he tripped over roots buried under a mound of melting ice.

Rufus tossed a handful of twigs onto the fire, shaking his head. "I don't know, Herb. Boyd's so hell-bent on revenge, he's not thinking straight. Maybe if we'd waited another month to escape, the trails would've been easier and there'd be more deer and elk to hunt."

"The timing was right, so we took it. Who knows if we'd have had a better chance later. The number of deer and elk don't matter 'cause Trask has no intention of stopping long enough for us to hunt. We'd have done better raiding the ranches we rode past." Tightening his coat around him, Herb hunkered down against the increasingly strong wind. "Fact is, we left with him. Now we've got to do the best we can until he's finished with the Thayer woman."

"If it were up to me, we'd get out of the Montana Territory as fast as possible, head south, and start over where no one knows us."

"It don't matter, Ruf. Now that we've escaped, our faces are going to be plastered everywhere."

Scrubbing a hand down his face, he looked up. "We could ride off without him." Rufus glanced toward the creek, lowering his voice. "No reason we have to stay with him. I'm telling you, Boyd isn't right in the head when it comes to the girl."

Swallowing the last of the dried meat, Herb stood, stretching his arms above his head. "I don't like the way he's obsessed with revenge any more than you, but I ain't leaving yet. He's got money hidden, and part of it belongs to us."

"What money?" Rufus sat up, his gaze hardening.

Herb glanced down at him, smirking. "What do you think happened to the money he made at his restaurant and selling most of the stolen cattle? It may not be much, but he's got it hidden someplace near the Pelletier ranch and I want my share."

Shaking his head, Rufus snorted. "The man ain't rich, Herb. That's why he blackmailed those brats.

Whatever you heard about a stash of money, you're wrong. Boyd's got no more money than me or you."

Hearing the rustling of bushes, Herb sat back down, ignoring Rufus's words as Trask walked toward them. "We gotta get some food tomorrow."

Trask scowled at Herb, but nodded. "We should be through the worst part tomorrow. From what I heard from other inmates, there are several small ranches on the other side of the forest. We'll get what we need from them."

"How far you figure we are from the Pelletier ranch?" Herb asked.

Trask thought a moment as he stared into the fire. "Three days. Maybe four."

"You know, they'll have gotten word about us escaping. Probably expect we'll ride their way." Rufus didn't look at Herb, focusing his attention on Trask. "We could be in Wyoming in a couple days if we head south, then ride on from there. Maybe Arizona. No one would be looking for us there."

Trask's lips twisted into a feral grin. "We head west, take care of business, then decide from there. I'm not leaving the area until I've settled some things with the Thayer girl."

Jumping up, Rufus paced back and forth, taking off his hat to run a hand through his hair. "It's a big risk, Boyd. They were waiting for us when we tried to get her in Splendor, and they'll be waiting for us at the ranch. We'll be riding into a trap."

"You afraid, Ruf?" Trask sneered.

"Damn right I am. Only a fool wouldn't be when they know someone's waiting for them to show up. The ranch is full of men who are crack shots. This ain't like blackmailing children, Boyd."

An uncomfortable silence fell between the three men. Rufus and Herb moved their hands to the handle of their guns, waiting for Trask to explode. The man wasn't used to being questioned. He'd be as likely to draw a gun and shoot as explain himself.

Herb stood, putting some distance between him and Trask. "Ruf's right. We got out of that hellhole and I'm not interested in going back. I don't see a purpose in going after the girl. What's done is done. I think we should get as far away from here as we can."

Trask's gaze narrowed on Herb, then moved to Rufus, but his hand didn't touch his gun. "I need sleep. We'll talk about this tomorrow." Leaving both men to stare after him, Trask grabbed his bedroll, shaking it out a few feet from the fire.

"You want us to keep watch, Boyd?" Herb asked, still not believing Trask yielded so easily. He hadn't agreed with them, but his response wasn't the angry contempt Herb expected.

Looking around, Trask shook his head. "There's been no sign of anyone following us. Bed down and get some sleep. We'll start early tomorrow." Laying down, he pulled a blanket over him, turning his back to the fire.

Rufus waited until he heard Trask snoring, then stood, motioning for Herb to follow. Moving to the other side of the horses they'd stolen their first day of freedom, he shot a look in Trask's direction.

"Something ain't right, Herb."

Stroking his chin, he nodded. "Yeah."

"What are we gonna do?"

Herb drew in a slow breath, his jaw working. "I don't know."

"He ain't the same man who brought us together a few years ago." Rufus tapped his head. "He just ain't right up here when it comes to that girl. Let's take our horses and ride out. He won't know we're gone until we've put miles between us."

Not a rash man, Herb hesitated. "We've been with him a long time. Maybe he wants to think on what we said."

Rufus shook his head. "I don't think so, and I ain't waiting around to find out. He's got a death wish, Herb. All that's gonna happen is him getting us killed."

Rubbing the back of his neck, Herb thought about the changes he'd seen in Trask since their first encounter years ago. Rufus was right. The man had changed from a hardened businessman to a calculating convict bent on revenge. The deterioration had been slow. As his businesses began to fail, he panicked, making irrational decisions, becoming suspicious of everyone. It had worsened during their time in prison. Now all he craved was vengeance, and Herb had no doubt he'd get them all killed before it ended.

"Let's go," he ground out in a flat voice.

"What about our gear?" Rufus glanced at their bedrolls near the fire.

"We can't take a chance he'll wake up and see us." Herb moved to his horse, glad they'd made the decision to keep them saddled, and swung himself up while Rufus did the same. "You ready?"

Rufus nodded, taking one more uneasy glance at Trask's sleeping form. "Where to?"

"We ride south."

Splendor

"You're certain you've told me everything, Wyatt?" Gabe Evans leaned his arms on his desk, his features unreadable, as were those of Dutch McFarlin, who leaned against the wall, his arms folded across his chest. Cash occupied a chair next to Wyatt.

Rubbing a hand down his weary face, Wyatt nodded. "Yes, sir. I'd captured Ned Baylor when Cash came to Arkansas to help Stephen Ramsey."

Gabe looked down at his notes. "You, Cash, and Ramsey served together, correct?"

"Yes, sir. We fought for the Confederacy. Ramsey and I served under Cash."

Nodding, Gabe motioned for Wyatt to continue.

"After the war, I went home to Tennessee to help my sister and her husband, decide what I wanted to do next. I'd thought of being a bounty hunter, the same as Cash, but wanted to spend time with family before deciding." Wyatt sucked in a breath, glancing around the room.

"Dutch, do you mind pouring Wyatt some coffee?" Gabe asked.

"Not at all." Grabbing a dented tin cup, Dutch filled it to the top, handing it to Wyatt.

"Thanks." Cradling the cup with both hands, he took a few sips, then set it on the desk. He blew out a breath, his face showing the misery he felt. "I'd gone into town to drink and play a few hands of cards. I got tangled up with one of the women and didn't make it back to the farm until late. I found my sister huddled in a corner, her dress torn, blood all over her." He looked up, his eyes haunted. "He raped her, then killed my brother-in-law. She couldn't handle it. Killed herself a week later." His voice hardened on the last. "I vowed to find Baylor and make him pay."

"How did you know it was Baylor?" Dutch asked, leaning his hip against the edge of Gabe's desk.

"My sister recognized him. He worked at the farm for a few weeks until Jerrod, my brother-in-law, fired him." Wyatt glanced up at Dutch. "Ned Baylor had cornered my sister in the barn, tried to force himself on her. Jerrod walked in, saw what was happening, and threw him out. Told him to never set foot anywhere near their place again. This was at least a year before I arrived. I didn't hear anything about it until my sister talked about it after Jerrod was murdered."

Gabe shook his head in disgust. "And you decided the best way to capture Baylor was to join his gang, gain his trust, then drag him to the sheriff. Good idea. Too bad it didn't work out."

Wyatt snorted, rubbing the healed injury on his left arm. "I got him within a day's ride of town when I was jumped, beaten, and left for dead. At least I think that was their intention. When I woke up, Baylor was gone. They left me in a pretty bad way. Broke my left arm, cracked some ribs, pistol whipped my face." He touched a scar on his left chin. "The good news was they didn't take my horse."

Cash chuckled. "He probably wouldn't let them get near him." He looked at Dutch, then Gabe. "Wyatt's horse is one of the best trained animals I've ever seen. He'd sit stone-still in the middle of cannon and rifle fire, then burst into action at a slight command from Wyatt. I don't believe I ever saw them more than twenty feet from each other. Even then, the horse kept his eyes glued to Wyatt."

Wyatt smiled, although it didn't quite reach his eyes. "My father gave me Rogue when he was a year-old colt. We've been together ever since."

"I can see why," Dutch said. "He's a beautiful horse with his black points and white markings."

"That's why my father bought him."

Gabe cleared his throat. "So you rode your horse to Little Rock."

"That's where I was taking Baylor. When I arrived, they arrested me for killing him. The sheriff said there were three men who saw it happen—all part of his gang. I figure they didn't plan to rescue him. They planned to kill him so he wouldn't give up their names." Wyatt shifted in the uncomfortable chair, leaning back. "I told my story, and for whatever reason, the sheriff believed me. The charges were dropped, he had the doc clean me up, and a week later, I left."

"Without the bounty money?" Dutch asked.

Wyatt glared at him. "I didn't care about money. The man was dead. That was good enough for me."

Gabe read his notes once more, then looked up. "Then you rode north."

"Cash mentioned Splendor, so I decided to take him up on his offer to visit. I took a few jobs along the way. Got as far as Denver when I saw the wanted poster. I'd planned to work a while, then continue.

Instead, I rode toward the Dakotas. A jail in a small town had the same poster outside the front door. By then, I was pretty much out of food with enough money to last a few days. I didn't wait around, heading straight to Splendor."

Gabe shook his head, leaning back in his chair. "You made it damn far, Wyatt. From what Cash said, you might not have lasted another day on the trail."

Wyatt looked at Cash and smirked. "Hell, I've made it through worse."

"Yeah, but you looked like hell when I walked into Dax's place." Standing, Cash walked to the stove and poured himself some coffee. "What's the best way to go about this?"

Gabe glanced at Dutch, who nodded. "I'll send a telegram to Pinkerton. It's the best way to find out who issued the poster without raising suspicions. Allan's working on the kidnappings and murders along the railroad lines and has contacts everywhere."

"What's your guess, Dutch?" Cash asked.

Rubbing his jaw, Dutch paced to the window, looking out at the street. "Somehow, Baylor's gang convinced another sheriff you were guilty of murder. I'm guessing they want to get rid of anyone who knew about their connection to Baylor. Gabe hasn't gotten anything on Wyatt, which is good. I'll help any way I can to get the thing tossed out. It just may take some time and persuasion from Pinkerton." Dutch snickered. "The man is tenacious."

Wyatt's shoulders relaxed, though his features stayed drawn. "I'd be in your debt."

"The hell you will. Get yourself together, find a place to stay and a job. I want Pinkerton to know you've settled down here with nothing to hide. I'm discovering this is a mighty fine town, Wyatt. Thinking of staying here myself." Dutch glanced at Gabe. Neither had told the other deputies they'd reached an agreement about Dutch working for him.

Cash sipped his coffee, looking over the rim of the cup at Wyatt. "The Pelletiers offered you work. With your skill training horses, I'd bet they'd have you work with Travis at the old Frey place."

Gabe stood, grabbing his hat from a hook. "It's way past suppertime and I'm starving."

"Wyatt's staying with Allie and me. At least for a spell." Cash glanced at Wyatt. "I'll take you back out to see Dax and Luke when you're up to it, and if working for them is what you want."

Pushing himself up, Wyatt tottered only a little before righting himself. "Food, rest, and work...in that order. Within a few days, I'll be ready for whatever comes next."

Gabe nodded, a scowl on his face as his thoughts drifted to Boyden Trask. He wouldn't rest easy, and neither would most around Splendor, until the man was captured and sent back to the territorial prison

in Deer Lodge. Then maybe everyone could get back
to life as usual.

Chapter Thirteen

Boyden Trask stretched his arms above his head, then stopped abruptly. Something felt wrong. Sitting up, he turned toward the fire, seeing nothing but ash. Then his gaze moved to the one lone horse and a roaring curse burst from his lips.

Jumping to his feet as the morning sun crested over the eastern hills, he dashed around the campsite, seeing no sign of Rufus or Herb. Shouting another curse, he hurried to pick up his gear. They'd left their horses saddled the night before, a precaution in case they needed to make a quick getaway. He mumbled a curse when he saw his saddle near a tree, the blanket tossed on top of it.

Taking a quick look around, he swung up on his horse. From the conversation the night before, he knew they'd head south. He didn't know how many hours were between them, guessing they'd left not long after he'd gone to sleep. All thoughts of Rosemary left him as he reined his horse left, taking a deer trail covered in fresh hoof marks. Trask would follow it until the tracks disappeared, then he'd continue south.

He had no idea where they'd end up. All he knew was when he found them, they were both dead.

The early-morning sun shone through the curtains, signaling another beautiful day, as Luke paced back and forth, waiting for Clay McCord to finish checking the baby.

"What do you think, Doc? Can I take my wife and son home?" Luke stopped next to the bed where Ginny sat holding Cooper André. He smiled down at them, knowing Dax would approve of the name.

Their father, Cooper, had been a strong presence in their lives, dying before either of them returned from the war. The youngest Pelletier brother, André, had stayed in Savannah to help with the family businesses. He'd succumbed to pneumonia the summer before the war ended.

"I don't see why not." Clay smiled at them as he packed up his bag. "I'll ride out later this week to check on both of you. I expect you not to overdue, Ginny."

Luke nodded. "Lydia and Rosemary will be there to help."

"Don't forget Selina and Margaret. They're going to want their turn helping with Cooper." Ginny looked at the bundle in her lap, lifting the blanket to see his face. "He is the most precious baby I've ever seen."

Clay smiled, seeing the glow on the face of each parent. "They're all precious, Ginny. But I have to say, Cooper is special." The baby had his father's strong features, his mother's soft green eyes and golden brown hair. Bigger than most newborns, Clay had no doubt Cooper would grow into an imposing man. "Do you need help getting ready to leave?"

"As soon as I let him know, Noah will take care of getting the wagon ready."

"I'll be glad to walk to the livery and tell him, Luke. You two take your time getting ready."

Luke reached out his hand. "Thanks, Doc."

Clay shook it, then turned to Ginny one more time. "I'm serious about you taking it easy. I'm letting you go home a little earlier than normal, trusting the wagon ride won't be too hard on you. Let the other women help out and give yourself time to recuperate."

Her face flushed a little at the clear message. "I will, Doctor. And thank you again, so much."

Clay nodded, a slow grin spreading across his face. "I'll see you in a few days."

Stepping into the clear morning, Clay was surprised to see Nick's daughter, Olivia, across the street, leaving the bank. Catching her attention with a wave and a shout, he crossed the street, joining her on the boardwalk.

Olivia's eyes gleamed as he stopped next to her. "Good morning, Doctor McCord."

Touching the brim of his hat, he nodded. "Good morning, Miss Barnett. You look lovely today. Of course, you look lovely every day. Have you had breakfast?"

Her face brightened. "Why, no, I haven't."

"Is there somewhere you have to be?"

A brow lifted, her head tilting to the side. "Not really."

"Wonderful. Would you care to accompany me to the livery while I speak with Noah, then join me for breakfast?"

Her gaze moved over his shoulder, landing on her father across the street, arms crossed as he leaned against the side of the hotel. The expression on her face alerted Clay, who glanced over his shoulder to see Nick scowl. Looking back at her, he lowered his voice.

"Would you prefer I ask your father for his permission?"

Her eyes darkened for an instant before she raised her chin, jutting it out in an act Clay recognized as defiance. "I'm twenty years old, Doctor McCord. Old enough to make my own decisions. I'd love to join you for breakfast." Without looking across the street again, she accepted the arm Clay held out.

As they walked toward the livery, Clay felt a pang of regret at not speaking with Nick before inviting his daughter to accompany him. Nick had become a good friend, not to mention a major benefactor in the new clinic. Clay owed him. Strolling down the boardwalk, he made a mental note to speak with him, asking his permission to court Olivia. He'd been considering it ever since he'd seen her, his heart stopping in his chest at her beauty. Yet he'd held off showing his interest for a good reason. He was a couple months shy of thirty, almost ten years older than Olivia. Back home, many marriages occurred between people who had an even bigger age difference. Here in Splendor, it didn't seem as common.

"Doctor McCord, are you all right?"

Blinking, he looked over at her. "Yes. Why?"

She grinned, leaning into him. "Because the livery is behind us."

Stopping, he shook his head, a laugh bursting from his throat. "Well then, I suppose we should turn around."

"That might be best." She smiled back at him, causing his heart to falter.

Clearing his throat, he turned back toward the livery.

"It's about time Clay released you." Dax bounded down the front porch steps, taking the lines from Luke so he could assist Ginny with the baby.

"We weren't gone that long." Taking Cooper from Ginny's arms, Luke glanced around in confusion, trying to figure out how to help his wife down.

"I've got her." Dirk ran up, carefully lifting Ginny and setting her next to Luke. "You look real good, Ginny."

"Why, thank you. I'm exhausted from lack of sleep, but very glad to be home." She started to turn away, then stopped. "Dirk, thank you for riding into town with us. I'm glad you were there."

He glanced away, not comfortable with praise he felt was undeserved. "I was happy to do it."

"Ginny!" Rachel threw the front door open.

"Rachel, you stay right where you are." Dax sent her a stern glare. "Ginny and Luke will bring the baby to you."

She did what he said, but if looks were fatal, Dax would've been mortally wounded. Rachel knew he wanted her to stay safe. Her delivery could come at any time, so he'd fallen into his ex-Confederate general identity, issuing her orders and expecting her to bow to his wishes. He'd been the same the last few weeks of her pregnancy with Patrick. She knew Dax would settle down once the baby came.

Waiting while Ginny slipped her arm through Luke's, Rachel strained to get a glimpse of the baby. She took a deep breath, pressing a hand against her stomach, trying to contain her excitement. Holding her arms out as they walked up the steps, she took him into her arms. Lifting the blanket, she stared into eyes the same color as Ginny's.

"He has your eyes." Rachel didn't take her gaze off the baby. "I hope they don't change."

"They change?" Luke asked, his brows drawing together.

Rachel nodded. "They could. His are light colored, so there's a decent chance they'll change. You'll know within a few months. Have you named him?"

Dax came up the steps in time to hear the question, wrapping an arm around Rachel's waist.

"We have." Luke glanced at Ginny, then Dax. "We named him Cooper André."

Dax's jaw slacked a little, his eyes clouding as he absorbed the significance.

"What do you think, Dax?" Ginny asked.

Pulling Rachel close, he cleared his throat. "I think it's a perfect name."

Rachel glanced up at him. "I've heard those names before. I remembered because you don't hear them often."

"Our father's name was Cooper. Our younger brother was André. Both died while we were away fighting the North." His chest tightened at the memory.

Rachel leaned up, kissing his cheek. "Well, I think it's perfect. Let's get inside. Lydia will be over any minute with Margaret and Selina. And I'm certain the boys will want to see Cooper." Noticing Ginny's tired expression, she touched her arm. "We'll keep the visits short. With Rosemary and the others, you'll be able to get plenty of rest."

Ginny nodded, her lips curving up into a faint smile. "I'm looking forward to it."

Splendor

"The stage is coming, Lena." Nick stood at the entrance of the Dixie, motioning to Gabe's wife, who stood behind the bar cleaning glasses. Setting the last one down, she wiped her hands down her apron before removing it. Hurrying to join Nick, she stepped onto the boardwalk.

"Do you think they're on it?" She felt almost breathless with excitement.

"I guess we'll find out in a minute." Nick adjusted the patch over his left eye. He hoped the extra patches arrived on the stage, too. "How many are you expecting?"

"Four." Lena vibrated with excitement. "I do hope they like it here." She held her breath as the stage came to a stop.

"Hey, Nick." The driver waved at them before securing the brake and lines, then jumping down as the guard climbed onto the top.

"Ervin. How are you?" Nick held out his hand, grasping the young man's.

"Can't complain." Ripping off his hat, he nodded to Lena. "Mrs. Evans. It's good to see you."

"It's very good to see you, Ervin. Do you have some passengers for us?"

Chuckling, Ervin settled his hat back on his head. "I sure do. Four young ladies. Friends of yours?"

"Not yet, but they will be." Lena moved aside to let him open the door, holding out his hand.

Nick scratched the back of his neck, leaning down close to her ear. "I sure hope you, Isabella, and my wife know what you're doing."

A brilliant smile broke across her face. "We most certainly do." The butterflies in her stomach belied the truth. Lena had no idea if this would work or not. Once the idea roosted in her brain, she couldn't get it out until she'd shared it with her close friends, Suzanne Barnett and Isabella Boucher.

"Tell me again where you found them?"

"Pettigrew's in Philadelphia. Isabella recommended them. She said they have a stellar reputation. Remember, Nick, she and her late husband lived in Philadelphia and were quite connected."

"Ah…makes sense." It didn't really, but Nick didn't want to stir anything up at this point.

Lena glanced behind her at the boardinghouse, then the hotel. "Oh, I need to let Suzanne and Isabella know the girls have arrived."

"You stay here. I'll let them know."

Nick shook his head before walking away. He couldn't believe his normally rational wife, Suzanne, would agree to such a harebrained scheme. Worse, the calm, sensible Isabella had gone along with it. When Nick had told Travis Davis, the man courting Isabella, of the women's idea, he'd thrown back his head and laughed. It was an unusual moment of levity for the quiet, somber Pelletier ranch hand.

"Take my hand, Miss, and I'll help you down." Ervin assisted each of the young women onto the boardwalk until all four stood wide-eyed, their hands clasping the bags the guard handed down. When a gust of wind came down the street, each struggled to hold their hats in place while keeping the anxiety off their faces.

Inhaling a deep breath, Lena moved forward, pulling a letter from a pocket in her skirt. "I'm Mrs. Lena Evans. Welcome to Splendor."

The tallest, a stout young woman with auburn hair, green eyes, and freckles across her nose, stepped forward. "Pleased to meet you, Mrs. Evans. I'm Miss Deborah Chestro." She looked behind her, motioning the others forward. "This is Miss Sylvia Lucero, Miss Tabitha Beekman, and the youngest, Miss May Bacon."

Lena glanced at the letter from Pettigrew's, nodding as Deborah mentioned each name, then looked up. "It's a pleasure to meet each of you. I hope the trip wasn't too tiring."

"Well, it..." Deborah's voice faded away as two older women stepped off the stage.

"I told you it wouldn't be so bad, Davinia. Look at this lovely town." Selma brushed dust from her skirt, then took off her bonnet to pat her hair.

"It was a miserable trip and you know it, Selma. We were stuffed in that rattling carriage for days." Davinia glared at Ervin and the guard, both turning away under her stare. "I hope they have a decent place to stay, but it's doubtful."

Lena looked at the young women. "Excuse me a moment." Walking over to the two older women, she cleared her throat, garnering their attention. "I couldn't help but overhear. If you need a place to stay, there is Suzanne's, which is the boardinghouse, and the St. James Hotel. Both are excellent and clean."

Davinia scanned Lena, her eyes narrowing. "Well, perhaps we'll try the St. James. What do you think, Sister?"

Selma nodded. "Very sensible, Davinia." She looked back at Lena. "I'm Selma Ritter, of the Boston Ritters, and this is my sister, Davinia."

Biting back a grin, Lena nodded. "I'm Mrs. Lena Evans. My husband is the sheriff in Splendor."

"See now, Davinia. This isn't at all populated by savages as you thought."

Lena could hear at least one of the young women behind her giggle. "Oh, we are quite civilized here, at least for a growing frontier town. When you speak to the clerk, please tell him you're friends of mine."

"That's lovely, Mrs. Evans. We'll do that." Selma glared at Davinia before her face softened. "Will the young women be staying at the hotel? They are all so sweet."

Lena noticed Davinia blanch at the description and wondered what it meant. Deciding to ignore it, she shook her head. "I'm afraid not. They'll be staying at the boardinghouse. If you're here for long, I'm certain you'll come across each other. Well, I'd better get them settled. It was a pleasure meeting you."

"You, as well." Selma looked down at the two trunks by their feet. "Do you suppose we can have the hotel come and fetch these?"

"Of course. Just tell the clerk there at the station. Have a good day, ladies." Lena turned back to the four young women, hearing Davinia's retort.

"Station," she harrumphed. "More like a dilapidated shack."

"Now, now, Sister. Remember what we decided. This is an adventure."

"Yes, it is. I just hope I survive it."

Ignoring them, Lena joined the others. "Do you have all your baggage?"

"We do," Deborah answered.

"Wonderful. Then let's get you settled in at the boardinghouse."

Sylvia stepped forward. "Excuse me, Mrs. Evans. Will there be something to eat at the boardinghouse?"

"More than you can imagine, Miss Lucero. If you're ready, I'll take you there." Lena led the way, unable to miss the number of people who stopped what they were doing to watch the five of them march down the boardwalk.

Their stares were nothing compared to what Lena suspected their comments would be when they discovered she, Isabella, and Suzanne had taken the bold step of paying for and transporting four mail order brides to Splendor. She grinned at the thought.

All they had to do now was find a way for the growing number of confirmed bachelors to meet the highly eligible young women...and soon.

Chapter Fourteen

"How far do we go before we make camp, Herb?" Rufus's back ached from being in the saddle over twenty hours with short stops to take care of personal business, eat the few berries they found along the trail, and allow their horses to rest.

Herb looked up, gauging the time by the location of the sun. "Two more hours should put us at the Wyoming border. If I remember right, there's a small town on our way where we can get some food."

"And what do we use for money?"

Herb snorted. "Who said anything about money?"

Rufus rubbed an itch on his arm, his mouth twisting into a sneer. "I don't care how we get food, but we can't leave the town without something to fill our bellies."

"We won't."

They rode in silence for a long time, glancing behind them every few minutes for any sign of a rider. Other than a couple ranch houses a good distance from the trail, they'd seen no one since they'd left Trask snoring in his bedroll.

"Boyd *will* come after us, Herb. He won't forgive us for leaving him behind, and he'll never forget. We may be looking over our shoulders the rest of our lives."

Herb pinched the bridge of his nose, then lifted a brow. "We're escaped convicts, Ruf. We'll always be looking over our shoulders. I'm thinking the safest place for us to go is the Arizona Territory. We'd be close to Mexico, able to get across the border if we're recognized."

"I don't know. I've heard the Apaches are vicious to the whites in the territory."

"We'll stay out of their way."

Rufus snorted. "It don't work that way with Indians. They'll kill and scalp us if we're caught. The same way Bloody Bill Anderson scalped the Union soldiers he killed."

Herb shook his head. "Anderson and his Confederate guerillas were sick sonsofbitches. I fought for the South, but I didn't mourn his death. Besides, I heard the Apaches don't scalp their captives."

"Maybe not, but I don't want to find out."

"You got a better idea than going to Arizona, Ruf?"

Scratching his chin, he shook his head. "I just don't want to go through Apache territory."

"Well, then, I guess we'll have to figure out a way around them." Although Herb had no idea how to avoid them.

He'd heard all kinds of stories. Some people claimed there were peaceful Apache in some parts of the territory, while others raided and took captives at will. The more he thought on it, the more he believed Arizona wasn't for him. All he knew for sure was they couldn't stay in Montana or Wyoming. Colorado wouldn't be safe, either. Maybe they'd head west to Utah. He'd heard about the Mormons around the Salt Lake area and how some men had several wives. He chuckled, wondering if they'd let them join.

"Salt Lake."

Rufus glanced at him, his eyes wide. "What about Salt Lake?"

"That's where we're going. We can change our names and the way we look. Might even take on their religion. Marry us some Mormon women. No one will ever think to look for us there."

"Marry? Hell, I have no intention of marrying, Herb."

He laughed, not caring if Rufus wanted to marry or not. "Let's see what you decide once we get there. Perhaps you'll change your mind when you see men with several wives." Herb looked at him, raising a brow.

Taking off his hat, Rufus ran a hand through his hair. "*Several* wives?"

"That's what I hear. The Mormons allow their men to have as many as they want."

The disgusted look left Rufus's face as he thought over the advantages. Settling his hat back on his head, a wicked grin split his face. "Don't seem as we have much to lose. I say we give Salt Lake a try."

Herb nodded. "Thought you might feel that way."

Redemption's Edge

Rosemary sat at the supper table, pushing food around her plate to look as if she had an appetite, which she didn't. Ever since Ginny and Luke arrived with Cooper, she'd been splitting her time between helping with the baby, preparing food for supper, and keeping a watchful eye on Rachel. It wouldn't be long before her baby would come. Then the house truly would spiral into a whole new level of chaos.

All the changes and added work weren't what crippled her appetite. She knew Dirk would make good on his declaration to learn about her past. When he did, everything would change between them. He'd made it plain he wanted nothing from her beyond keeping her safe from Boyden Trask. After what she had to say, he might ask Bull or one of the other ranch hands to take on that duty.

It pained her to think he believed himself incapable of love after what had happened with his wife. Melissa and his brother had hurt him in a way no man should experience. Rosemary wished she had more experience, knew what to say to change his mind, but she didn't.

"Not hungry?"

She startled at Dirk's words. He sat beside her, and although his plate was empty, he hadn't eaten with his usual relish. Shaking her head, she folded her hands in her lap.

"I guess I'm more tired than hungry." She glanced around the table, seeing everyone else lost in their own conversations, ignoring the two of them. "When Lydia finishes her supper, I'll help her clean up, then head to bed. It won't be long before Rachel's baby will come and work will increase even more."

"When you've had time to rest, we'll talk."

A lump formed in her throat. She'd known he wouldn't forget. "Talk?"

He cocked his head, raising a brow. "Have you forgotten you have a story to tell?"

Her shoulders slumped. "Oh, that."

Leaning close, he lowered his voice. "I want to hear it all."

His breath washing over her cheek sent a jolt of recognition through her, causing heat to form, her heart to pound. She had no doubt her face had flushed, announcing her discomfort.

Pursing her lips, she squirmed in the seat. "There really isn't much to tell, Dirk," she hissed, hoping no one heard her.

"Then it won't take long for you to tell me, will it?"

Gripping her hands so tight her knuckles turned white, she sighed. "No. I suppose not."

Rosemary did her best to prolong cleaning up after supper, visiting with Lydia until everything had been put away. When Bull came into the kitchen to escort his wife home, she followed them onto the porch, surprised to see Dax, Luke, and Dirk relaxing as they sipped whiskey. Thinking she'd been given a reprieve, Rosemary nodded at the men, ready to go back inside.

"Rosemary?"

Her heart stalled, steps faltering when she heard Dirk's voice. Ignoring the way her breath hitched, she raised her gaze to meet his.

"Yes?"

Standing, he set his empty glass on a table. "Do you have a few minutes to speak with me?"

She shot a quick look at Dax and Luke, relaxing when they continued in their own intense conversation, ignoring her and Dirk. Nodding, she walked down the steps, stiffening slightly at the feel of Dirk's hand on her lower back.

Instead of guiding her to the barn, he turned her toward a pasture filled with the horses they'd brought to fulfill the army contract. She had little time to admire them and found herself relaxing as they moved farther away from the house. Stopping next to the fence, she stepped up on the bottom rung, resting her arms on top.

"They are beautiful," she breathed, watching one horse chase another, then lose interest in the game and turn away.

Stepping up beside her, Dirk followed her gaze. "Too beautiful for the treatment they'll get in the military."

Frowning, she looked at him. "What do you mean?"

He continued to stare at the small herd. "Once we pass them off, they'll be put to hard use. The soldiers aren't cruel, and the horses will be taken care of as best as possible in a remote location. They simply won't be treated as well as the horses we use at the ranch."

They fell silent, Rosemary wishing what had become a comforting time outside could continue, knowing it wouldn't.

"Did you grow up on a ranch?" Dirk didn't turn to look at her when he asked.

"A farm. We did have two horses. One my pa used in the fields and to pull the wagon. The other he used to ride into town." Glancing over at him, she felt the old pain return. "He went into town often. Most nights after supper, he'd change clothes and ride out. My brother and I saw little of him as we'd be in bed by the time he returned."

His gaze met hers. "Your mother didn't mind?"

"I didn't think so until I got older. More than once, I came downstairs late at night and she'd still be up, waiting for him to return. I didn't bother her, just watched from the living room, knowing she'd scoot me off to bed if she knew I was up. Each time he returned, he'd take off his boots, then go upstairs, not ever acknowledging her. She'd watch until she heard their bedroom door close, then follow him. The stench of whiskey, smoke, and perfume surrounded him most of the following day."

Turning to face her, Dirk leaned against the fence. "Didn't she ever ask him where he'd been?"

"She used to when Ben and I were younger. He'd either yell at her or ignore her questions. She finally stopped asking. By the time I was thirteen, I began to understand what my mother already knew."

Dirk understood, remaining silent as one emotion after another passed over her face. Licking her lips, she met his gaze.

"My father was a hard man. If anyone questioned him, they'd feel his wrath."

Dirk straightened, his face twisting in anger. "He hit you?"

"On occasion. He'd treat Mama horribly, as if she were a slave to his needs. I can't recall a time he praised her for anything. He seemed to enjoy beating her down, making her cower with words, if not fists. When I got older, I began defending her, sometimes getting between them when I thought he might hurt her. That's when he'd hit me or shove me aside. Mostly, though, he used threats to get us to bend to his will. I can't tell you how many times he threatened to ride away, leaving us all behind. He'd taunt us with how it would be if he left. No money, no food, no one to protect us. God forgive me, but I grew to hate him, praying he'd leave and never return."

She looked back at the horses, but not before he saw pain flicker across her face. "When Pa got into one of his moods, Mama and I had no one to help us. Ben was so much younger than me, and even though he tried, he couldn't stand up to our pa. Then, for a while, life got better."

Dirk's brows drew together. "What happened?"

"Pa came home one spring afternoon with a young man who'd been working at a nearby farm. They'd run out of work, so Pa offered him a job." She swallowed the lump the memory caused. "I had just turned fifteen. He was eighteen, taller than Pa, and refused to be intimidated. The one time I saw Pa raise a hand to him, Elias grabbed his wrist and pushed him away. After that, Pa left him alone."

Dirk waited, seeing something flicker across her face. "Then what?"

Crossing her arms, she turned away, her gaze latching onto the horses. When she opened her mouth to speak, her throat closed. Clearing it didn't help. It felt as if she were suspended in time, unable to say more about the past.

Moving up to her, he raised his hand, lifting her chin with a finger. It was then he saw the moisture in her eyes. "You don't have to say any more. Whatever happened is in the past."

A tear escaped, slipping down her cheek before Dirk caught it with his finger. Pushing aside the guilt she'd never been able to escape, she continued.

"Pa seldom took us to town. Mama schooled me because Pa wouldn't let me take the horse. We seldom went to church, so I'd spent little time around boys." Drawing in a shaky breath, she glanced at Dirk, who nodded for her to go on. "Elias was so, well...I don't know...handsome, charming. He talked to me, made me feel special. Pa warned him away, but most of the time, Elias ignored him. Mama always set a plate for him, so we shared every meal together. When Pa went into town, Elias would stay with us for a while. Sometimes, he, Ben, and I would walk outside, check on the animals. Ben would usually get bored and run back to the house. As the summer passed, Elias and I spent more and more time together."

Dirk stiffened, already getting a sense of what she might say.

She stared into the pasture, as if she were seeing the past. "We talked of the future. He hated my pa and wanted to get me away from him. One night, he told me he loved me, wanted to take me with him when he left. He said we'd go west and he'd get work at another farm." She blinked, as if suddenly remembering Dirk next to her. "I was young and stupid, believing everything he said. By the end of the summer..." Her voice trailed off on a ragged breath.

Dirk placed a comforting hand on her back. "You don't have to say more."

Shaking her head, she refused to stop. He needed to hear it all. "By the end of summer, I was pregnant. The way he spoke of love, told me he wanted me, I thought Elias would be thrilled. The day after I told him, he disappeared. I never saw him again."

Dirk turned away, mumbling a curse before running a hand down his face. "What did your pa do?"

She watched his face, looking for any sign of disgust, but saw nothing. Shaking her head, she gripped the top rail of the fence. "He never found out. Neither did Mama."

Dirk's eyes widened. "How could they not know?"

Her shoulders tensed at the harsh tone.

Stroking a hand down her face, he leaned forward, placing a soft kiss on her cheek. "Tell me what happened."

"A few nights later, Pa lost the farm in a card game. He came home drunk, angry, telling us we had to leave. Within days, we were on the trail with a group of other wagons heading west. Pa didn't tell us where we were going. I knew Mama and Ben were scared. So was I, but not for the same reason. Three months had passed since Elias left. I was gaining weight and had no other clothes. By then, I'd accepted my fate, even began to get a little excited about having a baby...something all mine that Pa couldn't take away. Then the storm hit."

Dirk moved his hand down, threading his fingers through hers.

"We could barely see through the rain. The trail turned muddy, almost washing out in some places. The wagon master didn't stop. As the rain increased, one wagon broke down, then another. People stopped to help each other, but Pa kept going, driving off the trail to avoid the other wagons. The storm continued, lightning strikes hitting all around us. I don't know exactly what happened next. There was a loud bang, the wagon tipped, and when I woke up, I was on the ground, clutching my stomach." Her voice broke, a quiet sob escaping before Dirk wrapped an arm around her.

"Shhh. You don't have to say any more, sweetheart."

Shaking her head, the disjointed words tumbled out. "I...lost...lost the baby."

Turning her to face him, Dirk tucked her head under his chin, stroking her back as she sobbed out her agony. Silently, he cursed Elias and her pa, wishing they were here so he could take out his anger on them.

As the crying subsided, he pulled back, using his thumbs to wipe away the tears.

"I'm so sorry, Dirk. I know what you must think of me. I disgraced myself by believing what Elias said."

Placing a finger over her lips, he kissed her forehead. "I think you're a strong, courageous woman, Rosemary. You shouldered a burden no girl should have to bear at fifteen. Elias was the coward. He used you, then walked away, afraid to take any responsibility. He's the one disgraced, not you."

Staring at him, wanting desperately to believe his words, she leaned up, kissing him on the mouth. "Thank you."

Tightening his arms around her, he squeezed, then pulled back. "Come on. I'll walk you to the house. Tomorrow, we'll go for a ride. Would you like that?"

Covering her mouth to stifle a hiccup, she nodded, garnering a chuckle from Dirk.

"I guess that's a yes."

Walking to the house, she glanced up at him, her eyes red, the corners of her mouth tilting into a slight grin. The sight stilled his heart. Dirk looked away to clear his mind. She was the most beautiful woman he'd ever known, and without any doubt he wanted her. Now more than ever.

Chapter Fifteen

Bull walked into the barn, seeing Dirk saddling Banshee and a gentle mare Rosemary usually rode. "Where you off to?"

Dirk didn't look up. "The boys think we have a group of horses lost somewhere in Courage Canyon. I'm going to ride over and see."

"We have men for that. If they think the horses wandered that way, I'll send Mal and Tat to bring them back. No reason for you to go."

Dirk snorted. "No reason except I need to get out of here for a while. I'm taking Rosemary with me."

Crossing his arms, Bull leaned against the stall. "Do you think that's a good idea? We don't know where Trask and his men are."

"I'll be careful."

"I know you will, Dirk, but you're just one man. It'd be better to take Mal and a couple others with you."

"Not this time." Finishing with both horses, he grabbed the reins, leading them outside.

"Hold on, Dirk." Bull stepped in front of the horses, stopping him from leaving. "Is there a reason you don't want to take men with you?"

Glaring at Bull, he blew out a frustrated breath. He didn't have a good reason for putting Rosemary in possible danger, other than he wanted more time alone with her. Riding out without considering her protection was foolish...and selfish.

"You're right. Let Mal and Tat know. We'll be leaving in thirty minutes."

Bull nodded before leaving for the bunkhouse.

Staring at the front porch, waiting for Rosemary to appear, Dirk chastised himself. He'd invited her on a ride with him, not thinking beyond his desire to continue the conversation they'd started the night before.

When the men came in the evening before, they'd been angry about their count being off by a few horses. They'd searched everywhere, but hadn't found them. Mal talked about losing horses and cattle in Courage Canyon the previous spring. The problem was, the canyon was miles from where the herd had been grazing.

Dirk latched onto the idea. They expected Trask to come in from the north. The canyon was southwest, heading into the mountains. Lying on his bunk last night, Dirk had thought it a good place to ride with Rosemary. Now, he knew he'd been deluding himself.

"Hey," Rosemary said as she came down the steps, pulling his thoughts back to the present.

"Morning." He took in the sight of her. Unlike last night when he'd left her with red eyes and sullen expression, she glowed this morning, an infectious smile tugging at his heart.

"Where are we going?"

"South. Mal thinks we may have some lost horses holed up in a canyon down that way. He and Tat will be going with us."

If the thought of having the ranch hands ride with them bothered her, she didn't show it.

"We could be gone most of the day."

She glanced toward the bunkhouse, seeing Johnny, his recovering leg resting on a stool. She waved at him, then at Mal and Tat as they stepped outside. "Then I'll get food for us to take along."

"Morning, Boss." Tat stopped next to Dirk, his appreciative gaze following Rosemary as she walked up the steps and into the house. When he turned to face Dirk, the smile slid from his face. "Uh...Bull said you want us to go with you to search Courage Canyon, see if we can find the missing horses?"

"That's right. Rosemary's coming with us. Do you think you can keep your eyes to yourself?"

Mal's lips twitched before he looked at the ground.

Glaring at his friend, Tat nodded. "Sure, Boss. I can do that."

"Good. She's packing food for us to take. Go get your horses ready. We'll leave as soon as Rosemary comes back." Leaving the men to get ready, he led the horses to the front of the house, then leaned against a rail as he waited.

He'd slept little after Rosemary revealed her past. His gut twisted when he thought of what she'd gone through. She'd already told most everyone at the ranch about arriving in Splendor on a wagon train with her mother and brother. By then, their father had abandoned them, taking off with some woman he'd met along the way. When their mother became ill, they'd left the train, finding sanctuary in an abandoned shack not far from town.

There was no money for a doctor, so Rosemary did what she could to help their mother. It hadn't been enough to reverse the illness. She died with Rosemary on one side of her and Ben on the other. Dirk wondered if that was when she decided to become a nurse, vowing to ask her at some point.

She had a hard life, making up for it with determination, hard work, and courage. Rosemary had taken what life threw at her and turned it around, doing her best to not only feed and clothe Ben, but two other orphans, Teddy and Jimmy Odell. He admired her more than she knew.

"I have everything." She bounded down the steps, her radiant smile punching a hole in his gut.

Clearing his throat, he looked away, glad to see Mal and Tat walking up.

"Looks like we're ready." He helped her onto her horse, knowing she didn't need his assistance, but needing to touch her. When she'd settled in the saddle, he finally dropped his hands away, instantly missing the contact.

Tat glanced at Dirk, then touched the brim of his hat, nodding at Rosemary.

Mal stifled a chuckle. Tat didn't get intimidated often, but seems Dirk made it happen. "Good morning, Miss Rosemary."

"Good morning." She nodded at Tat and Mal.

Dirk swung up on Banshee. "Mal, you and Tat lead the way."

Kicking their horses, they moved out ahead of Rosemary and Dirk, heading south toward the mountains.

Splendor

"It sure has been quiet the last couple weeks." Deputy Mack Mackey leaned back in his chair in the sheriff's office, looking at his cards.

Caleb Covington nodded, checking his own cards. "I can't recall the last time we played cards in the jail."

"That's because you haven't been a deputy long enough to remember," Cash joked, shaking his head.

"Don't get used to it, gentlemen." Gabe picked up his coffee, taking a slow sip as he studied his hand. "The quiet never lasts long."

Beau Davis strolled in, taking off his hat. "Hey. What am I missing? If I would have known you planned to play cards this morning, I'd have been here sooner." Heading to the stove, he grabbed a cup, filling it with coffee as the door opened.

Gabe set down his cards when he saw who entered. "Ah. The man I've been waiting for."

Dutch nodded at the others. "Looks like you have a full house this morning."

"There's always room for one more player, McFarlin. Do you want in?" Mack asked.

Dutch shook his head. "My mind isn't ready to match wits with you degenerates this early in the morning."

"Neither are ours, but that hasn't stopped us." Caleb took another sip of his coffee as Gabe tossed down his cards.

"I asked Dutch to come in early for a reason."

Each man stilled, setting down their own cards to look at Gabe.

"You're all aware Dutch has been thinking of making a change. Splendor's growing faster than we can keep up with, especially with all the mischief going on."

Cash looked at the cards spread out on Gabe's desk. "Today notwithstanding."

"True." Gabe nodded. "Back to the reason Dutch is here. We need to expand the hours we patrol the town and have two men on watch each night. Until now, we haven't had enough men to do it. Now we do." Gabe nodded at Dutch. "I've offered him a job as deputy and he's accepted." Pulling out a badge, he handed it to him.

"Well, hell, that is good news." Mack stood, extending his hand to Dutch. "Glad you're here."

Each of the others did the same, mocking him about his choice in bosses, before the room quieted and all but Dutch and Beau sat back down.

Beau clasped Dutch on the back. "Guess you're going to have to come up with some more chairs, Gabe."

"I think I can manage that."

Mack stood. "Gabe, if you don't mind, I think I'll head over to the boardinghouse and grab some breakfast."

Gabe gestured toward the door. "Go ahead. We have nothing else going on here."

Caleb stood. "I think I'll join you."

"Do you two mind a third?" Dutch asked.

"Not at all." Mack looked at Beau and Cash. "You two interested?"

"Nope." Cash patted his stomach. "Allie made a big meal for me this morning."

"I'm good." Beau thought of his fiancée, Caro, who'd been asleep when he left the house. She deserved the rest. For the last few months, they'd been getting their separate ranches merged together while planning their wedding. In a couple weeks, she'd be his. "I'm going to start my rounds, Gabe."

"I'd best get on with mine, too." Cash set his empty cup on the stove and followed the others outside. "You men enjoy your meal." He nodded at Mack, Caleb, and Dutch as they made their way across the street, avoiding wagons and men on horseback.

Beau walked up to his longtime friend as the men walked into the boardinghouse. "You know why they're headed over there, right?"

Cash shook his head. "Other than being hungry?"

Beau grinned. "The young women the ladies brought to town are staying there."

Cash threw his head back and laughed. "The mail order brides?"

Beau cocked his head. "Is that a fact?"

"Allie's not providing details, but she's pretty tight with Lena, Suzanne, and Isabella. The word is they brought the young women to town because the number of single men is far outpacing the available women. I'm surprised Caro hasn't said something to you."

Beau crossed his arms, his mouth twisting in a wry grin. "Not a word, but she's been busy getting ready for our wedding."

Cash's face sobered. "Did you ever think when we rode into Splendor that we'd find wives and settle down?"

Beau chuckled, shaking his head. "Not once. I thought I'd be saddled with sharing a cabin with you for the rest of my life."

Cash clasped him on the shoulder. "Me, too, my friend."

"Take seats anywhere you want, gentlemen." Suzanne smiled at the three men as they walked in, noticing the badge on Dutch's shirt. "Am I looking at the newest deputy?"

Taking off his hat, he nodded. "You are, ma'am."

"Well, that is good news. And, please, call me Suzanne. Your breakfast is on the house this morning, Dutch. I'll get three coffees."

As the men took seats, the sounds of laughter drew their attention to the stairs. An instant later, the four young women appeared, their curious gazes scanning the dining room.

"Good morning, ladies." Suzanne emerged from the kitchen holding three cups of coffee. She looked for an empty table, nodding to them. "Follow me."

The men watched as Suzanne set their cups in front of them, then indicated the ladies should take the table next to them.

"I don't believe you gentlemen have met the ladies who arrived on the stage."

The three stood, Caleb the first to speak. "No, ma'am. We haven't had the pleasure."

"Ladies, these are three of Splendor's deputies. Mr. Mack Mackey, Mr. Caleb Covington, and Mr. Dutch McFarlin. Gentlemen, meet Miss Tabitha Beekman, Miss Sylvia Lucero, Miss May Bacon, and Miss Deborah Chestro. They're going to be making Splendor their home. Well, I'd better see to the other customers."

"It's a pleasure meeting you, ladies," Dutch said, his slight southern drawl smooth as molasses. "May I ask where you all are from?"

As usual, Deborah spoke first. "Philadelphia, Mr. McFarlin. And you? You have the voice of a southerner."

"Guilty, I'm afraid. I was born in Charleston, as was my father and his father before him. He and my mother still live in the house I grew up in."

"I suppose you fought for the Confederacy then."

His features stilled, the charm falling away. "The war is behind us now, Miss Chestro. At least it is for me. If you'll excuse me." Turning, he raised a brow at Mack and Caleb before sitting back down.

"Enjoy your breakfast, ladies." Mack bowed slightly, then sat next to Dutch.

"It was a pleasure meeting you." Caleb turned to take his seat, but not before taking one more glance at Tabitha. Something about her golden caramel eyes, soft brown hair, and unaffected smile drew him in a way he hadn't experienced in a long time. Picking up his coffee, he took a long swallow.

"Well, that seemed to go well, Dutch." Mack's somber expression told of his true thoughts.

"Unfortunately, there are many people who feel the same. Even though it's been four years, they can't put the war behind them. It seems Miss Chestro may be one of them."

Mack nodded. "I wonder how the other ladies feel."

Tabitha bit her lower lip, trying to stop the sharp rebuke she wanted to give Deborah. Within minutes of meeting the outspoken woman, she'd learned of her hatred for anyone from the South. It was a sentiment Tabitha didn't share. To her knowledge, neither did May nor Sylvia, at least not to Deborah's unfathomable degree.

"You were quite rude to Mr. McFarlin, Deborah." Sylvia shot her a cool look.

Tabitha nodded. "I agree. He was trying to be pleasant, and as usual, you couldn't keep your thoughts to yourself."

Deborah's lips drew into a thin line. "I don't care a wit if I was rude. Anyone from the South deserves the scorn directed at them, and that includes Deputy McFarlin."

May cleared her throat. The youngest and the most shy, she seldom gave her thoughts. "Perhaps you might consider saying nothing when you're unable to be gracious, Deborah. Remember, we're here to find husbands, not alienate everyone."

Deborah blinked several times, surprised at May's candor. Although soft-spoken, her words caused Deborah's chest to squeeze. "You may be right, but it isn't easy for me."

The others nodded, already knowing her history and how she'd lost her father and brothers at Gettysburg. Still, they'd all lost family and their homes. It was why they were in Splendor. They had nowhere else to go.

Chapter Sixteen

Southern Montana Border

Trask knelt, staring at the trail, trying to decide if the tracks he'd been following belonged to Herb and Rufus. Cursing his lack of tracking skills, he stood and looked around. With the meager amount of food he'd been able to forage, he had to make a decision. If he turned north now, he might be able to make it to Big Pine.

He knew the territorial capital well. There were a few people who might still consider him a friend. People he'd done favors for and might be willing to help him. Trask also knew where several storekeepers hid their cash boxes at night, and which ones lived in houses away from their businesses instead of apartments above.

Mounting his horse, Trask took one more look south. He had a choice to make. Follow Herb and Rufus, repaying them for their betrayal, or continue to Splendor, taking out his revenge on Rosemary.

He couldn't be certain which direction his ex-partners rode, although he was fairly certain they'd head toward the Arizona Territory and the Mexican border. Trask had heard stories of the Apache, and none of them were good. His skills as a gunslinger were marginal, his ability to survive in the rough desert conditions insignificant.

His chances of getting to Splendor were much better. Trask knew Rosemary would be at one of two places—the clinic or the Pelletier ranch. This time, he'd be more cautious, go after her when she was alone. If they'd gotten word of his escape, they'd know Herb and Rufus escaped with him. They'd be looking for three men, not one. He could take her by surprise, maybe a couple of the other brats, too. When he was done, he'd leave the territory and never return.

As he reined his horse north, another thought crossed his mind, causing his lips to twist into a sneer. Herb and Rufus were both ignorant enough to enter Apache territory, ignoring the danger in their panic to get away from him. With any luck at all, the Apache would take care of Trask's vengeance for him.

Splendor

"I must say, Sister, the accommodations at this hotel are much better than I anticipated." Davinia touched the corners of her mouth with her napkin, glancing down at her empty plate. "The food is quite good. Almost as good as the meals we had in New York."

"Yes, I believe you're right. I didn't expect fine china in a town such as this." Selma sipped her tea, glancing around at the other diners. "There are more people in Splendor than I expected."

"I agree. The fact we traveled here with those young women means there must be a number of eligible men here. At least young ones."

Selma snickered. "Yes, Sister, I believe there must be a good number of single men." Her gaze moved to the window next to them. Looking outside, her eyes widened. "Oh my. Look who is walking on the boardwalk across the street."

Davinia squinted, focusing on a young man and his companions. "Why, it's Mr. Cullin. I don't recall him saying anything about coming this way, do you?"

Selma shook her head. "Not a word."

"Well, I don't like it. Neither he nor his friends can be trusted, Sister. I'm quite certain they're drinkers and gamblers, and probably reprobates."

"Now, Davinia. There's no need to be so harsh. Mr. Cullin seems like a nice gentleman, and quite obviously from a good family."

Davinia's brows arched. "Those are the most dangerous kind, Sister. The ones you least expect can do the most harm."

Selma's hand flew to her mouth. "Oh, goodness. I do believe they're coming into the hotel."

"Perhaps they won't notice us." Davinia shifted in her seat, putting her back to the entrance. "Have they seen us?"

Selma's cheeks darkened. "Why, yes, Sister. They have...and they're coming toward us."

"If it isn't the lovely Ritter sisters." Willard Cullin took off his hat, giving the ladies a slight bow. "Gentlemen, you remember the ladies from the train."

His companions removed their hats, nodding at them.

"Mr. Cullin, it's a pleasure to see you again." Selma glanced at Davinia, pursing her lips at the scowl on her sister's face. "We didn't know you had left the train."

Willard glanced at the men behind him. "We almost didn't, Miss Selma. My friends convinced me to head north once we reached Salt Lake City. There are several ranchers around Splendor my companions would like to meet."

"And what *exactly* is your business, Mr. Cullin?" Davinia did nothing to hide the derision in her voice.

Willard's gaze narrowed on her, his eyes gleaming.

"Would you gentlemen like a table?" A young man dressed in white and black walked up to them.

"Yes, we'd appreciate it. Ladies, I'm certain we'll see you again before leaving Splendor." The men gave another slight bow before following the young man to their table.

"Davinia." Selma's gaze darted between her sister and Willard. "What is wrong with you?"

"We know nothing of his business. It seems wherever we travel, Mr. Cullin and his friends follow. Does that not seem strange to you?"

"A little, perhaps." Selma did believe it odd, but didn't dare give Davinia fuel for her temper. "I believe we should enjoy our time in Splendor, then continue with our plans. I don't want Mr. Cullin's appearance to ruin our journey."

Davinia shook her head. "Oh, nothing will ruin our journey, Sister. On that I am certain."

"The canyon is a couple miles up the trail, Dirk," Mal called over his shoulder.

Nodding, Dirk kept his eyes roaming, looking for any sign of the missing horses. So far, they'd seen nothing.

Rosemary followed his gaze. "I thought all the horses for the army were in the pasture near the house."

"They are. The missing horses are from a separate contract with another fort south of here.

We'll be taking them when we drive the cattle to Salt Lake. The fort is on the way to where the cattle buyers want to meet."

"When are you planning to leave?"

"Depends." Dirk didn't want to tell her part of the decision had to do with Trask. Since Bull had a wife and child, Dirk planned to lead the drive. Now he wasn't sure he could leave Rosemary if Trask wasn't back behind bars. "First, we have to find the missing horses."

Throughout the ride, neither mentioned Rosemary's past nor the ordeal Dirk lived through after his wife's murder. The stories were a lot to absorb. Their experiences didn't change the obstacles Dirk saw before them.

At thirty, Dirk felt used, washed up, with little to offer a young woman of twenty. He knew she'd be better off with someone closer to her age who wasn't as jaded and distrustful. Tat had been attracted to her since she'd arrived at the ranch, not bothering to hide his interest. Rosemary had always been friendly, never encouraging Tat's advances. Her aloof manner never discouraged him, though. Dirk wondered if the time had come to persuade her to seek a future with someone else.

"Here we are." Mal had shifted to look behind him, pointing ahead.

Within minutes, they'd entered the canyon, Rosemary's eyes going wide at the majestic sight.

"I had no idea something so beautiful was hidden a few miles from the house. You've never been here before?" she asked Dirk.

He shook his head. "Never had a reason to ride over here. We usually send Mal and some of the boys."

"Looks like an old cabin up ahead."

Dirk followed her gaze, seeing an old, weather-beaten cabin with a rock fireplace on the side. "Mal tells a story about pioneers who moved here at least thirty years ago. Several families started out from around St. Louis, seeking a better life. One family made it this far, determined they weren't going to let the elements beat them. Over time, it became known as Courage Canyon."

"What happened to the family?"

"According to Mal, they made it through the first winter. In the spring and summer, they built a place not far from where the Pelletier house now sits. Rumor has it Pat Hanes bought it from them while he was a Texas Ranger."

Rosemary's lips parted. "The man who died and left the ranch to Dax and Luke?"

Dirk nodded. "That's the rumor."

"Have you ever asked them?"

"Yep. They never heard who Pat acquired the ranch from, and never dug any further into it, although they'd heard the tale of Courage Canyon.

Maybe someday they'll talk to Horace Clausen at the bank about it. There must be records somewhere."

A beautiful smile curved the corners of Rosemary's mouth. "It's a wonderful story, though."

Dirk nodded. "Yes, it is."

"Found them." Tat's shout had them riding forward to join him and Mal. "They're all here."

"Good work, men. Get them together and we'll head back."

"Not until we've eaten, Dirk." Rosemary patted the saddlebag on her right. "I can't imagine a better place to rest for a bit."

Shaking his head, Dirk looked at the men. "You heard the lady. We'll eat, then get the horses back to the herd."

An hour later, they moved the horses out of the canyon and along the trail. When they reached the spot where they'd go north toward the herd, Dirk and Rosemary headed east toward the ranch.

"You sure you don't want to ride along with us, Dirk? It might be safer than going the rest of the way by yourself."

"I'm certain, Mal. We're about two miles from the ranch and we've seen no sign of anyone following or watching."

Mal glanced at Rosemary, who didn't seem concerned, then nodded. "All right. We'll see you later today."

Dirk kept the pace steady, continuing to watch the area around them. They hadn't gotten far when Rosemary's horse stumbled, then began to favor one side.

"Rein up, Rosemary. I want to check her hooves." Dirk slid to the ground, then helped her out of the saddle, lingering an extra few seconds before letting his hands drop from her waist.

"Let's see what we have." Lifting the right front leg, Dirk picked out a large stone from the mare's hoof. "She'll be all right, but you'll need to ride with me."

Unlike the last time they rode together, he settled her in front of him this time, wrapping his arms around her waist.

"Are you all right?" he breathed against her cheek, feeling her body tighten.

"Yes. Fine."

Dirk realized it had been a mistake to have her in this position. Before, he felt her chest against his back, her arms around his waist. This time, the warmth and weight of her between his thighs had his body hardening. He tried to ignore how good she felt, concentrating on watching the hills around them. It didn't work. When she shifted, he couldn't hold back a groan.

"I'm sorry. Did I hurt you?"

"No," he ground out, ignoring the fire building in him. A minute later, she shifted again, making him wonder if she was taunting him, trying to make him crazy.

"Rosemary, sit still."

"Oh. Sorry." Her tone wasn't the least bit apologetic. When she moved again, he reined Banshee to a stop. "What's wrong?"

Dirk didn't answer as he swung his leg over to dismount, then grasped her waist to bring her down beside him.

"Dirk—"

She didn't finish as his mouth descended upon hers in a crushing kiss that had her moaning. His lips played against hers, encouraging her until she opened. Within seconds, heat flowed through them, igniting the passion they'd ignored for too long. Wrapping his arms around her, he pulled her close, his mouth slanting across hers, deepening the kiss even more.

Rosemary moaned as his hands roamed her back, settling on the soft curve of her hips. Pulling his mouth from hers, he trailed light kisses along her jaw, down her neck, to the hollow of her throat. A quiver of sensation ripped through her, a tightness deep in her belly, making her feel as if she were on fire. Her head fell back, allowing him better access.

As his mouth continued its sensuous journey back to her mouth, she felt a sense of urgency, of need she didn't quite understand.

"Dirk..." she breathed out, not sure what she was asking.

"I have you, sweetheart." His breath caught on a groan as he slipped his arms behind her, lifting, carrying her off the trail. Finding a secluded spot, he laid her down, his mouth covering hers again as he stretched out beside her.

She felt his fingers play with the hem of her skirt before a warm hand moved up her leg to her thigh. His body was aligned with hers, his hands driving her insane, yet he still wasn't close enough. Reaching between them, her fingers worked the buttons on his shirt, opening one, then another before his hand settled over hers.

"Rosemary." His voice was ragged, needy. "Make sure this is what you want before you go any further."

Pulling her hand from his grasp, her breathing fast and uneven, she nodded, moving her hands back to the front of his shirt. Dirk didn't protest before his mouth descended on hers, his hands resuming their journey up her leg. As he moved closer to what he sought, he broke the kiss once more.

"There'll be no regrets."

She shook her head, eyes glistening with passion. "No regrets."

Lying in his arms, Rosemary couldn't remember a time she'd been so happy, so content. They were on a bed of leaves and twigs, yet she didn't care. They'd made love until they couldn't speak or move, their bodies tired and replete.

"I didn't intend for this to happen." Dirk kissed her forehead, his hand resting possessively on her stomach.

Her chest tightened, remembering his words. "I have no regrets, Dirk."

"Neither do I, sweetheart. It's just..." His throat constricted, not knowing what else to say.

"What do we do now?" She tried to make her voice light. The last thing she wanted was to make him feel trapped. Instead, she felt the rumble in his chest when he chuckled.

"Yeah."

Afraid to voice her question, she drew in an uneven breath, searching for courage. "What do you want to happen?"

His hand stroked her hair, then cupped her chin, lifting it so her eyes met his. "I want you, Rosemary. I just don't know if I'm what's best for you."

Shifting, she supported herself with her arm, looking down at him. "You're exactly who I want. Don't try talking yourself out of it now." She offered a shaky smile, having no idea how he'd react. To her surprise, he laughed.

"I'm so much older."

"I don't care."

"People back home believe I murdered my wife."

"I know you didn't."

Closing his eyes, he inhaled a deep breath, then opened them. "I have no home to offer you."

"We'll live in the shack in Courage Canyon."

Another chuckle rumbled in his chest. "You aren't going to let me talk you out of this, are you?"

Rosemary shook her head. "No, I'm not."

They were silent as she rested her head on his chest, a deep sigh escaping.

"Don't you have any doubts, Rosemary?"

She thought a minute, playing with the crisp hairs on his chest. "One."

He stilled, his breath hitching. "Tell me."

"After Melissa's betrayal, I'm afraid you'll never be able to trust me." She raised her head enough to see the struggle on his face. "I can see you aren't certain, either." Her voice trembled, a wave of fear ripping at her heart when he didn't answer. Pushing up, she stood, picking leaves out of her hair. Straightening her clothing, she closed her dress, her hands trembling as she worked the buttons. "We should start back before they begin to worry." Turning, she headed for the horses.

"Rosemary. Wait." Jumping up, he grabbed his shirt, then followed. "Stop."

Reaching Banshee, she felt strong hands on her shoulders, turning her to face him. At first, she couldn't meet his gaze. Blinking the moisture away, she glanced up.

He looked down at her, his emotions no longer hidden behind a mask of distrust. "I love you."

Blinking didn't stop the tears this time. Letting them fall, she cupped his hands with hers. "I love you, too."

Brushing a kiss across her lips, he smiled. "Then I'll find a way to forget my past, or at least not let it guide my future."

"Promise?"

Letting out a pent-up breath, he nodded, hoping he was true to his word. "Promise."

Chapter Seventeen

"Dirk, I can't stay at the ranch any longer. I need to return to the clinic." Rosemary looked up from where she worked at the kitchen counter, preparing a pie for supper. She needed to finish before the men came in for dinner.

It had been several days since they'd returned from the canyon. Although they'd said nothing to the others, everyone noticed the change between them. Rachel and Ginny had cornered her the night before, asking if she and Dirk were together. They'd been thrilled when she'd said yes.

Rosemary hoped she answered correctly. Even though they'd declared their love, he'd made no assurances of a future together.

"I know you're ready to get your life back, but it still isn't safe. There's been no word about Trask or the men riding with him. Gabe would've sent us a message if he'd heard anything."

Crossing his arms over his chest, Dirk tried to hide his agitation. She'd mentioned returning to the clinic before they'd left for the canyon, then had said nothing else until this morning. He wondered if she regretted what they'd done, needing distance from him.

Worse, he couldn't push away the slight thread of doubt eating at him, wondering if it wasn't the work she missed as much as Clay McCord. The direction of his thoughts angered him, knowing they were irrational. Still, they clung to him, like a shadow he couldn't evade.

She turned toward him, wiping her hands on a towel. "I know, and that's why I believe it's safe to return to work. If Trask were still after me, he would've shown up by now, don't you think?"

Walking to her, he placed his hands on her shoulders. "You can't outguess a man like Trask. Who knows what goes through the mind of someone who's blackmailed and threatened people to get what he wants. Maybe he won't ever come after you, Rosemary. Then again, maybe he's waiting in town for you to arrive at the clinic. I wish there was a good answer."

Pursing her lips, she rested her head against his chest, breathing in Dirk's unique scent. She'd know it anywhere—the heady aroma conveying the promise of love, security, and forever. Looking up, her gaze met his.

"I know you worry about me, and I'd feel the same if you were in danger."

Wrapping his arms around her, he kissed her forehead, tucking her head under his chin. "Would it help to consider how much Rachel and Ginny depend on you right now?"

Rosemary nodded against his chest. "Rachel's baby is due anytime, and with Cooper, Ginny wouldn't be able to offer much help. And Lydia..." Rosemary chuckled, thinking of Bull's wife. "She has baby Joshua, who's six months old, plus Margaret and Selina most days. And she's begun schooling the children while Ginny is taking care of Cooper."

"Which means you're needed here more than ever."

"The hard part is I'll always be needed here. With the orphans and babies, the work doesn't stop. It's hard because they are my family now, but in my heart, I want to complete my training as a nurse."

"And you will. Trask is a temporary obstacle, Rosemary. It won't be like this forever."

"I know you're right. It will be better once Rachel has the baby."

Dirk leaned away, kissing the tip of her nose. "And Trask is located."

She nodded. "And Trask is located."

Giving her one more hug, he dropped his arms to his sides. "Dax asked if I could go to town the day after tomorrow to talk with Noah about an order for the ranch. Come with me. You can go into the clinic while I meet with Noah, then speak with Gabe. We'll eat at the boardinghouse, then head back well before evening." As he spoke, her eyes widened, lips parting before her face broke into a smile.

Jumping into his arms, she almost knocked him over. Laughing, he looked into eyes bright with excitement. Before he could stop himself, he settled his mouth over hers, gratified at her moan of satisfaction.

Hearing someone clearing their throat, they pulled apart.

"Sorry to interrupt." Ginny tried to hide a grin. "Lydia isn't feeling well and asked if you would consider schooling the children today. She said it's only their math and writing." She glanced between Dirk and Rosemary. "Of course, if you're too busy..."

Rosemary felt her face flush as she shook her head. "No, it's fine. Let me finish the pie, then I'll go over and get the lessons from Lydia."

Ginny shifted Cooper in her arms. "There's no hurry. You can get the children together after dinner for a couple hours. That will give you time to finish up, um...whatever you're doing in here." Biting her lower lip, she left Dirk and Rosemary.

Looking up at him, she couldn't stop a laugh, causing him to laugh with her. Rosemary had rarely seen him smile or laugh. It was deep and rich, drawing her in, providing a glimpse of the man he was before the war and his wife's betrayal. *And his brother's*, she reminded herself, a bit of reality returning.

She glanced down the hall, making certain no one else was near. "I suppose we shouldn't have gotten so carried away."

Dirk shrugged. "Maybe not, but I refuse to feel bad about it. I need to ride out to check on the cattle. Will you be all right here?"

Clasping her hands in front of her, she nodded. "Of course, Dirk."

"Ellis and Joe are mending fences around the barn, and Johnny is sitting outside the bunkhouse, working on broken tack. They'll keep watch while I'm gone."

Walking to him, she leaned up, kissing his cheek. "I'll be fine. Go. I'll see you at supper."

Dirk snaked an arm around her waist, dragging her to him. "You'll see me before supper." Placing a quick kiss on her mouth, he walked out.

Splendor

Selma didn't try to hide her curiosity as she looked out the window of the hotel restaurant. Standing across the street, talking to a man who appeared to be the sheriff, was Mr. Cullin.

"I wonder what they're talking about." She didn't move her gaze from the two men.

"Who, Selma?" Davinia forked another piece of ham, placing it into her mouth with a flourish. "You really must try the ham, Sister. It is quite good."

Selma glanced at Davinia. "I find what is going on outside far more interesting than your ham."

Setting down her fork, Davinia glared at her sister. "Oh, all right. What is so fascinating outside that you won't allow me to eat my meal in peace?"

Selma ignored Davinia's mood, nodding toward the window. "Look for yourself."

Leaning forward, she blinked a couple times, focusing outside, then blew out an annoyed breath. "I don't see anything unusual, Selma."

"Oh, you can be so vexing, Sister. Look across the street."

"Fine." Standing, Davinia moved to the window, her eyes going wide when she spotted Mr. Cullin. "My word. I do believe that is Sheriff Evans he's talking to. I wonder what they could possibly have to say to each other." Shifting her gaze to Selma, she moved back to her seat. "I'm sure it's nothing, Sister. Mr. Cullin is simply being friendly."

"Perhaps, Davinia." Selma stared down at her food, taking one more bite.

"I believe it is time for us to explore the town before we decide to leave."

Selma choked on her small morsel of food. "I don't believe there is any more to see. Splendor is bigger than we first thought. Still, it has one main street with the lumber mill and school at one end, the hotel at the other."

"I've heard they're building a new clinic behind the bank."

Resigned, Selma folded her napkin. "And I suppose you'd like to see it."

"I'd hate to leave Splendor without seeing all it has to offer. Don't you agree, Sister?"

Seeing the determination, and something else she understood from years of living with her, on Davinia's face, Selma nodded. "Yes. I think it would be quite wise, Sister."

"Thank you, Bernie. This is the message I've been waiting for." Dutch read the telegram once more before tucking it into a pocket.

"Do you want to send a reply?"

"Not now, Bernie. I'll let you know."

Dutch stepped outside, still surprised to see the increase in activity since the first time he came to Splendor. If it hadn't been for his association with Luke Pelletier, another former Pinkerton agent, he might never have set foot in this place. Noticing Wyatt sitting outside the Dixie saloon, he walked across the street.

"Morning, Dutch."

"Wyatt. You're looking better every day. Allie Coulter must be feeding you well."

Patting his stomach, he nodded. "Too well." He motioned to the chair next to him. "Have a seat."

Pulling over a chair from a few feet away, Dutch lowered himself into it. "Are you still thinking of working for the Pelletiers?"

"Considering it. I can't make any decisions until I've figured out why those wanted posters are still out on me."

Reaching into his pocket, Dutch pulled out the telegram, handing it to Wyatt.

Reading it over, a slow grin formed on his face.

"Appears you can do whatever you want."

Wyatt nodded. "So it seems." He reached out a hand. "Thanks, Dutch. I appreciate all you've done."

Grasping Wyatt's hand, he shook his head. "I didn't do anything except make a request to Allan. It's incredible how many contacts he has and what he's able to do by sending out a few inquiries." Dutch watched as wagons and riders rode past, wondering why someone would send out bogus wanted posters. "I'm guessing someone isn't too happy about you not being charged with murder. It's the only reason I can think of why they'd go to the trouble of preparing and sending out false posters. If you hadn't noticed them, it may have been too late to make things right before some overzealous lawman or bounty hunter recognized you."

"And hauled me in?" Wyatt asked.

"I doubt you would've made it to a jail." Dutch grinned. "Sorry. I forgot you made your living as a bounty hunter."

Wyatt snorted. "Never did like it. Shortest profession I ever had."

"Gentlemen." Gabe walked toward them, grabbing another chair. "Mind if I join you?"

"Sit down, Sheriff. Dutch just brought me some good news." Wyatt handed the telegram to Gabe. Reading it through, he gave it back.

"Does Cash know?"

"Not yet. I'll let him know tonight at supper. Tomorrow, I'll ride out to the Pelletier ranch, see if they were serious about offering me a job."

A corner of Dutch's mouth lifted when he saw Miss Chestro and the three other young women leaving the boardinghouse. "Dax and Luke wouldn't have offered if they weren't serious. Right, Gabe?"

His mind focusing on the telegram Bernie had given him a few minutes before, he didn't hear the question.

"Gabe?" Dutch prodded.

Gabe gave him a blank stare.

"You got something on your mind?" Dutch asked.

Nodding, Gabe took out the folded piece of paper, handing it to Dutch. Reading it, he whistled. "This the first you've heard of it?"

"It is."

Dutch shook his head. "I'm surprised Allan hasn't sent word to me."

Wyatt looked at them. "What are you two talking about?"

Dutch glanced at Gabe, who nodded. Handing the telegram to Wyatt, they waited, seeing his expression harden.

"Cash told me about the kidnappings and murders along the railroad line. I didn't know there were similar murders this far north. There are no railroads up this way, are there?"

"Not a single one," Gabe answered.

Dutch drew in a slow breath. "According to the telegram, a young woman's body was found near Moosejaw, then another outside Big Pine. Whoever is doing this is coming our way."

Gabe stood, shoving the chair back against the building. "Whoever is doing this is already here."

Gabe spent the early afternoon talking to his deputies, telling them what he knew of the additional murders. They agreed to a new schedule of rounds, discussing a way to spread the word without causing panic. Everyone felt the urgency. A decision needed to be made right away.

"We have to let everyone in town know, Gabe. It may frighten them, but I doubt they'll panic." Mack stared out the window of the Dixie, the perfect place for them to talk while keeping watch on the town.

"I agree. Mack, I want you, Dutch, and Caleb to go from business to business, tell them what's been happening. Beau and Cash will ride to the ranches and farms close to town."

"How far out, Gabe?" Beau asked, his mind already going to his fiancée, Caro, who stayed at her place several miles from town.

"As far out as Redemption's Edge. From what Dutch and I have been able to learn, all the women were abducted while close to town, and all were alone. I want all young women to be inside by sundown and not on the street again until nine in the morning. No female, no matter her age, is to go anywhere alone."

"I don't think the women outside of town should be leaving their homes until we've caught whoever's doing this," Beau said.

Caleb nodded. "Or another murder is discovered well beyond our borders."

"Dutch, you said Pinkerton is involved. Do they know anything about who's doing this?" Mack asked.

"I know he has agents working on it. They were traveling on the railroad, went as far as Salt Lake City before they got word of a similar murder near Moosejaw. The good news is it seems most lawmen between Boston and San Francisco have heard about what's going on and are more vigilant than when the first murders occurred. Unfortunately, they haven't been able to discover anything about the murderers. We don't know if it's one man or several working together. No clues have been found near the bodies, and there doesn't seem to be any motive."

"And the women aren't connected?" Caleb asked Dutch.

"Not that they can determine. The murders have baffled everyone."

Gabe stood, placing his hat back on his head. "Enough talk. We need get out there and warn the town. I want them to tell one of us of anything they believe is suspicious."

Beau cleared his throat, looking at Gabe. "I want Caro to stay in town until this has been resolved."

Gabe nodded. He and Caro had been friends growing up in New York. It had been his invitation that inspired her to stop in Splendor on her journey to San Francisco.

"I'll let Nick and Lena know we need a room made up for her at the hotel. Let me know if you need help convincing her to leave the ranch."

Beau chuckled. "I might need to take you up on that."

"I'm going to talk to Noah about the murders. He may want to consider bringing Abby and Gabriel to town. Now that she's pregnant again, I doubt he'll want to leave her at the house alone." He looked at all his men before they walked outside. "I don't want any woman staying alone."

"Isn't Sarah Murton, the school teacher, single?" Dutch asked.

"Not by choice," Cash chuckled.

Beau shook his head, stifling a grin. "What he means is yes, Miss Murton is single and lives alone."

"My suggestion is one of the married men talk to her," Cash suggested.

"I'll speak with her," Gabe offered. "All right. Let's get started."

Chapter Eighteen

"I'm sorry I wasn't feeling up to helping you and Ginny with supper." Rachel sat down at the kitchen table, drawing in the fragrant aroma of Rosemary's pies. "I can help set the food on the table, though."

Rosemary stirred the stew, looking over her shoulder. "Don't even think about helping. Ginny, Lydia, and I can take care of it. You could let the men and children know we're ready."

"I'll do that now." Pushing up from the table, Rachel left the kitchen, both arms bracing her expanding belly.

Ginny watched her leave, a frown forming on her face. "I don't know how much longer she can go. Doc Worthington said she should have delivered her baby before I had Cooper."

"That's what Doc McCord thought, too. I think he only mentioned it to me." Rosemary ladled the stew into a large serving bowl.

"She could go into labor at any time." Lydia walked past Rosemary and Ginny, carrying a large basket of bread. "I hope it's soon. I'm beginning to worry about her."

Ginny nodded. "And the baby."

Rosemary tried to push aside her own concerns, reminding herself how inaccurate guesses could be when estimating when a baby would arrive. "Rachel is strong. She'll be fine."

"Rachel is as huge as a cow." Rachel came back into the room, lowering herself into a chair with a groan. "I do wish this baby would come. I don't remember being so big with Patrick."

"Did someone say supper was ready?" Dax walked in, leaning down to kiss Rachel as a loud clap of thunder shook the house. "This sudden storm isn't letting up."

Rachel glanced out the kitchen window at the pouring rain, shuddering as more thunder rocked the room. "A few more minutes." She looked down at her husband's mud-encrusted boots, wrinkling her nose. "You have plenty of time to change and wash up."

"I'll just get dirty again after supper."

Shaking her head, she motioned to the back porch.

"Yes, ma'am." Giving a mock salute, he walked through the kitchen to the back entrance where the women did the laundry and the men dumped their dirty clothes.

"Everything's ready." Rosemary carried the bowl of stew into the dining room, her gaze darting around. Everyone was there...except the one person she most wanted to see.

Cursing for the hundredth time, Dirk groaned under the weight of the fallen tree. The storm had come on so fast and strong, he hadn't had a chance to find shelter before a bolt of lightning hit the ground a hundred yards away. Seconds later, the sound of thunder ripped through the air, followed by another bolt of lightning and more thunder.

Banshee had reared back, tossing Dirk to the ground an instant before a third bolt of lightning shot straight down, hitting a large tree near the trail. He had no time to move before the trunk split, part of the tree crushing him into the thickening mud.

An hour later, he still hadn't been able to budge the trunk. Each time he tried to dislodge himself, excruciating pain shot up his leg and into his back. He didn't have the leverage or strength to move it.

Banshee stood to one side, nudging Dirk's face with his nose, as if the horse expected him to free himself. He had to figure out a way to escape. Taking a deep breath, he sat up, positioning his hands on the log when more lightning brightened the dark sky. Rearing up again, Banshee's hoofs pounded to the ground before his horse took off, leaving Dirk to take care of himself.

Heaving a sigh of relief, Dirk fell back, praying Banshee continued in the direction he ran—straight toward the ranch.

"Are you certain Dirk wasn't planning on going anywhere except to check on the cattle?" Dax leaned forward, resting his arms on the table, a clear indication of his concern.

Rosemary shook her head. "All he told me was he was going to check on the cattle."

"Bull?"

"Dirk checked on the herd in the northwest pasture while I did the same in the northeast, Dax. He didn't plan to be gone long—a few hours at most." Bull glanced at Rosemary, then back at Dax. "Like all of us, he's concerned about Trask showing up."

"The storm came up fast. It may have surprised him." Luke reached over to take Ginny's hand, squeezing it. "He probably found shelter where he could wait it out."

A loud knock had Dax standing, moving to the front door. Opening it, he motioned Mal to come inside. Looking over Dax's shoulder, Mal spotted Rosemary, then shook his head.

"Best you come outside with me, Boss."

Grabbing his slicker, Dax followed Mal outside.

"Dirk's horse just showed up...without him." Mal pointed to the barn. "Tat is taking care of him. He was pretty spooked."

"I want four men left behind to watch the women and children. Everyone else is to be ready to ride in fifteen minutes."

"I'll have them saddle your horse and Luke's."

"Bull's, too."

"Yes, sir."

Going back into the house, he didn't bother to hang up his slicker as he stepped up to the table. "Dirk's horse showed up without him." He looked at Luke and Bull. "I've got men saddling the horses. We need to leave right away. Bull, you'll be in the lead. You'll have a better idea which trail Dirk would take."

"What of the women?" Bull asked, standing.

"Four men are staying behind to guard the house. I want all the women and children inside." Dax knelt next to Rachel. "I don't want to leave, but—"

Rachel placed a finger over his lips. "I'm fine. You need to find Dirk."

Nodding, he gripped her hand in his, kissing her fingers, then stood. "Rosemary, I'll trust you to watch over the others while we're gone."

She hadn't spoken a word since Dax made the announcement about Banshee. Her mind raced over the possibilities, fear clutching at her as she settled on the worst possible outcome.

"Rosemary?" Dax's stern voice had her looking up.

"I'm sorry. Did you ask me a question?"

His face softened. "I know you're worried about Dirk, but I need you to keep watch over the women and children."

She nodded, her throat closing up when she tried to speak.

Dax stepped closer, placing a hand on her shoulder. "We'll find him, Rosemary. We won't come back until we do."

Montana temperatures always dropped along with the sun, and tonight seemed to have plunged lower than normal. Dirk felt his body seize up in the cold, his teeth chattering and body aching. At least it numbed his leg, helping to ease the pain.

The storm had come and gone within hours. Looking up, he saw no sign of the menacing clouds, nothing to indicate the damage left behind. The brightest moon he'd seen in a long time shown down on him, illuminating the site of his accident.

As his body shivered, an image of Rosemary filled his mind. By now, she'd be worried. If Banshee returned to the ranch as he hoped, she'd be frantic. After all she'd been through, he hated putting her through more anguish.

The howl of a wolf caught his attention, followed by the yaps of what he assumed to be the rest of the pack. Living in Montana, he'd learned wolves often traveled in groups of at least three, sometimes as many as ten. For the first time since the tree pinned him, Dirk felt a wave of fear. He'd rather face a group of outlaws, knowing he had some chance of survival, than a pack of wolves.

Hearing the barking again, he sat up, trying to use his dwindling strength to dislodge his legs. Trying over and over, he finally exhausted himself, his heart racing. When the howls stopped, his gaze darted around. The quiet bothered him more than their howls.

A slight rustling sound had him looking into the bushes. His gaze collided with a pair of yellow eyes— bright, clear, and threatening. Refusing to give in to fear, Dirk reached as far as he could, his fingers touching but failing to grasp a large rock. Shifting his weight, he tried again, this time wrapping his hand around it.

When he looked back to where he'd first spotted the wolf, three pairs of yellow eyes glowered at him. He couldn't get them all, but he might be lucky enough to get one. Sucking in a deep breath, he drew his arm back as far as possible.

Gunshots and loud shouts stopped his movement. Before he could fully register the chain of events, a group of riders swooped in, some chasing off the wolves, others dismounting, surveying the damage.

Bull knelt beside him. "You've really done it this time, Dirk."

Luke and Dax walked up, each carrying ropes, studying his position, the tree, and the surrounding area.

"Lightning?" Luke asked.

Dirk nodded. "Did Banshee make it back?"

"He did," Luke answered. "That's why we're here. Now, let's get you out from under there."

It took less time than Dirk estimated to free him, no thanks to any effort on his part. He couldn't move his leg before they arrived and he still couldn't. Bile rose in his throat at the sight of bone sticking through his pants.

Bull studied the leg, letting out a low whistle. "We won't be able to take him back on a horse. We'd better have someone fetch a wagon."

"Tat." Dax motioned for him to come closer. "We need a wagon."

Rolling up his rope, Tat looked down at Dirk's leg, wincing at the sight. "Yes, sir. I'll go right now."

"Take one of the men with you," Dax added. "And let Rosemary know we found him and he'll be all right."

Bull walked over to his horse, pulling a bottle of whiskey from the saddlebag. Kneeling next to Dirk once more, he offered him the bottle. "Now, we'd best see to that break."

Rosemary stood at the porch rail, refusing to leave until Dirk returned. Tat had dashed into the house, delivered the news, then hurried out. He helped another ranch hand hitch up the wagon, then drove off. When asked, Tat had said it would take at least four hours to bring Dirk back.

At least he's safe, Rosemary reminded herself.

She turned, ready to sit in the porch swing, when a loud scream startled her. Rushing inside, she ran down the hall to where Dax and Rachel had slept the last months of her pregnancy. Shoving the door open, she rushed inside. Rachel was on her hands and knees, taking deep breaths, a puddle underneath her.

"I...believe the...baby...is coming."

"Don't move." Stepping back into the hall, Rosemary ran to the base of the stairs, yelling up. "Ginny, Lydia, I need your help." Dashing to the bedroom, she helped Rachel shift into a sitting position on the floor against the bed. Grabbing a pillow, she stuffed it behind her back for support. "What happened?"

"I felt something happening and tried to get off the bed. My feet slipped and I fell forward.

Somehow, I got my hands out in front of me." She glanced at Rosemary. "Is there any chance you can help me back to the bed."

"We can all help." Ginny rushed in, followed by Lydia.

Once they got Rachel settled, Rosemary hurried outside to have the men prepare a wagon. She cast an impatient glance in the direction Tat had driven, wishing she didn't have to leave before Dirk returned. If his injury was as severe as Tat indicated, they'd be taking him to the clinic, which was where she would be with Rachel.

Returning to the bedroom, she saw Ginny and Lydia had already dressed Rachel for the trip to town. As she approached the bed, another round of labor pains hit, causing Rachel to yell, ending with a mumbled curse.

"Rachel!" Ginny burst into laughter.

Groaning, Rachel forced herself to breathe as her body recovered. "Sorry. Sometimes, well...my time in the battlefield medical tents returns."

"No need to apologize. If it helps, yell as loud as you need." Rosemary smiled. "And if it's punctuated with more colorful words, I'm certain none of us will tell."

"Not me," Lydia said as she helped Rachel stand. "We should get you into the wagon before the next round of pain starts."

Rachel nodded. "Then we'd best hurry. I think this baby is coming fast."

Within a few minutes, she was in the back of the wagon, wrapped in blankets, pillows behind and around her. Rosemary sat next to her. Ellis held the lines, his rifle next to him. Joe would ride alongside. Two other men would stay to watch over Lydia, Ginny, and the children.

"Are you certain you want to go alone, Rosemary?" Lydia leaned over the side of the wagon, her worried gaze focused on Rachel.

"I'm not alone. Ellis and Joe are going. Plus, Bull and Luke would have a fit if either you or Ginny came along. Don't worry. We'll be fine."

Ellis glanced over his shoulder. "Are you ready, Miss Rosemary?"

"We are."

"All right then." Ellis slapped the lines, going as fast as he could given Rachel's condition.

Before they made it past the large boulder signaling the entrance to the ranch, another labor pain gripped Rachel. Rosemary wiped her forehead with a damp cloth, reminding her to breathe.

As the pain subsided, Rosemary looked up at the sky, thankful the storm had passed, praying Dirk's injuries weren't any more serious than what Tat indicated. She knew they wouldn't waste time getting Dirk to the clinic. And once Dax learned

Rachel had been taken to town, nothing would stop him from getting to her.

"Rachel's in labor?" Dax stood in the entry, his hands fisted at his sides. "I need to see her." He tried to slide past them when Ginny grabbed his shoulder.

"Rosemary took her to the clinic, Dax."

"Alone?" His voice thundered through the house, waking Cooper, Joshua, and Patrick. He looked up the stairs, torn between going to Patrick and rushing to town.

Ginny touched his arm. "Your son is fine, Dax. Lydia, Selina, and Margaret are with the babies. And no, she did not go alone. Ellis and Joe are with her. Now, you need to get to town."

He hadn't planned to ride along with Mal and Tat when they continued to the clinic with Dirk. His plans had changed.

"It's started raining again." Luke walked in, shaking water off his slicker.

"Luke!"

Ginny hurried into his arms, kissing him, then pulling away. "How is Dirk?"

"He's in a lot of pain. We're trying to keep him dry until we leave for town." He looked at Dax. "They're ready to go. With the weather turning again, I'm thinking I should go with them."

"No. I'll go." Dax scrubbed a hand down his face. "Rachel went into labor and Rosemary took her to town."

Luke's eyes narrowed. "Alone?"

Ginny shook her head, her hands resting on her hips. "For heaven's sake. Do all the men here think the women are dimwitted?" Turning, she walked up the stairs.

Luke's startled expression locked on Dax, his brows drawing together in a frown.

"Ellis and Joe are with Rachel and Rosemary. I'll go in with Dirk, if you'll stay here with the others." Dax smirked. "It will give you some time to mollify your wife."

Luke shook his head. "I still don't know what I said, but fine."

"I'll get word to you about Rachel and Dirk as soon as I know anything." Settling his hat on his head, he clasped Luke on the shoulder. "Take care of everything until we get back."

Chapter Nineteen

"She's in with Doc Worthington, Dax." Clay McCord stood aside.

"Dirk Masters broke his leg. He's in the wagon."

"Rosemary told us. Rachel's uncle will deliver the baby and I'll patch Dirk up. You go ahead and let them know you're here." Clay held open the door so Tat and Mal could carry Dirk inside.

"He's been passed out most of the last couple hours, Doc." Mal glanced at Clay.

"Probably a good thing. Put him on the table in the room to the left."

"I think he may have finished Bull's bottle of whiskey." Mal pushed his hat off his forehead, grimacing when water splattered onto the wood floor.

Cutting Dirk's pants, Clay nodded. "I would've done the same with a break like this."

"Is he in here?" Rosemary stood in the doorway, her gaze landing on Dirk. "Oh, my God." She placed a hand over her mouth, her eyes wide.

"I can take care of Dirk. If it comes to it, Mal and Tat can help me. You need to be in with Rachel."

She glanced at Mal and Tat, who stood inside the small room. "Doc Worthington says it could be a while before the baby comes. If it's all right, I'd like to help in here until he needs me."

Clay looked up from pulling away Dirk's bloodied, dirty, and wet pants. "Boys, why don't you take a seat out front? I'll let you know if I need you."

"Yes, sir." Tat nodded at Rosemary as he left the room.

Mal touched her arm. "Call out if you need anything."

"I will." Her voice shook. Looking down at Dirk, Rosemary gasped. She'd known it would be bad, but had no idea how horrible the damage would be until she saw it up close.

"He's alive, and if I have my way, he'll be back walking again within weeks."

"You're an excellent doctor. If anyone can fix him up, it's you."

Dirk chose that moment to jerk awake, his arms flailing as he tried to sit up.

Clay put a hand on Dirk's shoulder. "It's all right, Dirk. You've been injured. The men brought you to the clinic."

His eyes, red-rimmed and glassy, fluttered open. Blinking a couple times, his gaze latched onto the one person he wanted to see most.

"Rosemary..." he whispered, his throat thick.

Leaning down, she brushed hair from his face. "I'm here, Dirk."

He held up his hand for her to grasp. "My leg..."

"I know. Doc McCord is going to fix it. He says you'll be fine."

Dirk's lips twisted. "I know it's bad." He gripped her hand tighter, his eyes panicked. "Don't let him take my leg."

"Shhh. He isn't going to take your leg." She glanced at Clay. His features were still, unreadable, making her heart sink.

"Dirk, the men did the best they could under difficult circumstances, but I need to reset the break. It's going to hurt. Do you want more whiskey or chloroform?"

"Neither." Grimacing, he forced himself to continue. "I want to know what's going on."

"If you're sure."

"Just do it, Doc."

Clay nodded at Rosemary. "Get his shoulders."

She licked her lips, hesitating a moment.

"Would you like me to call for Mal and Tat?"

Shaking her head, she settled her hands on Dirk's shoulders. "No, Doctor. I can do it."

Studying her face, he adjusted his grip on Dirk's leg, then gave her one quick nod.

"Sonofab—" Dirk bit back the rest of the word as the door flew open.

"Everything all right in here?" Mal looked at Dirk, then Clay.

"We're fine," Clay answered, noticing Dirk had passed out. Figuring it would be temporary, he concentrated on finishing the task of setting the leg.

"All right then. I'll, uh...be right out here." Mal closed the door on a soft click.

Clay worked quickly, finally looking up at Rosemary. "I've got this. Why don't you check on Rachel?"

She swallowed, not wanting to leave Dirk's side. "Are you sure?"

Clay tilted his head. "Rosemary?"

As if suddenly remembering Clay was her employer, she straightened. "Of course, Doctor. I'll go right now."

"If you aren't needed with Rachel, come back here. I'm sure Dirk will want to see you when he regains consciousness."

Her shoulders relaxed. "I will. Thank you, Doctor."

A baby's cry greeted Rosemary as she stepped into the larger room. Dax stood next to the bed, holding Rachel's hand. She looked exhausted, her face bathed in sweat. Still, a serene smile curved the corners of her mouth.

Closing the door softly behind her, she watched as Doc Worthington finished checking the baby. Stepping up to him, she looked down, her lips parting at the beauty before her. She tilted her head at the doctor, a question in her eyes.

"Another boy," he whispered, his eyes crinkling in amusement. Lifting the baby, he turned toward Dax and Rachel.

"Who would like to hold your son first?"

"A boy?" Dax's jaw went slack.

Rachel touched his arm. "I told you I thought we were having another boy. This time, you get the honors first, sweetheart."

"All right, General Pelletier. You've done this before." Doc Worthington held out the baby.

"*Ex*-general."

"Regardless, Dax. Take your son."

Rosemary stood off to the side, watching with her heart in her throat, feeling emotion swell inside her. No one would ever doubt the love between Rachel and Dax. The same could be said for Luke and Ginny, Bull and Lydia, and so many other couples in Splendor. Without a doubt, she wanted the same kind of love, and she wanted it with Dirk.

"Has he woken up yet?" Rosemary stepped next to the bed, touching Dirk's face.

"Not yet. Perhaps he's been waiting for you to return. How is Rachel?"

She smiled. "They've added another boy to the family."

Clay chuckled. "There must be something magical at Redemption's Edge. All the babies since I've come to town have been boys."

"Rosemary..." Dirk groaned, his eyes opening to slits. "My leg?"

"Is going to be fine, Dirk. The doctor was able to reset it." She gripped his hand, threading her fingers with his as Clay stepped next to her.

"You'll have to stay off your leg for at least a month, Dirk. Then you'll be able to use a crutch for a few more weeks—as long as you continue to keep your weight off it."

Dirk began to shake his head, then stopped when Clay held up his hand.

"This is *not* a suggestion, Dirk. At first, I thought you'd lose your leg. I believed it had taken too long to get you to the clinic, opening your leg to infection. I checked it thoroughly. When I saw no sign of infection, I decided to reset it. Right now, the wound is clean. If you want to keep your leg, it's important it stay that way." He looked at Rosemary. "You'll need to be his private nurse for a while, checking his leg several times a day. If there's any sign of infection, you must get him back here right away. For now, though, I want you to stay here at least two days, Dirk, so I can keep a close watch on how the wound is healing."

Rosemary nodded. "I know Rachel and Dax will let him stay in the house as long as needed."

"I'll stay with the men in the bunkhouse."

Rosemary glared at him. "No, you won't. You'll stay in the house where I can check your leg as often as needed without going to the bunkhouse."

"Rosemary..." he ground out.

Lifting her chin, she crossed her arms, scowling at him. "Don't you dare argue with me, Dirk Masters. You'll stay in the house and that is final." Glancing at Clay, she turned, stomping out of the room.

Dirk stared at the closed door, his mouth drawn into a thin line, the pain in his leg momentarily forgotten.

"She is one stubborn woman," Clay said.

"You have no idea."

"It's going to be hard to get away with anything."

Dirk's eyes narrowed. "Yeah, I know."

"She may be the only thing keeping you from losing your leg." Clay's gaze fixed on Dirk, a brow lifted.

Dirk let out a breath, feeling tired and defeated.

"And if I'm not mistaken, she loves you."

Dirk's mouth quirked up at the corners. "Yeah. I think you may be right."

"It's a glorious morning, Sister. The storm yesterday cleared the air. I think it would be a good day for a walk." Selma sat in her usual chair, watching wagons and horses navigate the muddy street.

"I do believe you've come up with a very good idea. After breakfast, we'll change into our day dresses and start out."

"Ladies." Willard Cullin walked up to them, one of his usual companions next to him. "I hope you're having a wonderful morning."

"Sister and I were just talking about that, Mr. Cullin. We've decided to take a walk while the sky is so clear."

"I think that's a marvelous idea, Miss Selma. Perhaps my friend and I will join you." Willard inched closer.

Selma sent a worried look at Davinia.

"Such a wonderful idea, Mr. Cullin." Davinia touched her napkin to the corners of her mouth. "I believe, however, Sister and I would quickly bore you with the way we dawdle."

"Oh yes, Davinia. Mr. Cullin and his friends would most certainly tire of us within a few minutes. It would be quite intolerable for you, I'm afraid." Selma raised her gaze to Willard.

Nodding, he glanced at his companion, then back at the ladies. "Perhaps you're right. Another time then."

"Perhaps, Mr. Cullin. Although I'm not sure how much longer we'll be in Splendor."

His face sobered. "Don't tell me you're leaving so soon."

"We can't stay here forever. Can we, Sister?"

"Heavens no, Selma. We have so much more to see and accomplish."

"If that's the case, be sure to let me know when you plan to leave. My companions and I may join you on the stage." Willard made a slight bow, then turned, he and his friend strolling out of the restaurant.

"Oh dear. What do you think he means?"

"I'm certain I don't know, Selma. But I know I don't like it."

"Wyatt, I'm going to ask you a favor. Unless, of course, you've already spoken to the Pelletiers about a job."

"I haven't mentioned it yet, Gabe. I joined Mal and Tat for breakfast at the boardinghouse this morning. They said Rachel had her baby. A boy. She and Dax are still at the clinic."

Gabe looked up from his desk, a grin on his face. "I hadn't heard about it. I'll have to let Lena and Nick know."

"I figured to ride out there today, but given what's happened, I plan to wait a few days. So, what is this favor you want to ask?"

"I want you to follow some men who've been in town a few days. I'd have one of the deputies do it, but I don't want to spook them."

Wyatt nodded. "I'd be grateful to have something more to do than sit out front and watch the people go by. Tell me about these men."

"Sheriff!" Bernie Griggs dashed out of the telegraph office, waving a message in the air. "This just came for you. Seemed urgent."

Gabe walked down the steps of the St. James where he'd gone to talk with Nick and Lena. Taking the message from Bernie's outstretched hand, he read it, a muscle in his jaw ticking.

"It's good news, though. Right?"

Gabe shifted his gaze from Bernie to the street, moving from one person to the next, looking for one face, not seeing it. It should've been a relief. Instead, his sense of unease rose.

"Seems those two men who escaped with Boyden Trask were spotted in Wyoming. Doesn't seem Trask wouldn't be far from them, don't you think, Sheriff?"

Gabe frowned. "I'd never try to guess anything about Trask, Bernie."

"Do you think those two may have run out on him?"

"I wouldn't be surprised. If so, where is Trask?"

Bernie swallowed, his eyes darting up and down the street. "Guess I'd better get back inside."

Gabe didn't respond, vaguely aware of Bernie hurrying away. His gaze landed on Rosemary as she stepped out of the boardinghouse.

"Rosemary!"

Lifting her gaze, she saw Gabe coming toward her. "Good morning, Sheriff."

"I heard Dax and Rachel had their baby."

She grinned, her mind momentarily pulled away from her worry about Dirk. "Yes. It's a boy. I believe they're still in the clinic." Glancing down the boardwalk, she looked back at Gabe. "Did you hear about Dirk?"

Gabe's face sobered. "No. What happened?"

She explained, ending with a comment about Dirk needing to stay at the clinic a few more days.

"That's rough, Rosemary. I suppose you'll be staying in town, too."

"I plan to. It's doubtful Dax and Rachel will head back with the baby for a couple days. When I spoke to them before I left for breakfast, Dax said he's getting a room at the hotel—at least for one night."

Gabe remembered the reason he wanted to talk with Dax. "I'm going to head into the clinic. Are you coming in?"

She shook her head. "Doctor McCord mentioned the progress they've made with the clinic. I thought I'd walk over and see for myself."

"I'll go with you."

"That's silly, Gabe. You have work to do, it's the middle of the morning, and the clinic isn't any more than a hundred yards away. I'll be fine."

Looking up and down the street, he searched for his deputies. He knew they were busy spreading the word about the murdered women. Wyatt was on his own mission, and Gabe needed to speak with Dax right away.

"There should be men working on finishing the clinic. Make sure they know you're there, and don't be gone long. And don't go anywhere else."

"Sheriff, I'm perfectly capable of taking care of myself."

"Of course you are. Still, I'll have your word you'll go to the new clinic, then come right back. I don't plan to hold Dirk's hand any longer than necessary."

She laughed at the image he presented. "I wouldn't expect you to hold it at all."

"Exactly my point. If you aren't back in twenty minutes, I'm coming to find you."

Huffing out a sigh, she nodded. "Yes, Sheriff."

Dax paced back and forth in the front room of the clinic. Gabe had greeted Rachel, welcomed the new addition, then asked if he could have a word with him. They'd been grateful no other patients were waiting in the clinic.

"Do you think he's still coming this way?"

"Dax, I just don't know. It's still possible whoever spotted the other two men missed seeing Trask. If they're smart, they'll get as far away from Montana as possible."

"Trask has already proven he isn't as smart a man as he thinks he is." Dax massaged the back of his neck, exhaustion working to claim him. "I don't know, Gabe. My gut tells me Trask hasn't forgotten Rosemary or Splendor."

Stroking his chin as he looked out the front window, Gabe nodded. "I'm afraid I'd have to agree. I've got Mack, Caleb, and Dutch spreading the word in town about the kidnappings and murders. Beau and Cash are doing the same, riding out to the nearby ranches and farms. I've even enlisted Wyatt to help out. All of them know about Trask, but their focus will be on keeping the town safe from whoever is murdering those young women."

"If you're asking for more help in watching for Trask, I can get it."

Gabe shook his head. "You've got enough going on with the baby and Dirk's injury. Noah's going to bring Abby and Gabriel into town. He'll be available to keep watch."

Dax snickered. "That's you and Noah. You'll need a few more than that."

Gabe chuckled. "True. By evening, my deputies will also be able to take positions around town. Truthfully, I don't want to put the townsfolk in more danger than needed. My men get paid for this, the others don't."

"I understand. But remember, my men and I are available if you need help."

"Thanks, Dax. I won't forget."

Chapter Twenty

"It's looking so good." Rosemary walked around the bottom floor of the new clinic, marveling at the design and workmanship.

One of the workers walked up to her. "Yes, ma'am. Mr. Mason has us working long hours, but we're almost done."

She knew how hard Bull had been working to bring it to completion. Resting her hand on the handrail to the upstairs, she turned back to the man. "When will you be finished?"

"By the end of the week. The fact is, there isn't much left to do." He looked at the other men, then back at Rosemary. "We're going to take our meal break now. Will you be all right in here by yourself?"

She thought of Gabe's words, then shrugged off his concern. It was the middle of the day with people on the main street. "Please, go ahead. I'm going to take a few more minutes to look around, then I'll be gone."

"If you're sure, ma'am."

"I am. Enjoy your meal."

Continuing upstairs, she stopped at the top, taking a moment to appreciate the work. She couldn't believe the space they'd have for treating patients. As the town grew, there'd be room for at least one more doctor and another nurse. Rosemary couldn't contain her excitement, knowing she'd be a part of the growth.

Walking along the hall, she poked her head into a few more rooms, then turned to go back downstairs and stopped. The bell in the church tower sounded, alerting Splendor of some type of danger. Looking out a window, she saw a plume of smoke near Noah's livery. Picking up her pace, she hurried down the hall. She'd go straight to the clinic, preparing herself for the disaster threatening her town.

"What is it?" Allie Coulter asked no one in particular as she raced out of her seamstress shop and onto the boardwalk.

Horace Clausen, the town banker, came outside at the same time, his gaze widening at the plume of smoke at the other end of town. "My God." He looked at Allie. "I think the lumber mill is burning. Noah's saddle shop and livery are right next door." He took off at a run.

Closing and locking the door, Allie followed him down the street, seeing most of the rest of the town moving in the same direction.

"Allie!" Suzanne Barnett ran up to join her. They stood in the middle of the street, watching flames from the lumber mill engulf the large building.

"There's Sarah Murton. I'd better go see if she needs help with the children." The school teacher led a group of children away from the flames toward the creek behind the boardinghouse. "Do you need help, Sarah?"

Brushing hair off her face, Sarah shook her head. "I think we're fine, Suzanne. I'm going to send them home, but wanted to get them outside right away. I'm so afraid the wind will pick up and the fire will jump to the schoolhouse."

Glancing behind her, Suzanne watched as the men hurried to douse the flames in the lumber mill while also trying to protect Noah's property. Gabe and his deputies worked alongside the other men, shouting instructions.

"If you're sure, I'll see what I can do to help." Suzanne hurried to join Lena, Allie, and Abby Brandt, who filled buckets from water troughs and passed them to others.

"What can we do?" Tabitha Beekman, along with the three other young women, stood next to them.

"There are at least two more buckets behind the boardinghouse."

"I'll fetch them," May answered, running in the direction she'd come, followed by Sylvia.

"Deborah and Tabitha, see Dutch over there?" Suzanne nodded toward the creek. "They could use more people to fill the buckets."

Tabitha ran off, but Deborah hesitated. "Is there anything else I could do?"

Suzanne handed another full bucket to the first man in line, her chest tightening at the sight of the main beam of the lumber mill collapsing. "Working with Dutch and the other men is the most important thing you can do right now."

Huffing out a breath, Deborah glanced at the deputy, then back at Suzanne.

"If you aren't interested, feel free to go back inside the boardinghouse. You can watch out the window of your room." Suzanne turned away, filling another bucket. She didn't have time for more of Deborah's theatrics while the town was in danger. Taking a quick glance behind her, she shook her head in disappointment as Deborah disappeared inside the boardinghouse.

"Keep the water coming," Gabe yelled, drawing Suzanne's attention back to what needed to be done. The town and the safety of the people had to come before whatever petty issues Deborah found so important.

Two hours later, the lumber mill had been reduced to embers. At least they'd saved the other buildings in town, including Noah's saddle shop and livery. Abby stood next to Noah, his arm around her waist, surveying the damage when Gabe and Lena walked up.

"Anyone seen Silas?" Gabe asked.

Noah nodded to the other side of the street. The lumber mill owner sat on the edge of an empty water trough, his face buried in his hands. "I asked if he has any idea what happened. He said he didn't know."

"It'll need to be rebuilt." Gabe looked over the damage. "Until it is, this town will be scrambling for materials to build the houses already started."

"At least the clinic is finished." Noah placed a kiss on Abby's forehead.

Gabe turned in a circle, looking at all those standing around. "Has anyone seen Rosemary?"

Abby cocked her head. "I didn't know she was in town."

Gabe told them about Dirk's accident and the new Pelletier.

Abby spotted Clay McCord, his clothes covered in soot, standing next to Mack and Caleb. "She's probably at the clinic with Dirk."

"Maybe. I'm going to make certain." Gabe walked down the street, picking up his pace the closer he got. Shoving the door open, he almost collided with Doc Worthington. "Is Rosemary here?"

Charles glanced around. "Not unless she's with Dirk." Opening the door to where Dirk rested, he took a quick look. "No. She's not in there. I stayed with Rachel while Dax went to see what he could do. Perhaps that's where she is."

Gabe's gut clenched, the same way it did whenever he sensed danger. "I need to go."

Charles grabbed his arm. "Is there anything I can do?"

"Get word to me if she comes back. And don't say anything to Dirk."

The lingering smoke clouded the sky, making it appear like early evening rather than mid-afternoon. Gabe didn't stop to talk with anyone on his way to the new clinic. It didn't surprise him to find the site empty of workmen. Every available person had been hard at work battling the fire.

"Rosemary!" He stepped inside, going from room to room. "Rosemary!" He continued to call her name as he bounded up the stairs, concern rising when she didn't respond. Refusing to waste more time, he rushed back to the main street, rounding up his men. He hoped Beau and Cash saw the smoke and were on their way back to town. He could sure use their help.

"What is it, Gabe?" Mack jogged up, wiping a sleeve across his face.

"You're just making it worse," Caleb joked, seeing the soot smear across Mack's face.

"You need me, Gabe?" Dutch looked at the others, then down at his own clothes. "Guess I'm going to need a new shirt."

Gabe's grave expression didn't change. "We have a...situation."

The three deputies quieted, all their joking forgotten.

"Rosemary is missing." Gabe's jaw tightened. It was his fault for not going with her, trusting she'd be all right going by herself.

"Missing?" Mack asked.

Gabe nodded. "She headed over to the new clinic about fifteen minutes before the fire started. I thought she'd be safe with all the men working on it. I just went over to the clinic and she isn't there."

Caleb looked behind him, scanning the crowd still milling about. "Maybe she left to help with the fire."

"Did any of you see her?" Gabe asked.

Each man shook his head.

"We need to start a search for her." Gabe turned at the sound of someone shouting his name. "Cash. I'm glad you're here." He explained the situation. "Fan out. I want to go from business to business. Check everywhere. Cash, I want you to start at the clinic. You're the best tracker we have. I need you to look for anything that would indicate where she went."

Cash nodded, taking off at a run for the clinic.

Gabe watched him go, then turned back to the others. "I'm going to find Noah, Nick, Wyatt, and anyone else I can to help search."

"Everyone will want to help, Gabe. There isn't anything they can do for the lumber mill today, but they can help search for Rosemary."

"I sure hope you're right, Dutch."

Rosemary pulled again at the bindings on her wrists and ankles. All her efforts did nothing except tighten them further. Her head throbbed, her eyes burning with unshed tears at the pain. Blinking to squeeze away the moisture and relieve the discomfort, she tried to focus. Nothing looked familiar in the dank darkness.

Trying to recall what happened was useless. She remembered the bell ringing and seeing smoke, then everything went black.

The sound of voices drew her attention. Blinking again, her eyes adjusted until she could see a tiny ray of light coming from beneath what appeared to be a door. She might not be able to loosen the bindings, but she could scoot as close as possible to the door. Maybe she could recognize the voices.

"Rosemary!"

People shouted her name over and over, getting nothing in return. Dax had sent Bernie Griggs to the ranch to let Bull know what had happened and bring back a few men. Even with his fear of horses, the mild-mannered telegraph operator was happy to do whatever he could to help.

As the afternoon sun sank behind the western range, Stan Peterman handed out lanterns from his general store. Suzanne at the boardinghouse and the staff at the hotel made gallons of coffee. The Dixie and Wild Rose closed, sending their people out to help search.

"What's going on?" Beau rode up to where Cash knelt near the new clinic, Caro reining her horse to a stop next to him.

Standing, Cash shook his head. "Rosemary is missing."

Caro's hand covered her mouth, her eyes widening in concern.

"Most of the town is trying to find her. She was last seen here. I'm trying to find a trail."

"Let me get Caro settled at the hotel, then I'll come back here to help you."

"I'm not going to the hotel, Beau. I want to help."

"Caro..."

She looked away from her fiancé to Cash. "Who else is helping?"

Wincing, he looked at Beau, then back at Caro. "If you're asking if Lena, Abby, Allie, and Suzanne are helping, yes, they are." He sent an apologetic shrug to his closest friend.

Caro didn't try to hide her smug smile. "I'm staying. Tell me what to do."

Resting her weight against the wall by the door, Rosemary listened. The voices were muffled, as if those on the other side had moved away. She waited, her eyelids heavy. Rosemary knew if she passed out, she might never live to see another sunrise, and the future she'd hoped for with Dirk would be lost.

Her stomach twisted at the thought of him, injured and in immense pain. By now, Gabe would know she hadn't returned. He would've gathered a group of men—his deputies, friends, and anyone else willing to help—to search for her.

She didn't know if her captors had stashed her in a secret location in town, or whether they'd ridden miles from Splendor. Something told her it was the first.

Hearing the voices again, she tensed, licking her lips as she concentrated on identifying her kidnappers. The muffled sounds gave her no clue as to how many held her or what they planned to do.

She grimaced, realizing not knowing her fate caused more distress than the blow to her head.

Straightening her back against the wall, she summoned whatever courage remained. Rosemary refused to be a victim, cowering at the threat before her. Strengthening her resolve, she took in the room. Now that her vision had adjusted, she noticed shelving against one wall held a variety of canned goods, bags of flour and sugar, and extra pots.

Her first thought was they held her beneath the boardinghouse, but that made no sense. Rosemary had worked for Suzanne, had been in the root cellar many times. A room such as this didn't exist. She considered the other businesses. The saloons wouldn't store such a vast array of supplies and pots.

She closed her eyes, trying to think of where else they would've brought her. If they were still in Splendor, the location had to be close to the clinic. And it would have to hold the supplies before her.

Her eyes flew open. *The general store.*

Rosemary had never been in the back room, but she'd heard Stan Petermann had a basement below the store. The location made sense, as did the slight smell of smoke coming in through the gaps in the door. Learning her whereabouts provided a renewed sense of hope. Now all she needed was to find a way to alert those looking for her without warning the kidnappers.

Chapter Twenty-One

"Rosemary?" Dirk's rough voice could be heard by no one except him. Opening his eyes, he looked around, already knowing he was alone. A sharp pain jolted him, eliciting a series of curses that should only be voiced in private, or in a group of other men.

He couldn't afford to have a broken leg, and neither could the ranch. In a few days, they'd be taking the horses to the army, then not long afterward, a large herd of cattle to Salt Lake. Being laid up for weeks wasn't an option, yet it was now his reality.

Dirk's back and arms ached to stretch, feel something beneath them other than the hard examination table. Straining to rise, he rested on his forearms, getting a measure of relief. If only he could shift his weight enough to sit up.

"I see you're awake." Doc Worthington walked in, a frown creasing his forehead. "You're supposed to be lying flat."

"My entire body hurts, Doc. I need to sit up."

Charles nodded. "Let's see what we can do." Leaving for a few minutes, he returned with a stack of pillows, using them to support Dirk's back. "Is that better?"

"Yeah. Thanks, Doc." He rested an arm over his eyes, then lifted it. "Where's Rosemary?"

Charles didn't meet his gaze, feigning renewed interest in Dirk's injury. "Looks pretty good right now."

"Good. Where's Rosemary?"

"With luck, you'll get through this without infection."

Dirk let out a frustrated breath. "That's good news. Now, where is Rosemary?"

"Well, now...while you were out, there was a fire at the lumber mill. People scattered, trying to help."

"And Rosemary?"

"She, uh...well, they're looking for her."

Finding strength he didn't know he had, Dirk pushed up, forcing one leg over the edge of the table, then hesitating on the one held together with splints and bandages.

Charles tried to steady him. "It would be madness to try and walk on your broken leg. You could do permanent damage."

Eyes full of fury and fear gazed back at him. "I don't care about the leg, Doc. If Rosemary has disappeared, I'm going to find her."

"Dirk, listen to me. You'll do more damage than good trying to help. Gabe and the entire town are looking for her. I don't know that there's anyone *not* searching."

"Then I need to be out there with them."

Charles glanced behind him, knowing the only other people in the clinic were Rachel and her son.

Even Dax was out searching, along with several men Bernie had fetched from the ranch. Settling his hands firmly on Dirk's shoulders, he increased the pressure, keeping his voice calm and firm.

"Listen to me. If you tear up your wound, infection could follow. Once there's infection, the chances of you keeping your leg are slim, but the chance of you dying is worse. Think about Rosemary, son. If she were standing right here, what would she say?"

Closing his eyes, Dirk breathed in through his nose, letting the air out in a whoosh. "She'd tell me to stay still and listen to you." His troubled gaze searched Doc's. "But she isn't here and I have to do what I think is best. Even with the town looking, they don't need to find her as much as me. I've got to be out there."

Studying Dirk's face, Charles could see there'd be no dissuading him. "All right. I'll help you outside and into a chair where you can watch what's going on. Then I'll find Gabe. As God is my witness, I will not allow you to put your life in danger. You will be in once piece when they find Rosemary. You defy me on this and I'll get men to tie you down."

Dirk sent him a warning glare.

"You can be mad at me all you want, son. That young lady is going to have a man to come back to when they find her. And believe me, I'm more scared of her than I am of you."

"Where is he?" Clay looked where Charles pointed at the clinic down the street. "I should've known he'd do something foolhardy when he learned about Rosemary. Well, as long as he stays put with his leg elevated, he should be all right. Is that Gabe with him?"

Charles nodded. "Gabe and Dax. They're trying to calm Dirk down."

"I'd better go talk to him myself. I hate to gang up on a patient, but..." Clay dashed off, leaving Charles to follow.

"There are close to a hundred people looking for her, Dirk. If you want to stay out here, that's fine, but you cannot walk on that leg." Dax knelt beside him, knowing how his foreman felt, wishing there was more that could be done.

"Gabe!" Beau hurried up to them, pointing behind him. "You'd better come with me. Cash found something." Gabe wasted no time following Beau.

Dirk tried to push up, but Dax's strong arms held him down. "Don't even consider moving, Dirk. I'm not above putting you in a wagon and having someone haul your sorry ass back to the ranch."

Scrubbing his face with both hands, Dirk mumbled a curse. "Go with them. Come back and tell me what Cash found."

Dax nodded. "I'll do that."

By the time he found them, Cash was pointing to something on the ground, then walked several steps away, pointing to something else as Clay joined them.

"Does anyone know if Petermann has a basement?" Cash asked.

"He does," Clay answered. Before the town learned of him being a doctor, Clay had worked for Petermann in the general store, gaining a reputation as a man who could be trusted. "He seldom goes down there. It's doubtful anyone but Stan, his family, and me know about it."

"Someone else does. See these tracks?" Cash knelt beside them. "Appears two people tried to carry a third, stopping every few feet to adjust the weight. It's why it took me so long to figure it out. At first, the footprints made no sense, seemed like any others. Then I began to study them." Standing, he walked to Petermann's back door. "They came here, then the tracks disappear."

Clay looked at the others. "Stan has been busy helping put out the fire, then with the search. It would've been easy for someone to get down to the basement."

"Beau, get Mack, Dutch, and Caleb...and Wyatt, if you can find him. I want everyone in place before we go down."

Beau nodded at Gabe, then took off.

"Clay, would you mind letting Dirk know what's going on?" Dax asked. "I don't want him getting edgy and trying to follow us."

"I'll go right now."

"What about the rest of the people searching?" Dax looked at Gabe.

"We won't say anything. I don't want to alert whoever has her that we may have found them."

Rosemary jolted awake, surprised she'd drifted off. Her head still throbbed, her wrists and ankles ached from being bound.

She wondered what woke her. The voices had ceased before she fell asleep. Rosemary remembered trying to make her way to the shelving, thinking if she could tip the unit over, others might hear it and come to her aid. The prospect seemed slight. Still, it was better than sitting here doing nothing. Before she could go more than a couple feet, the voices stopped her and she inched back to her place against the wall, which was where she'd fallen asleep.

Scooting a few inches, she stopped, listening. When she heard nothing, Rosemary continued, stopping every foot until she sat to the right of the shelving. If her wrists weren't bound behind her, it would be a simple task to leverage herself to a standing position. Even with her ankles tied, she could lean against the wall and shove the shelving to the ground.

Still, she had to try before whoever took her returned. Settling her back against the wall, she tucked her legs under her enough to get into a crouch. Pushing with her legs, she slowly edged upward, her hands scraping against the rough walls. If she could stand, she might be able to get her weight behind the unit, toppling it forward.

Rosemary always thought herself physically strong. As a nurse, she needed to be. Pushing upward, her legs began to shake with the effort, her arms and back burning from scraping against the ragged surface of the wall. Ignoring the sound of tearing fabric, she continued, determined to reach her goal. Taking one more deep breath, she pushed with every ounce of strength left, exhaling when she stood next to the shelves. Now she just had to keep her balance long enough to dislodge the shelving.

"I want you to stay up here, Stan. Let me and my deputies take it from here." Gabe checked the bullets in his gun, glancing at his men as they did the same.

"I won't argue with you, Sheriff." Stan backed up a few steps, then walked out the front door, feeling no shame in letting the lawmen do their job.

"Is everyone ready?" Gabe looked at each man, waiting for them to nod. "You all know what to do." Gabe started toward the back stairs, stopping when Dutch grabbed his arm.

"Let me go first." He pinned Gabe with a meaningful gaze.

"I know what you're trying to do."

"Then let me do it. You've got Lena and a son to think about."

"I'm still the sheriff, Dutch."

"That's why you're delegating me to go first." Without waiting, Dutch took long strides to the back stairwell, then quietly opened the door. He started down, one slow step at a time.

The stairs were old and in need of repair. As he looked down, he saw nothing except darkness. Placing his boot on the next step, he froze at the sound of splintering wood. The next instant, his weight broke the weakened board, sending him down to the floor.

At the exact same time, a crashing sound echoed through the room. Landing hard, his gun in front of him, his jaw slackened at the sight before him.

"What in tarnation?" He glanced around, grateful for the lantern resting on a barrel near the wall.

"Are you all right, Dutch?"

"Yeah, Gabe. Fine. But you'd better get down here."

He began to lower his gun, then instinct warned him not to as the frightened eyes of the women before him signaled their intention. Seeing the gleam of a rifle, he shook his head.

"I wouldn't, Miss Ritter. I assure you, I have no qualms about shooting a woman if she threatens me."

The sisters gave him a venomous glare, but didn't move, keeping their mouths clamped shut.

Dutch nodded. "Wise choice."

"Help!"

Gabe dropped to the ground, Cash and Beau close behind him, the scream piercing their ears.

"Rosemary?" Gabe shouted, his gun steady on the women as he moved past them to another door. "Rosemary, are you in there?"

"Gabe...help me!"

He turned the knob. Finding it locked, he stepped back and kicked it open. Relief flooded him. Across the room, tottering on legs bound at the ankles, stood Rosemary. Holstering his gun, he rushed forward, letting her sag against him.

"You found me..."

Getting Rosemary and the Ritter sisters back up the stairs was no easy task. They'd broken partway down, leaving three feet of open space.

"It's a good thing Mack and Caleb stayed up top or we'd never get these women out of here." Beau swiped an arm across his forehead.

"Who would've ever thought?" Cash pushed Selma Ritter from behind and into Mack's formidable grip. He looked behind him at the small stash of weapons and paraphernalia they'd found on the elderly sisters. Rope, chloroform, a knife, two revolvers, a rifle, and a thin coil of wire. He shuddered at what they intended to do with it.

Dutch settled his hands on his hips, shaking his head. "Not who I thought."

Beau still looked stunned. "I thought it might be that Willard Cullin guy who came in on the stage with a couple other men."

"About those men, Beau. Sorry Gabe and I couldn't say anything, but they're Pinkerton men. Allan would only provide information to me if I kept their identity a secret."

Beau snorted, clasping Dutch on the shoulder. "You did a fine job. I began to have my doubts about Cullin when I saw him and his men helping us put out the fire, then doing all they could to find Rosemary."

"They wanted to do more, but Gabe was afraid they'd blow their cover before we found her."

"What will happen to the Ritters now, Dutch?"

"My guess is Cullin will escort them back to Boston. Their crimes crossed state and territorial lines, but it all started in Boston."

"You boys going to gab down there all day, or do you want some help up?"

Chuckling, Cash moved to the bottom of the steps, grinning up at Mack. "We're on our way."

"Oh no, you don't." Clay pushed Dirk back down into the chair when they spotted Gabe and Rosemary on the other side of the street.

"Dirk!" She ran across the street, grateful for the lack of wagons and horses. "What are you doing out here?" Rosemary dropped next to him, wrapping her arms around his neck.

Groaning, he hugged her back. "Easy, sweetheart." He pulled back, looking at the tears in her eyes, his nostrils flaring in anger. "What happened?" He looked up at Gabe.

"She was taken by the Ritter sisters."

Dirk's gaze darkened. "Who are the Ritter sisters?"

Gabe explained, Dirk's hold on Rosemary tightening the more he heard. "They're the ones who've been kidnapping and murdering the women."

Dirk closed his eyes, kissing Rosemary on the cheek before she stood, continuing to rest her hand on his shoulder. "What of Trask?"

Gabe shook his head. "Seems he may still be out there. The two men who escaped with him were spotted in Wyoming. The last message I received said they'd gotten away."

"Trask wasn't with them?" Rosemary asked.

"He wasn't seen. It doesn't mean he wasn't with them." Gabe looked down at his hands still black with soot. "Time for me to clean up. Do you need some help before I leave?"

Rosemary touched Gabe's arm. "Thanks, but I believe you've done enough for one day. Go home to Lena and Jack." She glanced down at Dirk, who nodded.

"You know where to find me." Turning to leave, Gabe glanced over his shoulder. "Don't forget, Trask is still out there."

Boyden Trask lay on his back at the bottom of a ravine, fighting to catch his breath, his horse long gone. Staring up at the night sky, he knew his time was short.

He'd been so careful—conserving his water, eating sparingly, watching the trail for danger as he headed through the arid grassland on his way to

Splendor. Then his horse had spooked. He'd started to rise, then stopped at the unmistakable sound of a prairie rattler. His heart seized. The only snake he knew about in Montana that could kill a man.

When the hissing started again, his horse took off as he hurried to scoot away. If it hadn't been so dark, he'd have seen the ravine behind him. Instead, his instincts to run kicked in as the rattler struck. The bite went through his shirt, into the soft skin of his stomach. A scream tore from his lips, his feet struggling for purchase to get away.

He reached behind him. Instead of finding a solid surface, open air greeted him at the same time he shoved himself backward. There'd been nothing to stop his fall. Landing on his back, the air knocked from his lungs, the venom began to take effect.

Trask bellowed out a last heart-wrenching roar of anger, knowing he'd never be found and never find his revenge.

Epilogue

Several weeks later...

Gabe watched the newlyweds, Beau and Caro, talking with Reverend Paige and his wife.

Dutch joined him, following his gaze. "Glad that's over with. I've never felt comfortable at weddings."

"You ever been married?"

A look of horror crossed Dutch's face. "Not me. I'm not the type. Besides, who's to say she wouldn't turn out like one of those Ritter sisters."

Gabe took a slow sip of punch, nodding. "I doubt we'll ever know the full story now that they've been sent back east for trial. Must've been a lot of hate in the house they grew up in for both to turn into unrepentant killers."

"There's got to be a story there, and I'm guessing it'll all come out at the trial. No matter. Neither are right in the head." Dutch looked at Rosemary and Dirk, standing in one corner of the room. "At least we got Rosemary back unharmed. Seeing her now, you'd think nothing ever happened." He motioned with his drink toward the couple.

Rosemary stood next to Dirk, who stayed upright with the help of crutches.

She placed a hand on his arm. "I don't think Beau would've waited any longer to marry Caro." They watched the bride and groom laughing at something Cash said.

"He waited a long time for Caro. It's time they made it official." Dirk cleared his throat, the muscles in his jaw twitching. "Would you mind going outside for a few minutes? I could use some air."

"Not at all."

Wyatt watched Dirk struggle on the crutches, refusing help from those he and Rosemary passed on their way outside. The day after the fire, Dax and Luke repeated their offer of a job working with the horses. This time, Wyatt accepted. He'd been at Redemption's Edge for weeks, working with Travis at the old Frey ranch. From what he'd heard of Dirk's experience breeding horses, it still surprised him the man chose to work with the cattle.

"How are you, Mr. Jackson?"

A slow smile spread across his face as his gaze settled on Gabe's sister, Nora. He'd met her while staying in town, forcing himself to show disinterest, even though he'd been attracted to her right away. Desiring the sheriff's sister didn't seem smart when he had so little to offer and too much of a past.

"Miss Evans. Are you enjoying the wedding?"

"Very much. You?"

He chuckled. "As much as any man can enjoy seeing another man give up his freedom."

Her brows furrowed. "Is that how you see it?"

"In some ways."

Nora watched the couples dancing, considering his comment. "It's amazing how, in a few short minutes, they can transform a solemn church into a place of celebration. Do you like to dance, Mr. Jackson?"

His mind spun at her change in direction. "At times, Miss Evans."

She glanced at him, her eyes sparkling. "Is this one of those times?"

Setting down his glass, he turned toward her, holding out a hand. "It is. Would you care to dance, Miss Evans?"

"Yes, Mr. Jackson. I believe I would."

It had been a long time since Wyatt had held a beautiful woman in his arms. His time with women over the last few years consisted of card games, whiskey, and brief couplings. He hadn't allowed himself more. As they moved around the dance floor, he began to realize what he may have missed.

"Have you been married before, Mr. Jackson?"

He'd been taught to dance at a young age, hearing the rhythm and picking up the steps easily. Her question caused him to stumble.

"My apologies," he mumbled, recovering quickly.

"None needed. I've been told I ask too many questions."

Glancing down at Nora, he shook his head. "No."

"No?"

"I've never been married."

When the music ended, he held her an instant longer than necessary before escorting her off the floor. "Thank you, Miss Evans. It was a pleasure."

"As it was mine, Mr. Jackson." Turning, she walked away, looking back to see his gaze still on her.

"She's a handful."

Wyatt startled at Gabe's voice. "I wouldn't know. Your sister and I barely know each other."

"Good afternoon, Mr. Jackson." Lena walked up, slipping her arm through Gabe's.

"I'd prefer you call me Wyatt."

"Wonderful. Please, call me Lena. You are quite the dancer."

Wyatt chuckled at the compliment. "Rusty would be a better description of my skills."

"Regardless, Nora seemed to enjoy it. Well, I'm going to go talk with the young ladies. It's time to introduce them around." Lena kissed Gabe on the cheek, then left in the direction of Tabitha, May, Deborah, and Sylvia.

"Is the rumor true, Gabe?"

"What rumor is that?"

Wyatt grinned. "I heard Lena led the effort to bring the mail order brides to Splendor."

Gabe held up his glass, taking a sip, then laughed. "She did, along with a few other women.

Seems they believe we have too many bachelors and not enough single women."

"Should I be scared?"

"Absolutely."

From across the room, Travis watched Wyatt and Gabe talking before his gaze moved to see Dirk and Rosemary as they walked back inside, their faces full of happiness.

"What is it?" Isabella, the woman he'd been courting, the woman he loved, stood next to him. "Is something wrong?"

He looked at her, his features softening. "Everything is fine."

Travis had never been a man who expressed himself in grand terms, talking of love or emotions. His late wife used to say their horses spoke more to her than he did, causing their daughter to laugh. They were both gone now, as was their horse ranch in Tennessee. All casualties of the war.

Isabella nodded, used to his taciturn manner. "Look, Travis."

He followed her gaze to where Dirk spoke to Beau. In the next instant, Beau grasped Dirk's shoulder, then leaned over to kiss Rosemary on the cheek before turning to the other guests.

"Ladies and gentlemen. Dirk Masters would like to make an announcement."

Holding her hand, Dirk faced the crowd, clearing his throat.

"Uh, Rosemary and I are getting married."

"What's that?" Luke called out from across the room.

Clearing his throat again, Dirk faced Luke. "Rosemary and I...we're getting married."

"Sorry, Dirk. I still didn't hear you." Bull, his face neutral, stared at his friend.

Mumbling to himself, Dirk hobbled forward, pulling Rosemary along with him. Lifting his face, he spoke in a clear, bold voice.

"I've asked Rosemary to marry me, and she said yes."

"About time." Bull lifted his glass. "To two people who are perfect for each other. Let the fighting begin!"

Thank you for taking the time to read Courage Canyon. If you enjoyed it, please consider telling your friends or posting a short review. Word of mouth is an author's best friend and much appreciated.

Watch for book nine in the Redemption Mountain series, Forsaken Falls!

Please join my reader's group to be notified of my New Releases at:
https://www.shirleendavies.com/contact-me.html

I care about quality, so if you find something in error, please contact me via email at
shirleen@shirleendavies.com

About the Author

Shirleen Davies writes romance—historical western romance, contemporary romance, and romantic suspense. She grew up in Southern California, attended Oregon State University, and has degrees from San Diego State University and the University of Maryland. Her passion is writing emotionally charged stories of flawed people who find redemption through love and acceptance. Having been on numerous bestseller lists, Shirleen has over thirty books in print. She now lives with her husband in a beautiful town in northern Arizona.

I love to hear from my readers.

Send me an Email
Visit my Website
Sign up to be notified of New Releases
Check out all my Books
Comment on my Blog
Follow me on Amazon

Other ways to connect with me:

Facebook Fan Page
Twitter
Pinterest
Google+
Instagram

Books by Shirleen Davies

Historical Western Romance Series

MacLarens of Fire Mountain

Tougher than the Rest, Book One
Faster than the Rest, Book Two
Harder than the Rest, Book Three
Stronger than the Rest, Book Four
Deadlier than the Rest, Book Five
Wilder than the Rest, Book Six

Redemption Mountain

Redemption's Edge, Book One
Wildfire Creek, Book Two
Sunrise Ridge, Book Three
Dixie Moon, Book Four
Survivor Pass, Book Five
Promise Trail, Book Six
Deep River, Book Seven
Courage Canyon, Book Eight

MacLarens of Boundary Mountain

Colin's Quest, Book One,
Brodie's Gamble, Book Two
Quinn's Honor, Book Three
Sam's Legacy, Book Four
Heather's Choice, Book Five, Coming next in the series!

Contemporary Romance Series

MacLarens of Fire Mountain

Second Summer, Book One
Hard Landing, Book Two
One More Day, Book Three
All Your Nights, Book Four
Always Love You, Book Five
Hearts Don't Lie, Book Six
No Getting Over You, Book Seven
'Til the Sun Comes Up, Book Eight
Foolish Heart, Book Nine
Forever Love, Book Ten, Coming next in the series!

Peregrine Bay

Reclaiming Love, Book One, A Novella
Our Kind of Love, Book Two

Burnt River

Shane's Burden, Book One by Peggy Henderson
Thorn's Journey, Book Two by Shirleen Davies
Aqua's Achilles, Book Three by Kate Cambridge
Ashley's Hope, Book Four by Amelia Adams
Harpur's Secret, Book Five by Kay P. Dawson
Mason's Rescue, Book Six by Peggy L. Henderson
Del's Choice, Book Seven by Shirleen Davies
Watch for more books in this series!

Find all of my books at:
https://www.shirleendavies.com/books.html

Tougher than the Rest – Book One
MacLarens of Fire Mountain Historical Western Romance Series

"A passionate, fast-paced story set in the untamed western frontier by an exciting new voice in historical romance."

Niall MacLaren is the oldest of four brothers, and the undisputed leader of the family. A widower, and single father, his focus is on building the MacLaren ranch into the largest and most successful in northern Arizona. He is serious about two things—his responsibility to the family and his future marriage to the wealthy, well-connected widow who will secure his place in the territory's destiny.

Katherine is determined to live the life she's dreamed about. With a job waiting for her in the growing town of Los Angeles, California, the young teacher from Philadelphia begins a journey across the United States with only a couple of trunks and her spinster companion. Life is perfect for this adventurous, beautiful young woman, until an accident throws her into the arms of the one man who can destroy it all.

Fighting his growing attraction and strong desire for the beautiful stranger, Niall is more determined than ever to push emotions aside to focus on his goals of wealth and political gain. But looking into the clear, blue eyes of the woman who could ruin everything, Niall discovers he will have to harden his heart and be tougher than he's ever been in his life...Tougher than the Rest.

Faster than the Rest – Book Two
MacLarens of Fire Mountain Historical Western Romance Series

"Headstrong, brash, confident, and complex, the MacLarens of Fire Mountain will captivate you with strong characters set in the wild and rugged western frontier."

Handsome, ruthless, young U.S. Marshal Jamie MacLaren had lost everything—his parents, his family connections, and his childhood sweetheart—but now he's back in Fire Mountain and ready for another chance. Just as he successfully reconnects with his family and starts to rebuild his life, he gets the unexpected and unwanted assignment of rescuing the woman who broke his heart.

Beautiful, wealthy Victoria Wicklin chose money and power over love, but is now fighting for her life—or is she? Who has she become in the seven years since she left Fire Mountain to take up her life in San Francisco? Is she really as innocent as she says?

Marshal MacLaren struggles to learn the truth and do his job, but the past and present lead him in different directions as his heart and brain wage battle. Is Victoria a victim or a villain? Is life offering him another chance, or just another heartbreak?

As Jamie and Victoria struggle to uncover past secrets and come to grips with their shared passion, another danger arises. A life-altering danger that is out of their control and threatens to destroy any chance for a shared future.

Harder than the Rest – Book Three
MacLarens of Fire Mountain Historical Western Romance Series

"They are men you want on your side. Hard, confident, and loyal, the MacLarens of Fire Mountain will seize your attention from the first page."

Will MacLaren is a hardened, plain-speaking bounty hunter. His life centers on finding men guilty of horrendous crimes and making sure justice is done. There is no place in his world for the carefree attitude he carried years before when a tragic event destroyed his dreams.

Amanda is the daughter of a successful Colorado rancher. Determined and proud, she works hard to prove she is as capable as any man and worthy to be her father's heir. When a stranger arrives, her independent nature collides with the strong pull toward the handsome ranch hand. But is he what he seems and could his secrets endanger her as well as her family?

The last thing Will needs is to feel passion for another woman. But Amanda elicits feelings he thought were long buried. Can Will's desire for her change him? Or will the vengeance he seeks against the one man he wants to destroy—a dangerous opponent without a conscious—continue to control his life?

Stronger than the Rest – Book Four
MacLarens of Fire Mountain Historical Western Romance Series

"Smart, tough, and capable, the MacLarens protect their own no matter the odds. Set against America's rugged frontier, the stories of the men from Fire Mountain are complex, fast-paced, and a must read for anyone who enjoys non-stop action and romance."

Drew MacLaren is focused and strong. He has achieved all of his goals except one—to return to the MacLaren ranch and build the best horse breeding program in the west. His successful career as an attorney is about to give way to his ranching roots when a bullet changes everything.

Tess Taylor is the quiet, serious daughter of a Colorado ranch family with dreams of her own. Her shy nature keeps her from developing friendships outside of her close-knit family until Drew enters her life. Their relationship grows. Then a bullet, meant for another, leaves him paralyzed and determined to distance himself from the one woman he's come to love.

Convinced he is no longer the man Tess needs, Drew focuses on regaining the use of his legs and recapturing a life he thought lost. But danger of another kind threatens those he cares about—including Tess—forcing him to rethink his future.

Can Drew overcome the barriers that stand between him, the safety of his friends and family, and a life with the woman he loves? To do it all, he has to be strong. Stronger than the Rest.

Deadlier than the Rest – Book Five
MacLarens of Fire Mountain Historical Western Romance Series

"A passionate, heartwarming story of the iconic MacLarens of Fire Mountain. This

Connor MacLaren's search has already stolen eight years of his life. Now he is close to finding what he seeks—Meggie, his missing sister. His quest leads him to the growing city of Salt Lake and an encounter with the most captivating woman he has ever met.

Grace is the third wife of a Mormon farmer, forced into a life far different from what she'd have chosen. Her independent spirit longs for choices governed only by her own heart and mind. To achieve her dreams, she must hide behind secrets and half-truths, even as her heart pulls her towards the ruggedly handsome Connor.

Known as cool and uncompromising, Connor MacLaren lives by a few, firm rules that have served him well and kept him alive. However, danger stalks Connor, even to the front range of the beautiful Wasatch Mountains, threatening those he cares about and impacting his ability to find his sister.

Can Connor protect himself from those who seek his death? Will his eight-year search lead him to his sister while unlocking the secrets he knows are held tight within Grace, the woman who has captured his heart?

Read this heartening story of duty, honor, passion, and love in book five of the MacLarens of Fire Mountain series.

Wilder than the Rest – Book Six
MacLarens of Fire Mountain Historical Western Romance Series

"A captivating historical western romance set in the burgeoning and treacherous city of San Francisco. Go along for the ride in this gripping story that seizes your attention from the very first page."

"If you're a reader who wants to discover an entire family of characters you can fall in love with, this is the series for you." – Authors to Watch

Pierce is a rough man, but happy in his new life as a Special Agent. Tasked with defending the rights of the federal government, Pierce is a cunning gunslinger always ready to tackle the next job. That is, until he finds out that his new job involves Mollie Jamison.

Mollie can be a lot to handle. Headstrong and independent, Mollie has chosen a life of danger and intrigue guaranteed to prove her liquor-loving father wrong. She will make something of herself, and no one, not even arrogant Pierce MacLaren, will stand in her way.

A secret mission brings them together, but will their attraction to each other prove deadly in their hunt for justice? The payoff for success is high, much higher than any assignment either has taken before. But will the damage to their hearts and souls be too much to bear? Can Pierce and Mollie find a way to overcome their misgivings and work together as one?

Second Summer – Book One
MacLarens of Fire Mountain Contemporary Romance Series

"In this passionate Contemporary Romance, author Shirleen Davies introduces her readers to the modern day MacLarens starting with Heath MacLaren, the head of the family."

The Chairman of both the MacLaren Cattle Co. and MacLaren Land Development, Heath MacLaren is a success professionally—his personal life is another matter.

Following a divorce after a long, loveless marriage, Heath spends his time with women who are beautiful and passionate, yet unable to provide what he longs for . . .

Heath has never experienced love even though he witnesses it every day between his younger brother, Jace, and wife, Caroline. He wants what they have, yet spends his time with women too young to understand what drives him and too focused on themselves to be true companions.

It's been two years since Annie's husband died, leaving her to build a new life. He was her soul mate and confidante. She has no desire to find a replacement, yet longs for male friendship.

Annie's closest friend in Fire Mountain, Caroline MacLaren, is determined to see Annie come out of her shell after almost two years of mourning. A chance meeting with Heath turns into an offer to be a part of the MacLaren Foundation Board and an opportunity for a life outside her home sanctuary which has also become her prison. The platonic friendship that builds between Annie and Heath points to a future where each may rely on the other without the bonds a romance would entail.

However, without consciously seeking it, each yearns for more . . .

The MacLaren Development Company is booming with Heath at the helm. His meetings at a partner company with the young, beautiful marketing director, who makes no secret of her desire for him, are a temptation. But is she the type of woman he truly wants?

Annie's acceptance of the deep, yet passionless, friendship with Heath sustains her, lulling her to believe it is all she needs. At least until Heath drops a bombshell, forcing Annie to realize that what she took for friendship is actually a deep, lasting love. One she doesn't want to lose.

Each must decide to settle—or fight for it all.

Hard Landing – Book Two
MacLarens of Fire Mountain Contemporary Romance Series

Trey MacLaren is a confident, poised Navy pilot. He's focused, loyal, ethical, and a natural leader. He is also on his way to what he hopes will be a lasting relationship and marriage with fellow pilot, Jesse Evans.

Jesse has always been driven. Her graduation from the Naval Academy and acceptance into the pilot training program are all she thought she wanted— until she discovered love with Trey MacLaren

Trey and Jesse's lives are filled with fast flying, friends, and the demands of their military careers. Lives each has settled into with a passion. At least until the day Trey receives a letter that could change his and Jesse's lives forever.

It's been over two years since Trey has seen the woman in Pensacola. Her unexpected letter stuns him and pushes Jesse into a tailspin from which she might not pull back.

Each must make a choice. Will the choice Trey makes cause him to lose Jesse forever? Will she follow her heart or her head as she fights for a chance to save the love she's found? Will their independent decisions collide, forcing them to give up on a life together?

One More Day – Book Three
MacLarens of Fire Mountain Contemporary Romance Series

Cameron "Cam" Sinclair is smart, driven, and dedicated, with an easygoing temperament that belies his strong will and the personal ambitions he holds close. Besides his family, his job as head of IT at the MacLaren Cattle Company and his position as a Search and Rescue volunteer are all he needs to make him happy. At least that's what he thinks until he meets, and is instantly drawn to, fellow SAR volunteer, Lainey Devlin.

Lainey is compassionate, independent, and ready to break away from her manipulative and controlling fiancé. Just as her decision is made, she's called into a major search and rescue effort, where once again, her path crosses with the intriguing, and much too handsome, Cam Sinclair. But Lainey's plans are set. An opportunity to buy a flourishing preschool in northern Arizona is her chance to make a fresh start, and nothing, not even her fierce attraction to Cam Sinclair, will impede her plans.

As Lainey begins to settle into her new life, an unexpected danger arises —threats from an unknown assailant—someone who doesn't believe she belongs in Fire Mountain. The more Lainey begins to love her new home, the greater the danger becomes. Can she accept the help and protection Cam offers while ignoring her consuming desire for him?

Even if Lainey accepts her attraction to Cam, will he ever be able to come to terms with his own driving ambition and allow himself to consider a different life than the one he's always pictured? A life with the one woman who offers more than he'd ever hoped to find?

All Your Nights – Book Four
MacLarens of Fire Mountain Contemporary Romance Series

"Romance, adventure, cowboys, suspense— everything you want in a contemporary western romance novel."

Kade Taylor likes living on the edge. As an undercover agent for the DEA and a former Special Ops team member, his current assignment seems tame—keep tabs on a bookish Ph.D. candidate the agency believes is connected to a ruthless drug cartel.

Brooke Sinclair is weeks away from obtaining her goal of a doctoral degree. She spends time finalizing her presentation and relaxing with another student who seems to want nothing more than her friendship. That's fine with Brooke. Her last serious relationship ended in a broken engagement.

Her future is set, safe and peaceful, just as she's always planned—until Agent Taylor informs her she's under suspicion for illegal drug activities.

Kade and his DEA team obtain evidence which exonerates Brooke while placing her in danger from those who sought to use her. As Kade races to take down the drug cartel while protecting Brooke, he must also find common ground with the former suspect—a woman he desires with increasing intensity.

At odds with her better judgment, Brooke finds the more time she spends with Kade, the more she's attracted to the complex, multi-faceted agent. But Kade holds secrets he knows Brooke will never understand or accept.

Can Kade keep Brooke safe while coming to terms with his past, or will he stay silent, ruining any future with the woman his heart can't let go?

Always Love You– Book Five
MacLarens of Fire Mountain Contemporary Romance Series

"Romance, adventure, motorcycles, cowboys, suspense—everything you want in a contemporary western romance novel."

Eric Sinclair loves his bachelor status. His work at MacLaren Enterprises leaves him with plenty of time to ride his horse as well as his Harley...and date beautiful women without a thought to commitment.

Amber Anderson is the new person at MacLaren Enterprises. Her passion for marketing landed her what she believes to be the perfect job—until she steps into her first meeting to find the man she left, but still loves, sitting at the management table—his disdain for her clear.

Eric won't allow the past to taint his professional behavior, nor will he repeat his mistakes with Amber, even though love for her pulses through him as strong as ever.

As they strive to mold a working relationship, unexpected danger confronts those close to them, pitting the MacLarens and Sinclairs against an evil who stalks one member but threatens them all.

Eric can't get the memories of their passionate past out of his mind, while Amber wrestles with feelings she thought long buried. Will they be able to put the past behind them to reclaim the love lost years before?

Hearts Don't Lie– Book Six
MacLarens of Fire Mountain Contemporary Romance Series

Mitch MacLaren has reasons for avoiding relationships, and in his opinion, they're pretty darn good. As the new president of RTC Bucking Bulls, difficult challenges occur daily. He certainly doesn't need another one in the form of a fiery, blue-eyed, redhead.

Dana Ballard's new job forces her to work with the one MacLaren who can't seem to get over himself and lighten up. Their verbal sparring is second nature and entertaining until the night of Mitch's departure when he surprises her with a dare she doesn't refuse.

With his assignment in Fire Mountain over, Mitch is free to return to Montana and run the business his father helped start. The glitch in his enthusiasm has to do with one irreversible mistake—the dare Dana didn't ignore. Now, for reasons that confound him, he just can't let it go.

Working together is a circumstance neither wants, but both must accept. As their attraction grows, so do the accidents and strange illnesses of the animals RTC depends on to stay in business. Mitch's total focus should be on finding the reasons and people behind the incidents. Instead, he finds himself torn between his unwanted desire for Dana and the business which is his life.

In his mind, a simple proposition can solve one problem. Will Dana make the smart move and walk away? Or take the gamble and expose her heart?

No Getting Over You– Book Seven
MacLarens of Fire Mountain Contemporary Romance Series

Cassie MacLaren has come a long way since being dumped by her long-time boyfriend, a man she believed to be her future. Successful in her job at MacLaren Enterprises, dreaming of one day leading one of the divisions, she's moved on to start a new relationship, having little time to dwell on past mistakes.

Matt Garner loves his job as rodeo representative for Double Ace Bucking Stock. Busy days and constant travel leave no time for anything more than the occasional short-term relationship—which is just the way he likes it. He's come to accept the regret of leaving the woman he loved for the pro rodeo circuit.

The future is set for both, until a chance meeting ignites long buried emotions neither is willing to face.

Forced to work together, their attraction grows, even as multiple arson fires threaten Cassie's new home of Cold Creek, Colorado. Although Cassie believes the danger from the fires is remote, she knows the danger Matt poses to her heart is real.

While fighting his renewed feelings for Cassie, Matt focuses on a new and unexpected opportunity offered by MacLaren Enterprises—an opportunity that will put him on a direct collision course with Cassie.

Will pride and self-preservation control their future? Or will one be strong enough to make the first move, risking everything, including their heart?

'Til the Sun Comes Up– Book Eight
MacLarens of Fire Mountain Contemporary Romance Series

Skye MacLaren's life revolves around her family and the fierce bucking bull stock they provide to rodeos. She's competitive and competent, having no room in her life for a relationship—including one with a world champion rider and business competitor.

Gage Templeton's rodeo past and executive position with a national bucking stock supplier assures him of exciting work and nights with any woman he chooses. He'll let no one get close—until his company partners with a competitor, forcing him to work with the one woman who could turn his resolve upside down.

Knowing a relationship is the last thing either needs, both charge ahead, certain they can keep their explosive feelings for each other in check—and away from curious family and friends. Continuing their secret encounters becomes even harder when outside forces threaten both their businesses and the people they care about.

As Gage works to discover the threat meant to cripple his company, Skye's doubts increase. She wants more from the most magnetic man she's ever known, but protecting her heart must come first.

Desire, distrust, fear, and the pain of the past cloud their minds, even as they work together to identify the danger. Can two strong, determined people conquer the perils to their lives as well as their hearts?

Foolish Heart– Book Nine
MacLarens of Fire Mountain Contemporary Romance Series

Ernesto Salgado's life continues to change. An ex-Special Forces operative, he recently left the U.S. Marshals Service to start a new life—minus the woman who left him without an explanation or backward glance. Working as head of security for MacLaren Enterprises is the opportunity he needs to move on.

Paige Wallace made a choice that continues to haunt her every day and each night. The life she dreamed about, had at her fingertips, disappeared in one decisive moment. A new job with her longtime friend offers the break she needs, a chance to forget her biggest failure and start over.

No problem, right? Except Paige and Nesto now work for the same company.

And that's not the only issue. The family member she dropped everything to help has become embroiled in illegal dealings, doing business with those who would harm not only Paige, but the entire MacLaren family.

As head of security, Nesto's priority is to keep all employees and owners safe. He'll do whatever needs to be done to excel at the job, even when it includes protecting the woman who walked out of his life.

The more he digs, the deeper the threat becomes, affecting everyone. Nesto has to face a hard truth— the only way for him to succeed is with Paige's help.

How can he trust a woman he thought loved him but walked away, especially when they acknowledge the passion still burning between them?

As the threat increases, Nesto uses all the resources available to protect those he cares about. If he could only use the same resources to protect his heart.

Redemption's Edge – Book One
Redemption Mountain – Historical Western Romance Series

"A heartwarming, passionate story of loss, forgiveness, and redemption set in the untamed frontier during the tumultuous years following the Civil War. Ms. Davies' engaging and complex characters draw you in from the start, creating an exciting introduction to this new historical western romance series."

"Redemption's Edge is a strong and engaging introduction to her new historical western romance series."

Dax Pelletier is ready for a new life, far away from the one he left behind in Savannah following the South's devastating defeat in the Civil War. The ex-Confederate general wants nothing more to do with commanding men and confronting the tough truths of leadership.

Rachel Davenport possesses skills unlike those of her Boston socialite peers—skills honed as a nurse in field hospitals during the Civil War. Eschewing her northeastern suitors and changed by the carnage she's seen, Rachel decides to accept her uncle's invitation to assist him at his clinic in the dangerous and wild frontier of Montana.

Now a Texas Ranger, a promise to a friend takes Dax and his brother, Luke, to the untamed territory of Montana. He'll fulfill his oath and return to Austin, at least that's what he believes.

The small town of Splendor is what Rachel needs after life in a large city. In a few short months, she's grown to love the people as well as the majestic beauty of the untamed frontier. She's settled into a life unlike any she has ever thought possible.

Thinking his battle days are over, he now faces dangers of a different kind—one by those from his past who seek vengeance, and another from Rachel, the woman who's captured his heart.

Wildfire Creek – Book Two
Redemption Mountain – Historical Western Romance Series

"A passionate story of rebuilding lives, working to find a place in the wild frontier, and building new lives in the years following the American Civil War. A rugged, heartwarming story of choices and love in the continuing saga of Redemption Mountain."

Luke Pelletier is settling into his new life as a rancher and occasional Pinkerton Agent, leaving his past as an ex-Confederate major and Texas Ranger far behind. He wants nothing more than to work the ranch, charm the ladies, and live a life of carefree bachelorhood.

Ginny Sorensen has accepted her responsibility as the sole provider for herself and her younger sister. The desire to continue their journey to Oregon is crushed when the need for food and shelter keeps them in the growing frontier town of Splendor, Montana, forcing Ginny to accept work as a server in the local saloon.

Luke has never met a woman as lovely and unspoiled as Ginny. He longs to know her, yet fears his wild ways and unsettled nature aren't what she deserves. She's a girl you marry, but that is nowhere in Luke's plans.

Complicating their tenuous friendship, a twist in circumstances forces Ginny closer to the man she most wants to avoid—the man who can destroy her dreams, and who's captured her heart.

Believing his bachelor status firm, Luke moves from danger to adventure, never dreaming each step he takes brings him closer to his true destiny and a life much different from what he imagines.

Sunrise Ridge – Book Three
Redemption Mountain – Historical Western Romance Series

"The author has a talent for bringing the historical west to life, realistically and vividly, and doesn't shy away from some of the harder aspects of frontier life, even though it's fiction. Recommended to readers who like sweeping western historical romances that are grounded with memorable, likeable characters and a strong sense of place."

Noah Brandt is a successful blacksmith and businessman in Splendor, Montana, with few ties to his past as an ex-Union Army major and sharpshooter. Quiet and hardworking, his biggest challenge is controlling his strong desire for a woman he believes is beyond his reach.

Abigail Tolbert is tired of being under her father's thumb while at the same time, being pushed away by the one man she desires. Determined to build a new life outside the control of her wealthy father, she finds work and sets out to shape a life on her own terms.

Noah has made too many mistakes with Abby to have any hope of getting her back. Even with the changes in her life, including the distance she's built with her father, he can't keep himself from believing he'll never be good enough to claim her.

Unexpected dangers, including a twist of fate for Abby, change both their lives, making the tentative steps they've taken to build a relationship a distant hope. As Noah battles his past as well as the threats to Abby, she fights for a future with the only man she will ever love.

Dixie Moon – Book Four
Redemption Mountain – Historical Western Romance Series

Gabe Evans is a man of his word with strong convictions and steadfast loyalty. As the sheriff of Splendor, Montana, the ex-Union Colonel and oldest of four boys from an affluent family, Gabe understands the meaning of responsibility. The last thing he wants is another commitment—especially of the female variety.

Until he meets Lena Campanel...

Lena's past is one she intends to keep buried. Overcoming a childhood of setbacks and obstacles, she and her friend, Nick, have succeeded in creating a life of financial success and devout loyalty to one another.

When an unexpected death leaves Gabe the sole heir of a considerable estate, partnering with Nick and Lena is a lucrative decision...forcing Gabe and Lena to work together. As their desire grows, Lena refuses to let down her guard, vowing to keep her past hidden—even from a perfect man like Gabe.

But secrets never stay buried...

When revealed, Gabe realizes Lena's secrets are deeper than he ever imagined. For a man of his character, deception and lies of omission aren't negotiable. Will he be able to forgive the deceit? Or is the damage too great to ever repair?

Survivor Pass – Book Five
Redemption Mountain – Historical Western Romance Series

He thought he'd found a quiet life...

Cash Coulter settled into a life far removed from his days of fighting for the South and crossing the country as a bounty hunter. Now a deputy sheriff, Cash wants nothing more than to buy some land, raise cattle, and build a simple life in the frontier town of Splendor, Montana. But his whole world shifts when his gaze lands on the most captivating woman he's ever seen. And the feeling appears to be mutual.

finds refuge and a home at the sprawling Redemption's Edge ranch...and love in the arms of Bull Mason, the ranch foreman. For the first time since her parents' death, she feels cherished and safe.

In an instant their dreams are crushed...

Bull is resolute in his determination to track down and rescue Lydia's brother, kidnapped during the celebration of their friend's wedding. He's made a promise—one he intends to keep. Picking the best men, they are ready to ride, until he's given an ultimatum.

Choices can seldom be undone...

As their journey continues, the trackers become the prey, finding their freedom and lives threatened.

And promises broken can rarely be reclaimed...

Can Bull and Lydia trust each other again and find their way to back to the dreams they once shared?

Deep River – Book Seven
Redemption Mountain – Historical Western Romance Series

Beauregard Davis, ex-Confederate Captain and bounty hunter, has put his past behind him to focus on his future. He's a lawman with a purpose and a dream—do his job to the best of his abilities, and build a life with the woman he loves. Beau believes his life couldn't be better...until the day she boards a stagecoach, leaving him behind.

Caroline Iverson has a dream she won't deny. Traveling west, she expects to experience adventure. Instead, Caro finds a good man and unanticipated love. She never imagines the difficult decision to leave him behind would come back to haunt her.

After months of burying his pain in alcohol, Beau emerges stronger, determined to concentrate on a future without Caro. Doing his best to forget the past, he focuses his energy on work and preparing to build a home.

He never expected her to return, looking to recapture the love the two once shared.

Adding to Beau's concerns, two threats hang over him—outlaws have targeted his town, and he's being tracked by unidentified foes.

Keeping the town, Caro, and himself safe are his main priorities. He'll do whatever it takes to protect them. Guarding his heart is another matter.

How does a man ignore an all-consuming love without exposing himself to a threat worse than the physical dangers he already faces?

Courage Canyon – Book Eight
Redemption Mountain – Historical Western Romance Series

Dirk Masters, ex-Union Cavalry Captain, traveled hundreds of miles to put his past behind him. Finding Splendor and getting a job at Redemption's Edge seems the perfect opportunity to start over. His new life is predictable and peaceful...until a feisty young woman creates chaos in his orderly existence.

Rosemary Thayer has overcome more than one obstacle to achieve her dream of becoming a nurse. After a rough start, the people of Redemption's Edge have accepted her into their family—all except the rude and arrogant foreman who seems to enjoy making her life miserable. Soon, she'll have earned enough to leave the ranch for a place of her own.

But trouble continues to plague Rosemary. The unwelcome news of an escaped convict threatens to stall her plans of an independent life.

After months of anticipating her departure, Dirk is given an assignment he doesn't want, but can't turn down. Guard Rosemary from not one, but two possible threats. Could his life get any more complicated?

The last person she wants disrupting her future is now a part of it—every day, morning and night.

Not only is the escaped convict certain to come calling, another danger is inching its way toward Splendor, threatening young women, and no one can identify the attacker.

Worse, Dirk is fighting not only the threats, but his own internal desire. They're oil and water, meant to be as far apart as the Pacific from the Atlantic. So why does he crave her touch, seek any excuse to get close?

Reclaiming Love – Book One
Peregrine Bay – Contemporary Romance Series

Adam Monroe has seen his share of setbacks. Now he's back in Peregrine Bay, looking for a new life and second chance.

Julia Kerrigan's life rebounded after the sudden betrayal of the one man she ever loved. As president of a success real estate company, she's built a new life and future, pushing the painful past behind her.

Adam's reason for accepting the job as the town's new Police Chief can be explained in one word—Julia. He wants her back and will do whatever is necessary to achieve his goal, even knowing his biggest hurdle is the woman he still loves.

As they begin to reconnect, a terrible scandal breaks loose with Julia and Adam at the center.

Will the threat to their lives and reputations destroy their fledgling romance? Can Adam identify and eliminate the danger to Julia before he's had a chance to reclaim her love?

Our Kind of Love – Book Two
Peregrine Bay – Contemporary Romance Series

Selena Kerrigan is content with a life filled with work and family, never feeling the need to take a chance on a relationship—until she steps into a social world inhabited by a man with dark hair and penetrating blue eyes. Eyes that are fixed on her.

Lincoln Caldwell is a man satisfied with his life. Transitioning from an enviable career as a Navy SEAL to becoming a successful entrepreneur, his days focus on growing his security firm, spending his nights with whomever he chooses. Committing to one woman isn't on the horizon—until a captivating woman with caramel eyes sends his personal life into a tailspin.

Believing her identity remains a secret, Selena returns to work, ready to forget about running away from the bed she never should have gone near. She's prepared to put the colossal error, as well as the man she'll never see again, behind her.

Too bad the object of her lapse in judgment doesn't feel the same.

Linc is good at tracking his targets, and Selena is now at the top of his list. It's amazing how a pair of sandals and only a first name can say so much.

As he pursues the woman he can't rid from his mind, a series of cyber-attacks hit his business, threatening its hard-won success. Worse, and unbeknownst to most, Linc harbors a secret—one with the potential to alter his life, along with those he's close to, in ways he could never imagine.

Our Kind of Love, Book Two in the Peregrine Bay Contemporary Romance series, is a full-length novel with an HEA and no cliffhanger.

Colin's Quest – Book One
MacLarens of Boundary Mountain – Historical Western Romance Series

For An Undying Love...

When Colin MacLaren headed west on a wagon
train, he hoped to find adventure and perhaps a little
danger in untamed California. He never expected to
meet the girl he would love forever. He also never
expected her to be the daughter of his family's age-
old enemy, but Sarah was a MacGregor and the
anger he anticipated soon became a reality. Her
father would not be swayed, vehemently refusing to
allow marriage to a MacLaren.

Time Has No Effect...

Forced apart for five years, Sarah never forgot
Colin—nor did she give up on his promise to come
for her. Carrying the brooch he gave her as proof of
their secret betrothal, she scans the trail from
California, waiting for Colin to claim her.
Unfortunately, her father has other plans.

And Enemies Hold No Power.

Nothing can stop Colin from locating Sarah. Not
outlaws, runaways, or miles of difficult trails.
However, reuniting is only the beginning. Together
they must find the courage to fight the men who
would keep them apart—and conquer the challenge
of uniting two independent hearts.

Brodie's Gamble – Book Two
MacLarens of Boundary Mountain – Historical Western Romance Series

Brodie MacLaren has a dream. He yearns to wear the star—bring the guilty to justice and protect those who are innocent. In his mind, guilty means guilty, even when it includes a beautiful woman who sets his body on edge.

Maggie King lives a nightmare, wanting nothing more than to survive each day and recapture the life stolen from her. Each day she wakes and prays for escape. Taking the one chance she may ever have, Maggie lashes out, unprepared for the rising panic as the man people believe to be her husband lies motionless at her feet.

Deciding innocence and guilt isn't his job.

Brodie's orderly, black and white world spins as her story of kidnapping and abuse unfold. The fact nothing adds up as well as his growing attraction to Maggie cause doubts the stoic lawman can't afford to embrace.

Can a lifetime of believing in absolute right and wrong change in a heartbeat?

Maggie has traded one form of captivity for another. Thoughts of escape consume her, even as feelings for the handsome, unyielding lawman grow.

As events unfold, Brodie must fight more than his attraction. Someone is after Maggie—a real threat who is out to silence her.

He's challenged on all fronts—until he takes a gamble that could change his life or destroy his heart.

Quinn's Honor – Book Three
MacLarens of Boundary Mountain – Historical Western Romance Series

Quinn MacLaren has one true love...Circle M, the family ranch. He makes it a habit of working hard and playing harder, spending time with experienced women who know he wants nothing more than their company. He buries the love he feels for one woman deep inside, knowing he'll never be the man she needs.

Emma Pearce is a true ranch woman, working long hours to help keep the family ranch thriving. Feisty, funny, and reliable, she's the girl all the single young men want—after they've sewn their wild oats. Few know Emma has her heart set on one man. A man who may never grow up enough to walk away from his wild ways and settle down.

When tragedy strikes, Quinn's right where he doesn't want to be—as temporary foreman of the Pearce ranch. Stepping in to fill Big Jim Pearce's shoes isn't easy. Neither is keeping his feelings for Emma hidden and his hands to himself. Honor-bound to do what is right, Quinn meets the challenge, losing Emma's friendship in the process.

Adding to Quinn's worries, something sinister is working its way through the thriving town of Conviction. Unforeseen forces are at work. Debt builds, families lose their ranches, and newcomers threaten to divide not only the land, but the people—including the Pearce family.

As events unfold, Quinn faces the difficult challenge of keeping his feelings for Emma hidden and his honor intact. Doing what he believes is right couldn't feel more wrong.

After all, what's a man without honor?

Sam' Legacy – Book Four
MacLarens of Boundary Mountain – Historical Western Romance Series

Samuel Covington, ex-Pinkerton agent and deputy in the frontier town of Conviction, has come a long way from his upbringing in Baltimore. His job, and a particular woman, occupy his time and thoughts. His future is assured—until a message from home tears it all apart.

Jinny MacLaren loves the ranch, her family, and one particular deputy. Even though Sam's never said the words, she's certain of his feelings, envisioning a future as his wife—until the day he announces he's leaving without a promise to return.

His future no longer belongs to him. Sam never anticipated the news awaiting him, or the consequences of a past he'd left far behind.

Shoving painful thoughts of Sam aside, Jinny focuses on a life without him, allowing a friendship to grow with someone else. He's handsome, smart, and caring, yet in Jinny's heart, he'll never be Sam.

As both face an uncertain future without the other, neither anticipates the dangers stalking them.

Protecting what's his is Sam's calling. Reclaiming what he left behind may prove to be the biggest challenge of his life.

Find all of my books at:
https://www.shirleendavies.com/books.html